THE FIREARMS OFFICER

By

Cari Davies

Print ISBN 978-1-7384231-5-6

Published by
Llyfrau Cambria Books, Wales, United Kingdom.
Cambria Books and Cambria Stories are imprints of Cambria Publishing.
Discover our other books at: www.cambriabooks.co.uk

'There is a land of the living and a land of the dead, and the bridge is love, the only survival, the only meaning.' Thornton Wilder.

For Robin – The real hero.

Cover design by Carolyn Michel

CONTENTS

PART ONE

1

London - (August - 2021)

We forget that on the best of days the worst can happen. That when the sun is at its zenith dark clouds can gather and eclipse the light.

In the leafy London suburb of Wimbledon, Samantha Elliot was relishing the freedom to meander along the high street in the warmth of the midday sun. Her daughter was at preschool, and Sam felt relieved of any responsibility. Free to browse in a shop window and admire those Taylor jeans, rip at each knee, a white tank top to complete the outfit. Free to imagine going on a date again. Free to embrace a whole new beginning in life…

Until a scream splintered the air.

It sliced through the rumble of traffic and hushed the chatter of people. Sam spun around and saw, only a short distance away, a bearded youth, his face contorted, his eyes frenzied, a bloodied knife wielded above his head. A woman lay on the pavement beneath him, her white shirt crimson stained, as poised to strike again, he yelled, '*Allahu Akbar!*'

Bystanders tried to stop him, but he stabbed them also. A man reeled back clutching his stomach. A youth had his leg slashed. A girl was cut on her cheek. Traffic screeched to a halt as people fled in all directions, desperate to escape.

All except Sam, who couldn't flee anywhere. She couldn't believe what was happening in one of the safest suburbs in London. The reason she'd moved here. The sky was blue, the sun was shining, as blood trickled along the pavement…

The attacker spied her stillness. He fixed his hate filled eyes on her, and everything went into slow motion. She seemed to leave her body to hover in the chilling space between this world and the next, as he careered towards her, yelling, '*Almawt lilkafirin!* Death to the infidels!'

Around the corner, Jules Caron and Ted Rowlands, two members of the anti-terrorist unit, waited in an unmarked car, its engine running. A pair of undercover officers, they'd been operating surveillance on a low risk subject and hadn't been too worried when Ahmed had sneaked into an alleyway. They had expected him to reappear. Hearing screams coming from the high street they turned to one another in dread.

'*Merde!* We'd better hope that's not him,' said Jules.

Half English, half French, he was the younger of the two. Not long in the unit, he'd been concerned that the youth had been showing increased signs of fervour of late. But his partner had dismissed Ahmed's attendance at a mosque with an extremist preacher, as mere student curiosity.

'Better your foot down!' A now equally worried Ted urged.

Not needing to be asked twice, Jules pressed hard on the accelerator and raced them to the scene.

He skidded to a halt at the near end of the high street, and they leapt out. Both wore denim jeans, dark body-armour vests, trainers for speed of movement, and balaclavas, which they pulled on at the last minute. They snatched their Glock 17 pistols from their leg holsters and ran towards the commotion.

'*Mon Dieu,*' Jules was stunned to see that people were already injured, as a berserk Ahmed struck at random.

Ted barked into his mobile, 'Code red. Terrorist attack on Wimbledon high street. We need the emergency response team, the bomb disposal unit, ambulances and paramedics.' He listened for a second, then switched off. He turned to Jules. 'We follow Protocol - Confront, Contain, and Negotiate. If that fails – shoot the bastard.' He checked that his Bodycam was working, and they moved forward in stealth.

Jules had been a soldier before he joined the anti-terrorist unit. A sniper hiding on rickety town roofs in Afghanistan. It was easy for him to dodge around people and take the forward position. Hidden beside a parked car, he watched as Ahmed picked his next victim. The young woman, her back turned, stood, as if frozen, as the youth careered towards her bellowing, '*Almawt lilkafirin!*'

Jules wanted to shout, 'Run, Cheri!' but knew it was better he stayed unseen. It was ice he needed in his veins not emotion. He aimed his gun.

Pity, that in his haste to join him Ted stumbled into the side of the vehicle. The clang caused Ahmed to spot them both.

'*Alkhanaziru!*' the youth screamed.

'Yeah, *pigs!*' echoed a feckless teenager, who'd slyly leaned out of a café doorway and raised his phone to record the scene.

'Get out of here!' commanded Ted. But the teenager carried on as if he were making a movie.

For Sam it was all too real. She had a brief glimpse of the two masked men kneeling beside a car. She could only pray they were police officers, before she was grabbed, yanked around, strands of her hair pulled out by the roots, her cries ignored, as the attacker crushed her against his chest like a human shield.

'*Merde!*' Jules swore under his breath. It was hard not to be transfixed by her wide terrified eyes, her tumble of blonde hair, and fragile features. What if he shot her by mistake? He always felt a rush of anger seeing an imbalance of power between a man and a woman, a residue of feeling from his own abusive childhood, as she was held in a vice like grip.

'*Tashabuk alsalama!*' Ahmed growled.

Jules knew the words - *Peace be with you* - used in this context, meant exactly the opposite.

With murderous intent, Ahmed placed the knife across her throat, and began chanting, '*Allahu Akbar!*' in a rising crescendo.

Jules clicked off the gun's safety catch.

No time for negotiation. Ted went straight to the warnings. 'Drop the knife! Drop it! Drop it! Or, we'll shoot!' he hollered.

Ahmed merely tightened his grip and chanted louder.

For a second Jules hesitated. The task was all the harder because over the past weeks he'd learned about Ahmed. Knew for instance that the youth liked two spoons of sugar in his coffee. Knew he liked to sneak into the cinema to watch a movie of an afternoon, just as he did. Knew he was a student with a promising future in engineering. Knew what his death would mean for his family and the wider community...

Sam did not want her life to end either, and not like this. An image of Milly swam before her. How could she leave her daughter alone? She saw the officer with his gun aimed, his eyes two slits behind a balaclava, her life in his hands, as she waited for him to save her...

Jules saw her despair, but needed her to shift a fraction so he could hit Ahmed between the eyes, the two black holes now filled with hate. With a flicker from his own eyes he willed her to – *move!*

The blade cut into her skin. She jerked her head aside. The shot rang out. The knife clattered onto the pavement. Ahmed slumped down. So, did she.

Silence.

Sam lay uncertain whether she was dead or alive. She opened her eyes and saw the sky had darkened. Then turned her head to find the attacker sprawled out beside her, and knew, with a rush of relief, that it was he who'd left this earth, not she, a last look of incredulity on his youthful face.

At that moment a pigeon swooped down to stand with its head cocked and stare, just as she was doing, at the blood seeping from the hole between the eyes, before it flew off as if in fright.

Sam glanced up the street and saw other people were injured. She hauled herself up as bedlam broke out, people shouting that the danger was not over.

The officer who'd saved her, his gun put away, ran up and warned of a *suicide belt,* his words muffled behind his balaclava as he hustled her away.

The sly teenager stopped filming and scarpered, as, sirens blaring, vans full of police arrived. They were followed by bomb disposal experts, dressed like Martians, who went to check the attacker's body for explosives.

Sam, though at a safe distance, couldn't stop trembling as she watched them. The fear one might detonate and blow them to smithereens felt eerily familiar, the destruction too horrible to contemplate. 'Please God, no...' she whispered.

Jules placed a hand on her shoulder to steady her. It was the least he could do.

The gesture helped humanize the unidentifiable stranger who she was standing so close to. Close enough to smell his aftershave, a spicy aroma. She only hoped it overcame the metallic scent of the blood now oozing from the cut in her neck.

Jules pulled out his hanky, white pressed and clean, and handed it to her.

She held it to stench the flow, but blood seeped through, a crimson stain spreading, warm and sticky on her fingers. She felt a rush to her head, and with a defeated moan, she passed out.

Jules caught her before she hit the ground. He held her limp body until the, 'All Clear!' was called, and the explosive belt declared a fake. When the paramedics arrived and took her over, his job fulfilled, as discreetly as he'd arrived, he slipped away.

Sam came around inside an ambulance, still holding his now bloodied handkerchief. The only link she had to the man who'd saved her, a man she hadn't even thanked.

But she was alive, and for the moment it was all that mattered. Relief took over as she was driven from the street she'd been so happy in only a short while ago, now turned into a place of misery and carnage.

Jules drove away slowly, not wanting to draw attention to himself and his partner. When he reached a quiet street, he parked under a shady tree.

Ted ripped off his balaclava. 'Good job we had these on so neither of us can be identified.' He threw it onto the back seat.

Jules peeled off his own and reached for his hanky to wipe the sweat from his face. Then remembered he'd handed it to the woman to staunch the flow of blood. He shuddered, and used his balaclava instead, before chucking it next to Ted's.

His gun-holding hand started shaking. It wasn't the first time he'd killed someone. But he hadn't expected it to happen like this, so soon into his new job. In Helmand no one had ever used the word - *kill*.

Words like engaging, dropping, bagging, were intended to distance a soldier from the actual act, and as a sniper Jules had always used a long-range rifle. But today, using a handgun, it had felt personal. The woman's terror, the whiplash of the bullet through the air, the image of Ahmed slumping down, brought a rush of anguish.

Ted, angry that the youth had turned into such a monster, had no such qualms. 'You dispatched him like a true terminator. *Boom!*'

Jules winced at a word straight out of a movie. He rubbed his fingers across his now dry mouth and recalled the sly teenager who'd leaned out of a café doorway to film as if he was witnessing one. 'How could he do that?' he asked Ted.

'Callous, he was.' His partner rolled down his window and spat out of it. Then tapped his Bodycam 'Good job I have the official version recorded. It will see us through the enquiry.'

Jules felt his stomach lurch. 'There has to be one?'

'It's mandatory.'

'Mon Dieu.'

At that moment Ted's phone pinged. He relayed the message to Jules. 'We have to go to Wimbledon Police Station for the debriefing. The Commander's already on his way. We're to use the back entrance to avoid meeting any of the local officers.'

Jules knew of the rivalry between different forces, and could only hope he'd be backed by his own unit.

Sam arrived at the hospital to find other victims there ahead of her. Trolleys were being wheeled about, one man was screaming.

A woman, wearing a black gown and Hijab, lay with blood dripping to the floor. The attacker had struck out indiscriminately, hurting even his own.

Inside a curtained cubicle, the bloodied hanky shoved inside her pocket, a doctor tended her neck. He seemed young and inexperienced. A covid mask half covered his face. He told her an artery had only just been missed. And that because the knife had been serrated, the suturing of the wound would be more difficult.

He took his time doing it. Sam tried to think of other things to distract herself, like being home in time to fetch Milly from school.

'Will it leave a scar?' she asked, when he'd finished.

'Depends how well it heals.'

She felt like a marked woman anyway, the damage to her psyche of more concern.

He sprayed on anesthetic and set to work. He told her that the stiches were dissolvable and should disappear in a few weeks. That she should keep the wound warm and clean. He put an adhesive dressing on, and gave her a couple to take away. Told her the skin around the cut might go red and inflamed, but that was a sign it was healing.

'How will I know if it's not?'

'The bleeding will start again. The wound will reopen and pus will ooze out, a sign it's infected. Come back and see me if you're at all concerned.'

He shone lights into her eyes, and asked questions. Did she feel dizzy? Was she nauseous? Had she a headache?

She had all of these, but wanted to go home and be alone. She begged to be released, but she had to wait a good while before he granted permission.

She walked a little unsteadily along the corridor. At the hospital entrance a policewoman took charge. 'We'll give you a ride as we need to take your details.'

Sam sat in the back of the car, gave her name, age, how she'd celebrated turning twenty-four only last week, and finished with her address.

'How many others were injured?' she asked as they drove her away.

'Eight, including you. But at least no one died. Except the perpetrator of course.' The policewoman gave Sam a steady gaze. 'It was fortunate those officers were on hand.'

'Do you know the one who saved me?'

'No, I don't. And even if I did, I couldn't say. He must remain anonymous for his own safety. There'll be an enquiry about today and his actions will undergo scrutiny.'

'But he saved my life. He's a hero.'

'You can give a statement to corroborate that, when you feel able.'

7

Sam nodded. She'd do whatever she could to help him.

It was a relief to be taken home by way of the back route, avoiding the high street.

'Traffic has to be diverted as forensic teams are at work,' the policewoman told her. 'It'll be chaos for a while.'

Sam wondered if Wimbledon would ever be the same.

At least in her own street there was no sign of disruption. The Victorian red brick, semi-detached house, was a welcome sight. It was not large but suited just her and Milly.

'Is there someone waiting for you?' asked the policewoman.

Sam shook her head, and didn't elaborate. She didn't want to mention her divorce, or that she was a single parent, it was private.

'I'll get a squad car to drive by and check everything's okay.'

Sam thought of little Milly. 'Do you think it might not be?'

'Better to be on the safe side.' A card was produced. 'This might help, too.'

Sam looked down at the words - Victim Support. She hated being labelled one. She doubted she'd use it. She'd find her own way through this, if she could.

She went inside her home, slid down onto the cool of the hall floor, and howled. Her body racked by angry sobs.

It was a good hour before she could stop.

2

Jules and Ted arrived at Wimbledon Station and entered by the back entrance.

Their Unit Commander was waiting in the basement, in a room set aside from the usual police business. Jules handed his gun over. It was bagged for a thorough examination.

Evans was a solid muscular Welshman, and the man who had recruited Jules when he headed up the interview at Scotland Yard. There were those at Main Command who had felt Jules wasn't ready for the complexity of undercover work. That his French accent might be a hindrance. But Evans had waved their doubts away, declaring the unit could only benefit from someone with grit, determination, and ace shooting skills. That the police training would deal with anything else he needed to know. Jules could only hope that this belief in him still held, as his commander narrowed his eyes.

'How are you feeling, lad?'

Jules's leg started jigging. He had to clamp his foot down on the floor to hold it still. 'I'm shaken, sir.'

'I'm sure you are. It was a close call. You do know that counselling's available any time you want it.' Evans gave a nod of sympathy. 'Talking through things can help.'

Jules didn't answer. Last thing he wanted was someone stirring up his emotions. It was best he kept a stiff upper lip. He'd admired this about the British when he first came to live here, and so far, it had served him well.

Evans gave up and moved on. 'Let's get the formalities over with.' He switched on the recording machine placed at the end of the table and asked them to say how long they'd been part of the unit.

Ted had been there for years. Jules, but a few months.

For anonymity, they were to use pseudo names. Jules, was to be Officer Y. Ted, Officer Z.

Jules tried to recall every detail leading to the final shot. He spoke hesitantly as his memory felt spooked. When he reached the end, the relief was palpable. Even his leg calmed down.

Ted gave his version next and backed him up to the hilt.

Evans switched off the machine and nodded appreciatively at them both. 'Good job you were near and could race to the scene, however pissed the local response team are that you arrived before them.' He nodded at Jules. 'You're a hero in my book, lad.'

Jules wished he felt like one, and not like a cold-blooded killer.

'It's a pity that the police have received such bad press recently,' said Evans. 'Accusations of misogyny, racism, homophobia, you name it.'

Jules had seen for himself how some officers in the unit were indeed guilty of racism and misogyny. Insults were bandied about at anyone who looked remotely foreign, he'd copped a few himself. As for the pornographic pictures on the inside of locker doors, they spoke realms.

'You could come under fire for this incident,' Evans warned. 'The Independent Office for Police Conduct will be interviewing you both. They'll want proof you followed protocol.' He looked at Ted. 'Give me your Bodycam. It should give all the cover you'll need.'

Ted removed the camcorder from off his jacket, and handed it over.

Evans checked it out. He lifted his head, and looked at Ted. 'Something's not right. You did switch it on, didn't you?'

'Of course, I did.' Ted swallowed. 'Unless it got dislodged when I...' he looked at Jules, 'stumbled.'

'*Stumbled?*' Evans pressed the recorder button, but again nothing happened.

Jules felt a tremor of fear as Evans handed it back to Ted. 'I hope this isn't a cock up,' said the commander.

Jules couldn't help feeling a spark of anger. The recording would have vindicated him by showing exactly what happened.

'You did give clear warnings?'

'Of course, sir.' Ted was on the defensive.

'Did anybody else hear them?' Evans's tone was irritated now.

'The victim must have,' said Ted. 'Though Ahmed was shouting.'

'She's probably too traumatized to be of any use,' damned Evans. 'We'd do better to check the street cameras. Pity most need replacing and can't be relied on thanks to budget cuts.'

Jules told him of the sly teenager who'd filmed. 'His camera was working, sir.'

'Pity he scarpered with it,' said Ted.

Evans rubbed his lips with his fingers, his mood no longer friendly. 'Well, let's hope he comes forward. I'll get the Police Commissioner, in his TV update, to ask anyone who has any footage to hand it in.' He sat back and studied his two officers. 'Tell me, what did you miss about Ahmed's behavior prior to this morning. He must have been showing some agitation.'

Jules knew he hadn't missed anything. That he'd informed Ted about his fears. But as a member of the Church of England, his partner was keen on showing tolerance. Now, under the steely gaze from his Commander, Ted had more doubts. 'Jules had concerns, sir. I should have listened to him. I couldn't believe Ahmed would turn into a monster. He was just a youth.'

There was a withering sigh.

Evans leaned forwards and lowered his voice. 'Well, what's done is done. You must say you had no proof anything was being planned, or you'll look negligent.' He leaned back and became business like. 'They want to interview you first thing tomorrow morning. You at eight, Jules. Ted at nine. Separately.' He gave them a stern look. 'Loyalty between partners is everything at times like this. See you stick to the same story.'

His voice had a tone of regret as he added they'd have to be suspended from the unit, pending the enquiry. He offered an olive branch saying it would be paid leave. He told them to leave London until press interest had died down. To take a holiday and recover.

Jules's first thought was that he could return to France. Maybe go hiking in the alps. He hadn't been back since he'd left.

Pity Evans read his mind.

'You can't leave the country, lad. Not when you're under investigation. You must hand your passport in.' He stood up. 'Briefing terminated.' And he left the room.

Jules was damned if he'd hand in his passport. It would be like an admission of guilt.

'What happened to the presumption of innocence?' agreed Ted.

They sat in silence for a moment, the image of the dead Ahmed like a ghost between them.

'I'm not sure we can pin our hopes on the teenager who took the phone footage,' said Ted. 'He called us *pigs* if you remember.'

Jules shook his head not wanting to remember any such thing

They went outside. Ted drove off to his home in lower Wimbledon. Back to the bosom of the family he referred to as the most important part of his life. Jules drove in the other direction, to the neighbouring suburb of Putney, where he lived alone.

The apartment was on the top floor of a converted warehouse. It had spectacular views of the Thames. Barges and ferries meandered along, pushing aside stray logs, bottles, cans, and all kinds of litter carelessly thrown in. Murky secrets lurked in the deep, even bodies sometimes surfaced, which made it fascinating on any other day. But now his own life felt murky, Jules had no desire to even look.

He couldn't take his usual pride in his pad either. Bought with money his mother had left him, the apartment was open-plan and spacious, with few possessions to clutter it. He'd designed it himself, a bit of a man cave, he supposed, one he could bunker down in.

He needed a drink. He poured out a whisky, flopped down on the sofa, and switched on his audio streaming. Music could always change his mood, and he listened to Litvinovsky's – 'The Grand Cahier, La Foret et Riviere,' until a calm descended.

He took a long shower, the sweat and gore of the day, washed away, at least, momentarily.

He returned to the sitting room, a towel wrapped around his still wet skin, and switched on the television, only to find that the event on the high street was being relived. It was hard to listen as passersby gave accounts of what had taken place. His part in the ordeal was recounted by strangers. Some called him a hero, some felt he'd acted too hastily. 'He wore a balaclava and behaved more like a robot than a human being,' said a woman.

'Merci pour rien!' Jules shook his head, and sat down.

It was a relief when a clip was shown of the local Police Superintendent, uniformed and braided, a microphone set up outside Wimbledon station, where he announced that but for the actions taken by the two brave officers today more people would have been hurt, or could have died.

Then a journalist asked who these officers were, and Jules froze. Even though the superintendent said their identities were protected, more questions were asked. - *Why were they nearby? Was it because they were already conducting a surveillance on the youth? Were they undercover?*

The Superintendent said he couldn't comment, but that everything would be examined by the IOPC. It would be a fully independent enquiry. He asked for anyone who'd taken phone footage to hand it in as potential evidence, and closed the update down.

Jules took another swig of whisky as the news went onto to name the victims. He felt sorry for them as their identities were exposed somewhat recklessly. He peered closer at the photograph of the woman whose life he'd saved. She looked younger, only a teenager, but had the same tumble of blonde hair, and an inviting smile that drew you in. Jules remembered how terror had made her eyes luminous. How she'd connected with his and had moved just in time. How they'd synchronized.

Samantha Elliot, an actress, recently divorced, has a young daughter...

They seemed more interested in her checkered history, than the fact she was alive and saved from an almost certain death.

Jules switched off, preferring to read an Arch Comic on Architectural Evolution. The way things were built was a passion of his. *Yes, is More,* had sketchy new ideas, and revolutionary designs. He studied a photograph of the *Burj Khalifa* in Dubai, the tallest building in the world. The sheer feat of the engineering took the mind to a different sphere. The image of silver tiers rising ever upwards into the sky filled him with inspiration, and for a brief while, the hideous carnage he'd witnessed today, was eclipsed.

3

Alone in the hall, her tears abated for the time being, Sam pulled herself up from the floor and walked into the kitchen. Every part of her body ached. Any movement felt hard to execute. She may have survived her ordeal but her muscles hadn't registered it, they were weak and limp.

She gulped down a drink of water and looked out of the kitchen window at the garden in full bloom. Hollyhocks towered in the borders, busy lizzies fought for space, nasturtiums spilled onto the lawn in an array of colours she might never have seen again. The thought of dying in such a horrible manner had her touching her neck, doubtful the scar would ever fade. She fingered the dressing, then remembered the bloodied hanky was still in her pocket, and she pulled it out.

Not daring to look in case she fainted again, she went into the small utility room. She filled a bowl with cold water, added some stain removal, and dropped it in. Her eyes still averted, she rinsed until the hanky was returned to its purity.

It made her curious about the officer who'd handed it to her. He'd seemed young like she was, and might also be traumatized. Even if he had taken the shot like he was a machine. She recalled how afterwards he'd placed a hand on her shoulder in what had felt like an act of solidarity, the gesture comforting. That underneath that cold exterior, he was a human being.

She hung the hanky out to dry in the garden, where it fluttered in the breeze like a flag. A reminder of how near she came to not existing, and a warning to be more vigilant in the future. Life no longer felt safe, no longer felt free. Any chance for this had been dashed to smithereens on a bright summer morning, and a sob escaped her.

She went inside to call her mother, concerned she'd learn of the event on the television.

It was a while before Stella Elliot answered. She was probably outside doing the thing she loved most, painting. When her voice finally came on the line, Sam couldn't hold back the tears as she spoke of the horror that had taken place.

'You must leave London,' said her shocked mother. 'Get in the car and drive straight to Dorset. You should be with me. I can't have you and Milly living in a place where madmen attack innocent people.'

Sam knew her mother was probably right. She promised to think about going there, but didn't want Wimbledon turned into a place of evil either.

No sooner had she put the phone down than it rang again. This time it was her friend Andrea, who'd only just heard what had happened and wanted to warn Sam. 'There's been a terror attack in the high street. A maniac ran amuck, striking people down at random. One poor woman had a knife put to her throat. She could have been beheaded.'

Sam broke in. 'I know. It was me.'

A stunned silence. 'Oh my God, Sam. You must be traumatized. I'm coming straight over.'

'No, please don't. I can pull myself together better on my own. I have to pick up Milly soon.'

'For goodness sake, I can fetch her for you. You must stay put. She can have lunch with Polly at my house.'

Sam knew Andrea's daughter, a year older than Milly, was a kind girl. But she wanted to see Milly for herself, to hold her close. Added to which if she stayed indoors she might never dare go out again. 'I want things to be as normal as possible,' she explained. 'I don't want Milly to be terrorized. I have to show her that I've survived.'

'Well, if you insist. What a nightmare. Just when we've been freed from lockdowns and life was returning to normal.' Andrea drew breath. 'And for him to target you of all people, after what you've already been through. What with your divorce and your ex legging it to Canada.'

Her new friend didn't know everything. Sam didn't want her pity. She couldn't allow the fear of being helpless in the face of male aggression to return because she'd frozen in fright today. She couldn't succumb to becoming a victim all over again. 'It was I who ended the marriage,' she said defiantly, and ended the call.

She went into the sitting room, with its newly painted umber walls, rustic blue sofa, and oriental carpets. She sank to the floor and took up a yoga position, stretched out her spine, closed her eyes, and tried to ease the stress away as best she could, hoping she'd feel strong enough to fetch Milly.

She'd wanted her daughter to attend the preschool facility, offered over the long summer holidays, in preparation for primary school in September. So far, Milly had enjoyed the playground games and the walks on the common, but had complained that the children who already lived in Wimbledon had bonded together, and left her out.

Sam understood her daughter's position all too well. Newly arrived in the area, her own status as a single mother had seemed to make other mothers wary of her. As if she was the sore thumb amidst the suburban family bliss lived by everyone else. Andrea was the only real friend Sam had made so far.

A scarf sufficed to hide the dressing on her neck. It would also keep it warm, and make the cut heal more quickly she hoped. She didn't want anyone seeing it and asking awkward questions.

She set off for the school, bravely, but as she reached the gates, fear enveloped her again. A blackness descended, like a bird of prey had swooped her up into the ethos and kept her hovering there. It was a relief to find Andrea waiting at the gate. Her friend gave her such a big hug she came back to earth.

'You need all the support you can get.' Andrea reached into her pocket and pulled out a rape alarm. 'Here, take this.' She handed it over.

'You think someone will attack me again?' Sam feared the word, 'Victim,' was stamped across her forehead making her fair game for anyone.

'It's just a precaution. It makes an ear-splitting shriek and people will come running to your aid.'

Sam shoved it into her pocket, knowing her friend was doing her best to help. She could see the other mother's glancing over, but they stopped short of coming any closer.

'They know what's happened to you. But they haven't told the children. Milly doesn't have to know until you're ready to tell her. I suggested that they gave you space,' Andrea explained.

'That's all they've ever given me,' said Sam. 'I don't want to be treated like a leper.'

To her surprise two of them ventured forth.

'What a horrendous thing to happen,' said Nicola, the wife of a banker, who usually ignored Sam. 'It's bold of you to come here to collect Milly,' she said.

'I'm glad he was shot and killed,' said Olivia, a tall willowy model, with a loud voice. She glanced around at a group of Muslim mothers who were huddled together, protectively. 'I hope they didn't hear that, but it's only how I feel.'

Sam could see divisions were forming even though the attacker had struck at random, regardless of people's creed or culture. She was about to say something about this, when Barbara, the psychotherapist arrived, and took her aside.

'You'll need time to process what's happened. I can easily find you a counsellor trained for such needs. Milly could come on a play date with Lucy, while you pay one a visit.'

Sam felt she'd had her fair share of counselling when deciding to leave her marriage. She didn't feel the same need to talk about the attack. She wanted to banish it from her mind and blot out the images. At the same time, she knew playdates were something that Milly had longed for and didn't want to lose the kind offer.

Her daughter came running out. She was real, and tangible, the smell of pencils and rubbers on her skin. Sam held her close. 'It's so good to see you, sweetheart.'

Miss Potts, who was in charge, came up and whispered how shocked she was to hear what had happened. Then explained she'd also kept it from the children. That it was better they heard about such horror in the safety of their own homes, especially Milly.

Sam thanked her, and blinked back her tears, keen to rush her daughter away before someone accidentally blurted anything.

A still concerned Andrea offered beds at her home. Sam knew it was large and had plenty of room, but still declined. She wanted to be in her own house tonight. 'There'll be police officers patrolling outside,' she reassured her friend. 'We'll be fine.'

'Well, if you change your mind, call me.'

Sam fled back to the house, where she fed Milly a lunch of bake beans and fishfingers. She couldn't be bothered to follow good eating rules today. Sensing weakness in her mother, Milly pushed for more rules to be broken and tried to raid the sweet jar. Sam's firm *No,* had her daughter running out into the garden to use the swing. She went even higher than usual, her cheeks aglow, her curly hair awry, and her legs kicking out as she sang, 'Happy As You Know It,' to the skies.

Sam only wished she could be as carefree.

When evening came she sneaked a look into the street and saw a police car idling by. The two officers inside gave her a salute, which reassured her.

She gave Milly a lengthy wallow at bath time. Water was chucked everywhere. There was a lot of clearing up to do before her daughter finally climbed into bed.

Tucked in, Sam read from a favourite book - 'Charlotte's Web.' Milly loved the tale of Wilbur, the little runt of a piglet, destined to be killed, who was saved over and over. Sam too found it comforting on the very day someone else had saved her, even if he was a stranger she'd never know.

Exhausted by the effort to carry on as though everything was normal, she kissed Milly goodnight. She'd wait until morning to explain what had happened, and, at least, her still unaware daughter, went to sleep with a smile on her face.

Jules spent the evening in the quiet pub not far from his apartment, where he downed a glass of burgundy, and picked at his steak and chips. He'd not much appetite. Not helped by a couple sitting nearby who were hell bent on discussing the terrorist attack.

'Who'd have thought that would happen in Wimbledon of all places, 'The Land of The Wombles,' said an elderly man, sipping his evening pint. 'I mean that kid's book was ahead of its time being so eco-friendly. All about furry animals who collected rubbish left lying around, and recycled it underground.' He shook his head. 'Not like nowadays when litter is left everywhere. The police should be tougher, like those officers today, no messing with them, was there?'

'I'm not so sure,' said the younger woman. 'They may have overstepped the mark by killing him, Dad.'

Jules didn't wait to hear any more. He downed his wine and left.

It had made him more anxious about the meeting in the morning. He knew the independent conduct officers would be thorough, but hoped they'd also be respectful. He tried to reassure himself it was just a procedure.

Back home he ran the event through his mind more calmly, clinically, not leaving anything out up to the final moment, when Sam Elliot, held like a human shield, her death imminent, had waited in desperation for him to save her.

How could he not?

4

Sam didn't sleep well. She suffered a nightmare. *The attacker was holding a knife to her throat. A shot rang out, but the bullet entered her instead of him. It was she who slumped down dead.* She woke, bathed in sweat.

The moment she closed her eyes it happened again. In the end she lay propped up on her pillows afraid to sleep at all. Every sound made her tremble, the hoot of an owl, a car horn, a train rumbling in the distance. It was a relief when daylight filtered through the curtains heralding the morning, and she could go downstairs to make her usual cup of tea.

More out of curiosity than common sense, she switched on the television to find the coverage was still focused on the attack. It was disconcerting as strangers stepped up to recount the event. She had to sit down as her near-death experience was described in graphic detail.

Her privacy was intruded upon. Photographs were shown from her acting days, when she was only fifteen. She cringed to see images of the character being described as a -*Lolita,* a precociously seductive girl. They also mentioned the hasty marriage and later divorce. Though they didn't go into the details, which, thank goodness, had been kept confidential as part of the severance package.

The commentator moved on to question the actions of the officer who'd saved her. Instead of calling him a hero, he suggested he might have been trigger happy, and too eager to shoot.

Sam felt angry. She knew how the officer had waited until the very last moment, when he'd indicated for her to move. How she'd only responded just in time. She felt a rush of shame that she hadn't run away like everyone else. Then he wouldn't have to endure all this scrutiny.

She switched off the TV, rose from the sofa, and returned to the kitchen. She recalled how the policewoman, who'd ferried her home yesterday, had said she could give in a statement. Maybe she should do this soon, corroborate the evidence, and do her civic duty.

If she could find the courage. First, she had the onerous task of explaining to her innocent, trusting, five-year old daughter, that the world was not always safe.

She returned upstairs, dressed, and popped the scarf around her neck, before going to help Milly dress. It was best her daughter didn't know she'd even had a wound. Not yet anyway.

After a light breakfast they sat down together in the sitting room, and Sam, as sensitively as she could, told Milly what had happened. How a bad man had attacked people in the high street, and that one of them was her. But, that a policeman had saved her.

'How?'

Sam knew she couldn't fudge this. She took a breath. 'He…'

Milly finished for her. She screwed up her eyes, and put two fingers together like a gun. 'He shot him, didn't he? Like this – *Bam!*'

Sam was taken back. Her daughter couldn't have known this was exactly what had happened. But children were so aware these days, even at five. 'It's over now so there's nothing to worry about,' she tried to reassure them both. Her heart was missing beats.

Milly climbed onto her lap. 'You won't ever die, will you, Mummy?'

Hard for Sam to answer when she almost had. 'Not if I can help it.' She resolved to protect herself better in the future.

A quiet moment, Milly's thumb in her mouth, before the inevitable question. 'Does Daddy know?'

Sam tensed. 'We don't need to worry him now he's living in Canada.'

'But if he thinks we're in trouble he might come back.' Milly teared up.

Sam couldn't say she didn't want Simon to come anywhere near them. How she was glad he'd moved to another country, far away. How he'd treated her so badly she never wanted to see him again.

She held Milly close, and wiped her eyes with a tissue. 'You don't have to attend the school today. You can stay home with me. We can do a jigsaw and then some gardening, if you like.'

Milly put her thumb back into her mouth. She sucked for a while longer, before deciding she'd go, after all. 'I might miss making a friend, if I don't,' she said, poignantly. Then jumped off her mother's lap in a determined spirit.

Sam felt proud of her daughter. She fetched their coats and they went outside. No police car. It must be patrolling around the area.

She held Milly's hand as they walked along the few streets to the school. There was a church on one side, and a park on the other, which gave a peaceful atmosphere. After a quick kiss, her daughter ran bravely into the playground.

Sam saw other children staring at her daughter. They started whispering amongst themselves. To her relief, a small group walked over and surrounded Milly in a protective circle. She watched as they walked inside the school together.

It was a classic example of how good could come out of bad. She walked home feeling braver herself. Why not do her duty right now? Strike while she had the courage. Give in her statement and set the record straight. End this nightmare.

Jules avoided the reopened high street by using the back roads. He didn't need to relive the trauma before his interview.

He arrived in good time. He was dressed in his jeans, sweatshirt, and trainers, and hoped he looked professional enough as he made his way down to the basement, to the same room where the briefing with the commander had taken place only yesterday. Three chairs were laid out similarly, but this time, he sat in the one on its own.

It was a while before two men arrived. He stood up, but the older one, white haired and seemingly superior, indicated for him to sit again. There was no attempt to put an officer at ease, just a stony silence.

The younger man introduced himself by recording his name into the tape. Steve Sinclair had his fair hair smoothed back, and an officious manner. The older man, named Veer Patel, was more relaxed, though his inquisitive eyes homed in on Jules.

Sinclair stated, again for the benefit of the tape, that they were from the Independent Police Conduct Authority. Here to interview Officer Y, the shooter involved in the attack on Wimbledon high street.

'Age?' he asked Jules.

'Twenty six.' He'd soon be twenty seven, but he felt in no rush to say this. He felt old and weary already.

The interview began in earnest as Patel set out the ground work.

'We need to know about your earlier life as a youth. And as a soldier before you joined the unit. How this might have impacted on your decision to shoot.'

Patel had the cool look of a clinical observer, a psychologist perhaps. Someone who was used to weighing things up. He sat back and allowed the younger Sinclair to start questioning, under his older, watchful eyes.

'Your mother was English, but your father was French. He still runs a *casino* in Nice, correct?' said Sinclair.

Any mention of his father always unnerved Jules. 'I have nothing to do with him,' he said. 'We are estranged.' His father's dubious business dealings had already been scrutinized before he'd been allowed to join the unit. 'I left France when my parents divorced. I was fourteen. My father and I haven't spoken since.' He fell silent hoping to end this line of questioning. His own clean record and lack of contact with his father had seen him through before.

But Sinclair wouldn't let up. It was as if he was out to impress, Patel. 'So, your father wasn't at your mother's funeral two years ago?' He gave a sly smile.

How did he know this? Jules had asked the English relatives who were present to keep it under wraps. Someone must have slipped up. 'That was my father's one and only visit to England. His final farewell to my mother.'

The older Patel intervened. 'I expect he also said adieu to you. Left you some money, perhaps?'

'He left me his car, and vowed never to see me again.'

'What make?'

'A Merc.'

Patel let slip a smile.

Jules only just managed to stop himself enthusing about the six-speed manual gear box, the sports suspension, the convertible aspect, but couldn't hold back his look of pride.

23

Sinclair, who had no such pleasure in motor vehicles, moved on to another subject. 'You joined the army straight from school, correct?'

Jules nodded. He remembered how good it had been to find a place to channel the anger he'd accumulated over the years, as he was turned into a disciplined soldier.

'You did your first tour of duty when you were just nineteen in Afghanistan? When combat duties for British soldiers were coming to an end.'

2013. There'd been some fierce battles before the hand over to the Afghan Government forces, the following year. One skirmish had resulted in Jules being awarded a medal for bravery.

'It was the Military Cross,' said Patel. 'For saving a member of your patrol at grave risk to yourself.' He gave a nod of approval.

Sinclair's response was less enthusiastic. 'So, you're a hero twice over?' He frowned as though this couldn't be possible.

Jules didn't say that rescuing a mate was all that had mattered. That he'd had to blot out the bodies of the other dead soldiers, sprawled out, legs blown off, stomach entrails exposed, the skin on their faces peeled away, as he'd carried his comrade to safety. He doubted that Sinclair had ever seen any real action and therefore couldn't understand the intense loyalty between soldiers. How any one of them would have done the same for him. It was what made the job, noble.

Patel took over. 'You returned later, when the British had officially left, in a training capacity for the Afghan government forces. You spent a few more years there.'

Jules nodded. His acute eye sight had given him a skill as a sniper. He'd helped Afghan recruits to pick off insurgents from the rooftops, when surprise attacks were launched.

'You and your partner, Leo Henshaw, had a reputation as ace shooters.' Jules shrugged off the compliment. 'But your soldier days came to a premature end when your mother became ill.'

Jules still found it hard to talk about this. He took a breath. 'She was dying of cancer. I had to come home and nurse her. After she passed, I had a lot to sort out. I needed to make a home on my own. I opted to leave the army and settle in London.'

24

He didn't reveal how his grief had led to a near breakdown. How his childhood had caught up with him. As had the carnage he'd witnessed in Afghanistan. How only extreme physical exercise had saved him from oblivion. But no one knew about this. It was private.

'And then you joined the police,' said Sinclair.

'It felt a good fit.'

Sinclair looked dubious. 'Your skills may have been useful in Afghanistan, but the streets of London have their own challenges, when lone attacks are up close. You do know that by being the shooter, this is all on you.'

Jules blanched. He hadn't known any such thing.

'You had the assailant under surveillance, didn't you?'

Jules nodded.

'Was his behavior of concern?'

Jules knew he had to answer carefully. 'I was worried he was becoming involved in a more radical form of Islam, but I had no proof.'

'You must have felt you knew him,' intervened Patel.

'Perhaps, too well,' said Sinclair. 'So, he could slip under the radar and appear in a high street wielding a knife. Maybe he fooled you and you shot him to get even.'

Jules had to hold down the outrage he felt at this slur on his character. He strove to keep calm. 'Knowing him made no difference. He was like any other attacker who had to be stopped.'

'Being a sniper in Afghanistan, able to pick people off in a moment, might have made you hot headed,' said Sinclair.

'Hot headed? You have to be ice cold to calculate where to hit with precision.' Jules felt he was talking to an idiot.

'You could have gone for his legs. Better still his arm. You would have forced him to drop the knife, that way. He didn't need to die.'

'He was holding the woman in front of him as a human shield. I could have hit her by mistake if I'd shot at his body.' Jules's voice was rising. 'I had to neutralize him.'

'Why didn't your partner take the shot?' said Patel. 'He was senior after all, and you were new to the unit.'

'Ted was going to negotiate. I was in the forward position.'

25

There was a moment's pause before Patel spoke, his voice quiet but steely. 'You didn't know that the policy of *shoot to kill*, was under review?'

Jules felt his breath leave him. 'I did not. We were told to contain the situation, but if that failed...' he faltered, remembering the panic in his partner's voice. 'Ted shouted warnings but he was ignored. I had no choice but to shoot to kill.' He retreated into an icy silence.

In his youth in France Jules was often called a *moins courer* - a lad of little heart. His cold demeanour had started as a defence against his father's drunken rages to show he wasn't scared. When he'd moved to England he'd used it in response to school bullies. Now he used this against this belligerent interview technique.

Sinclair made one last swipe. 'Well, you did save a life. Let's hope she was worth it.' His phone pinged and he pulled it from his pocket, read a message, and whispered in Patel's ear. Then without any explanation he exited the room.

The remark about the woman felt wildly inappropriate. Jules looked at the older man. 'Can I go now?'

But Patel shook his head.

They sat in silence, waiting for Sinclair's return.

5

Before she lost her resolve, Sam went upstairs and changed into a formal suit, ready to visit the police station. She appraised herself in the mirror and tightened the scarf around her neck. It was likely to become a permanent fixture. She was determined to be taken seriously and not seen as some neurotic actress as had been suggested on the news.

Outside, she saw the patrol car was disappearing on its round of the area, as she drove away.

Wanting to avoid the now re opened high street, she took the back route to lower Wimbledon. She switched the car radio at the classical music channel, and Tchaikovsky's, 'Piano Concerto in D major,' blasted forth. It served to heighten her sense of purpose. She arrived at the station, parked at the front, and went quickly inside.

The duty officer, an elderly man, recognized her straight away, and was concerned. 'Shouldn't you be at home safe, after such a horrific event?'

'I want to put the record straight. They're pedalling lies on the news.'

Well, that's the media for you.'

A police siren blared outside, startling her.

The duty officer came from behind his counter and took her into a side room. 'You'll be alright in here. I need to alert a higher authority, but I'll be back soon.'

She waited. Then started pacing up and down. She was on the point of leaving when the door opened and a woman in a grey suit walked in.

She eyed Sam with interest. 'I'm informed you'd like to give a statement.'

No point backing out now, Sam took a breath. 'If it's convenient.'

'As it happens it is. Follow me.'

Sam was led down some stairs to a basement area. It was away from normal police procedures and felt more secretive. She heard raised voices, but couldn't make out where they were coming from. It made her wonder if someone else was giving in their statement as she was.

The room for her interview had chairs and a table, on which there was a glass and a jug of water. At the far end was an audio machine.

The woman indicated for her to sit, before sitting herself opposite. 'I'm Eve Preston from Scotland Yard.' She gave a quick smile. 'It's good of you to come in. This won't take any longer than it has to.'

She seemed important as well as sympathetic. Sam breathed a sigh of relief.

Then the door opened and in walked a younger man, who sat beside the woman.

'I'm Steve Sinclair, from the Police Conduct Authority,' he announced.

Sam wasn't sure what this conduct authority was, but Sinclair had a more confronting air that made her uneasy.

Eve Preston spoke first. 'The attack must have been a horrific experience. Are you sure you're ready to speak about it?'

'I want to tell the truth. They're saying things on the news that are misleading.'

Steve Sinclair gave her a cool look.

Odd how policemen were scary just because they were in the business of catching criminals. Under his gaze, she felt like a criminal herself just by being there. She'd address her statement to the machine and do her best to ignore this man.

Eve Preston pressed the start button. 'Ready?'

Sam nodded. She could hear the tape whirring as she confirmed her name, and age. After which all she could think of was an irrelevant detail. The pigeon that swooped down in the aftermath, its head cocked in curiosity, its eyes staring in shock, at the lad sprawled out on the pavement, dead. The bird had flown off moments later as if in fright. Which was exactly what Sam wanted to do now. Maybe she wasn't ready to do this.

Eve Preston switched off the machine and poured out a glass of water. 'Here, drink this.'

'Thanks.' Sam gulped it down.

28

'Would you prefer to come back another day?' Sinclair spoke in a tone that suggested he wished she would. That her presence was an inconvenience.

It made her rally to the cause. 'No. I want to get this over with.'

The machine was switched back on. Sam steeled herself against the stomach-churning revulsion that came with each recall. People screaming and running, the blood on the pavement, the shock, the coldness of the knife on her skin. She had to focus hard to use the exact words for the warnings given. ''Drop the knife! Drop the knife! Drop it! Or we'll shoot!' The officer yelled this,' she said. 'But the attacker ignored him.' Her fingers reached to remove the now obligatory scarf, and she revealed the dressing. 'He sliced into my neck, here.'

She saw Sinclair's eyes flicker at the size of the plaster, before she hid it again. 'If the officer hadn't taken the shot, I would have died.'

Silence.

Eve Preston switched off the machine.

Sinclair looked as though he was about to speak, but Sam didn't give him the chance as she was finding it hard to breathe. 'Am I done?'

'Yes, but are you okay?' Eve Preston looked concerned.

'Not really. It's brought it all back.' It took all her effort to push back her chair and stand up. 'I'd like to go now.'

Eve Preston rose. 'Let me escort you upstairs.'

Sam was glad to leave Sinclair behind.

As they walked along the corridor, Eve Preston tried to reassure her. 'We believe the attacker was a lone operator. You should be safe from now on. But just in case we'll keep a car patrolling in your area.'

Sam couldn't hear any voices in the corridor. All was silent now.

Once they'd reached the entrance hall she was thanked for coming in, before the woman from Scotland Yard disappeared. Sam was left with the elderly duty officer.

'We need more people like you to give statements on our behalf,' he said, his eyes fatherly.

His kindness brought tears to her eyes, and she made a hurried exit.

Sinclair returned and whispered a few words to Patel, before flicking his hand dismissively at Jules. 'You can go, Caron.'

'Go?'

Sinclair gave a disingenuous smile.

It was left to Patel to explain. 'It appears that the woman whose life you saved has backed up your version of the event. Other witnesses may shed a different light, of course, but for now, we don't need you.' He also indicated to the door.

Jules didn't waste any time. He pushed back his chair, went out into the corridor, and took the stairs two at a time, eager to reach his car. It was good of the woman to give her statement in so soon.

There was no sign of Ted outside. His partner had yet to go through his own interview, which, hopefully, would be kept short now their version of the event had received some back up.

Jules climbed into his Merc and vented his fury with Sinclair, banging his hand down on the steering wheel. *Batard! Batard!* Then he switched on the engine and drove out of the back entrance at speed.

At the same time Sam sped out of the front one, eager to get home. But as she entered the main road she forgot to look both ways, and almost caused a collision with a driver racing up behind her. He blared his horn in protest and knowing she'd been in the wrong she raised her hand in apology, before driving on.

Jules had to skid to a halt as a car coming from the front entrance zipped in front of him. The bloody nerve! He blared his horn in protest. Saw the driver wave a hand in an apology. A woman. He peered more closely and only then did he see who it was.

It was easy to recognize the victim whose life he'd saved. Particularly as she'd just given evidence on his behalf at the station. She'd probably found this as hard as he had found his interview. Any anger he'd felt dissipated and was replaced by a feeling of gratitude.

In a spirit of camaraderie, he stayed on her tail as she drove through Wimbledon. She took the back route to avoid the high street, something he'd also intended to do. They both meandered past the famous tennis grounds, recently packed with fans from all over the world, eager to watch players like Djokovic demonstrate his spectacular skill. A very different event to the violent one of yesterday.

He followed at a discreet distance as she drove up a road leading back towards the high street. He pulled into the side as she turned into a narrow street. Then watched as she eased her car under a leafy ash tree, its branches spreading over the roof of a Victorian semi, the first in a row. There was a flash of a slim leg as she climbed out, her movements graceful as she walked to a small front gate, unlatched it, and arrived at her door, green painted, with a colourful glass inset. Then she was safely inside and gone from his sight.

He sat for a moment relishing the satisfaction of seeing her home safely, before driving away.

6

Home again, Sam felt a need to be out in the fresh air. To take a stroll on the common as she usually did at this time of day. She'd been told the assailant was a lone operator and not to be worried, but dare she risk it?

Before her nerves got the better of her she ran upstairs and changed into her tracksuit and trainers. Other people would be out jogging, she reasoned, and she could tag along behind them safely. As a last thought she fished out the rape alarm, before heading down and out through the front door.

The police patrol car was parked, but the two officers inside were too busy talking to see her sneak across the road. She didn't want any fuss.

She had to dodge around a queue of cars to cross the main road. She walked over to the pond and stood for a moment watching families feeding the ducks. Normal life was going on as though nothing terrible had happened.

She headed for the track, which other runners were already pounding along. She tried to chase after them but found her limbs were still too weak. A slight drizzle started falling and she took cover under an avenue of trees.

The greenery gave a sense of tranquility. Cocooned in nature, she leant her forehead on the cool of a damp trunk. When she looked up and saw raindrops glistening in an array of spider's webs, the world still full of beauty, she felt tears pricking. Only these were ones of gratitude at being alive, and in moments she was sobbing with relief.

Jules was trapped in the queue of traffic on the main road. The smell of petrol fumes was nauseating. At the first chance, he turned off into a lane running alongside the common, and parked in a grassy layby.

The heathland was spread out invitingly before him. A run was too hard to resist. A slight drizzle of rain had started falling, so he reached into the back seat for his hoodie.

He climbed out, plugged in his ear phones and allowed, 'The Eye of the Tiger,' a song from his favourite rock band to propel him forwards, as he headed for the track in the distance.

He gave the damp ground a good drubbing. He was so relishing the chance to release the tension that he failed to see the puddle until he'd stepped into it and water had splashed onto his jeans. He stopped to brush it off. As he did his ear plugs fell out, and instead of hearing music, he heard crying. He raised his head and saw it came from a woman not far ahead, her head leant on a tree trunk, as she sobbed.

Merde! He couldn't just jog past and ignore her. He walked up slowly.

Sam heard him coming. She brushed away the tears, and turned to see a lone man.

As he came closer, Jules saw, to his alarm, it was she. He jerked to a stop. It was one thing to follow Sam Elliot in his car in a hidden gesture of camaraderie, but to come face to face like this was insanity. He could have kicked himself for even thinking of taking a run in this vicinity. He stood in confusion.

Sam felt a shiver go through her seeing a strange man glowering at her. She just wanted him gone. But he didn't move. He stood as though transfixed. She glanced around, saw that the other runners were far ahead, and felt a rising panic. She went hot and cold. Her heart started pounding. She reached into her pocket for Andrea's alarm and held it up. But before she could use it she felt an acute pain in her chest. Next thing she was doubled over, and gasping for breath.

Jules knew a panic attack when he saw one. He couldn't just leave her. He'd have to help her through it, particularly as he seemed to be the cause. He could only hope that the balaclava he'd worn during the attack had done its job, and that she wouldn't recognize him.

He took control and spoke in a firm but kind voice. 'I can help you through this, if you do as I say.' She wasn't in any position to argue, poor woman. 'Take shallow breaths and let the air out slowly.' She tried but choked. Her hand rose to her neck and touched the scarf tied around it, there, he surmised, to hide her wound.

He was reminded of the hell she'd been through. 'Try again,' he said, more gently, and she managed to snatch a breath. 'That's it. You're doing well. Take another. And another. Keep going. It will soon ease.' He focused on her eyes, pale and poignant.

Sam felt her head was swimming, but understood the man who'd scared her was now trying to help her. Maybe he was no one to worry about and she'd become paranoid. She clung to his eyes, dark and steady, and listened to his mellow voice, noting the slight accent – Was it French? Her brain wasn't working.

'Imagine you're lying on a sandy beach, waves lapping to the shore. The sun warming you...' It went on.

She clung to the image. Allowed her mind to drift, until the panic subsided, and she could relax a little. After a while she was able to straighten up and she let out a long breath of relief.

He smiled. 'Better?'

It was such a nice smile she risked one back. 'I think I may have over reacted.' She felt embarrassed now.

He shrugged. 'With no one else around it was understandable. But no need to be afraid, I'm just a tourist passing through.' The lie would have to do. She nodded anyway. 'I'm sorry I scared you.'

A slight breeze through the trees made the leaves rustle and for a moment they were suspended in time. An indefinable feeling passed between them, as if a bond was being formed, one that was elusive, but also compelling.

Jules recalled a Chinese Proverb that said - *if you save someone's life you are then responsible for that person* - and he felt the power of this.

Sam felt the warm rush of gratitude towards the tourist for calming her down.

A group of runners appeared. They were not alone anymore. Jules came out of his reverie, gave her a farewell nod, walked away, then broke into a run.

As Sam watched his figure disappearing she felt a strange sense of loss.

Desperate to be home again, she followed the group of runners back across the common. The traffic had eased by the time she reached the main road. A few streets on she was at her front door, the house, her only real sanctuary.

Jules returned to his car stirred up by the experience. He feared the lie he'd told about being a tourist might not hold. That he wouldn't get away with this another time. In future he'd stick to his usual haunt of running along the embankment in Putney. Stay in his own area. Better still he should leave London as the commander had suggested, and avoid meeting Sam Elliot ever again.

7

Sam went straight to the kitchen and drank a full glass of water. She was about to head upstairs and take a shower when both her phones rang simultaneously. She picked up her mobile first. 'Is that Samantha Elliot? I'm from the Sun newspaper.' She switched the wretched journalist off.

The same thing happened with the landline. She'd been found. When they both started ringing again she escaped upstairs, where she lay on the bed, sank her face into the pillow, and in a muffled voice begged to be left alone as panic hit again. She tried to allow the image of the sea to calm her but without the Frenchman's kindly voice it didn't work so well.

After a while she rose, peeled off her clothes, and opted for the comfort of a warm bath. But lying naked in the water, she felt like a piece of meat waiting to be sliced up, and she climbed out.

She dressed and went downstairs, where she looked out of the kitchen window at the Hollyhocks and sunflowers standing tall. She wished she could do the same. Not be reduced to a wilting wallflower, by panic and fright.

When Andrea's familiar voice shouted over the garden gate Sam ran to open it, using the key hidden under a flower pot. 'Am I glad to see you,' she cried. Maybe she couldn't survive this on her own.

'I couldn't get through on either of your phones. I was worried about you,' said Andrea.

'I had to switch them off as journalists were hounding me. Come inside.'

'The TV announcers are digging up your past,' said Andrea as they had a strong cup of tea. 'They've mentioned your divorce and your acting career. You never told me you were in a popular drama and had a following.'

Sam leant against the back of the kitchen sink. 'I was only sixteen. It's where I met Simon. We married a few years later.' She shrugged. 'He was the star of the show.'

'Really?'

Sam fell silent. Now, didn't feel the time to explain more.

'I can't imagine marrying a star. My husband's so ordinary.'

Sam knew Jeremy, an accountant by trade, spent his days adding up figures, and working all the hours god gave him on behalf of his family. Why couldn't she have picked an unpretentious man like him.

'I had a fright on the common,' she told Andrea. 'A lone man appeared and I had a panic attack. I pulled out your alarm but hadn't the time to use it.' She pulled out the hanky, the one the firearms officer had given her, and wiped away a tear. 'As it turned out the stranger wasn't harmful at all. Just a tourist who stayed to help me. There was something arresting about him. He calmed me down.' She shook her head. 'But it didn't last. I came home, felt safe for five minutes, but when journalists started calling and harassing me, I panicked again.' She broke down.

Andrea put an arm around her shoulder. 'Maybe you should go away for a while. To your Mum in Dorset, perhaps?'

'She wants me too, but why should I be driven out of Wimbledon when I've only just moved here.' Sam wiped her eyes, then blew her nose. 'I hate feeling so disempowered.'

Andrea sighed. 'I'll make us a coffee. We need to find a way to deal with this.'

Sam sat down at the table whilst Andrea glanced out of the window and admired the garden. 'You've made it such a haven.' She opened the window and breathed. 'The smell of the gardenia hedge is heavenly,' she praised. Then let out a cry of dismay, 'Oh god, a man's climbing over it with a camera around his neck.'

Sam went to peer over her shoulder and saw the shabbily dressed figure coming across the lawn towards them. 'Shit!'

'Duck,' cried Andrea, as he came up to the window, and she pulled Sam below it with her.

There was a tapping on the glass. 'Can I have one photo, please?' A voice called through. 'It could help revive your acting career, Samantha.'

Sam rose like Medea. 'I don't give a damn about my career. If you don't bugger off, I'll call the police.'

He slunk away.

'That feels better,' said Sam.

Andrea rose. She knew her friend needed to work and earn money. 'Maybe you should return to acting,' she suggested.

Sam shuddered at the thought. Acting would feel too exposing. Odd how a career that she'd spent most of her life working for seemed all wrong. All she wanted to do was to hide.

They retreated to the sitting room at the front of the house. The window looked out onto the street.

Andrea peeked. 'Dammit, there are news vans arriving. Journalists with microphones are piling out. 'They'll be at the front door any moment. You have to get away, Sam.' Andrea half pushed her friend back into the kitchen, where she plugged the landline back into the wall. 'Call your mother,' she commanded.

It seemed the only answer. When Mother gave her unwavering support, Sam put down the phone feeling fortunate to have a bolt hole. She made Andrea promise not to tell anyone where she was going, then rushed upstairs to pack a few clothes for her and Milly.

Andrea made mugs of steaming coffee, which she carried outside to the street. The journalists helped themselves, and ignoring their questions she returned indoors, leaving them to their speculations.

When Sam reappeared, her friend offered to help her to slip away unseen, as the press were now preoccupied. The pair headed out the back way. Sam's car was parked under the ash tree. The suitcase was slipped into the boot. Andrea sat in the driving seat, while Sam hid in the well behind it.

Her friend then eased the car into the road. The journalists looked over in surprise, and Andrea gave them a cheeky wave before speeding away. 'I feel like an actress myself,' she joked as one or two chased after them. When they realized that the person driving wasn't Samantha Elliot, they gave up. Andrea, delighted her rout had worked, headed for the sanctuary of her own home.

Once there, Sam took her place in the driving seat, and thanked her good friend for helping her.

'I'll let you know when it's safe to return.' Andrea waved her away.

Arriving at the school, Sam saw a couple of journalists at the school gates, so she sneaked around to the back. Miss Potter spotted her, and helped her slip in through a side door.

In the classroom the other children were agog at the subterfuge of Milly being spirited away.

'Where are we going, Mummy?'

'To Granny, by the sea.'

'Whoopie!' cried Milly, in an enviable mood of adventure.

Belted up they set off. Sam became nervous she was being followed as she headed out of London for the M 3. A car was hot her heels. She fretted a journalist was hounding them until the car disappeared up a slip road. 'Thank God, Milly, it's gone,' she said in relief.

But her daughter was too excited about seeing Granny to be worried about anything.

Sam only wished she could feel the same. She couldn't believe that in such a short space of time her plan for a new, happy, independent life in Wimbledon could have gone so awry. That instead she'd be fleeing to the depths of Dorset with no idea when it would be safe to return.

Back at his apartment, Jules stared out of his panoramic window at the river, the tide low enough to allow mud larkers to be out searching for hidden treasures - Roman coins, planks of old timber from ships, old clay pipes. It was fascinating what could be found. At any other time, he would have joined in, not hide inside like a wanted man.

His mobile pinged and Ted Rowlands started venting his feelings about his own interview.

'They blamed me for my bodycam jamming instead of admitting police equipment is old and fucking useless. They also suggested we had it in for Ahmed because he'd made us look incompetent by slipping under our radar. That you shot him in revenge with me encouraging you.' Ted took a breath. 'Sinclair's been watching too many movies on Netflix, if you ask me.' Jules smiled inwardly at this. 'Thank god that woman came in to give her statement. An angel of mercy is that actress.'

Jules mumbled his agreement but said no more, afraid he'd let slip about the brief meeting he'd just had with her.

'At least they've given us paid leave,' Ted continued. 'I'm taking the wife and kids to Brighton on our first holiday for years. Where are you going?'

Jules had only just started thinking about it. His idea of going to France had been stymied. Hiking in the French alps would have been glorious if he'd been allowed to leave the country.

Ted switched off and Jules was left to contemplate his options. He could visit his relatives in Colchester, but as he'd only been back a few times since his mother had died, he felt out of touch. He'd been more concerned to build a new life for himself in London.

The other choice would be to visit his sniper partner from his time in Afghanistan. Leo Henshaw lived on a farm in the wilds of the Salisbury Plain, near to the military base where they'd both trained. His loyalty was unquestionable.

Jules found his number and drummed his fingers on the coffee table, whilst waiting for him to answer.

His mate's jaunty voice barrelled down the phone.

'Strike me dead if it's not the lad who had my back in the worst place on earth. What the devil do you want, Jules? Are you tired of being a boring copper?'

Leo was a big man, with a big voice, and a big heart. Jules felt his spirits rise. 'If you must know,' he answered. 'The anti-terrorist unit is not unlike being in Helmand. All quiet until hell breaks loose.'

'And has it?'

'You could say.'

'Well, you'd better escape to my oasis in the middle of nowhere,' Leo boomed.

I'm on my way,' said Jules.

8

'Dorset'

Sam sped along the M3 in her Golf convertible. She'd bought it with money from the divorce settlement, wanting a car that would provide some light relief from the difficulties in ending her marriage. As they reached open countryside she rolled back the roof and let the breeze blow her troubles away.

Milly asked to sit in the front beside her, not entirely legal, but Sam relented, and drove in the slow lane.

She found some music. 'Fight Song,' soon had her singing with gusto, and Milly did her best to join in. Rachel Platten's lyrics about taking back one's life, of finding one's power, of proving you'd be alright, rallied them both.

Sam cruised through Hampshire. They bypassed the ancient city of Winchester, a place of spirituality and learning with its the medieval cathedral and historic buildings. Once the seat of 'Alfred The Great, it had a sense of perpetuity. Knowing it had survived through the ages revived her hope she could endure her own ordeal.

She'd soon crossed the border into Dorset where she headed for the coast.

When the sea came into view across the cliff tops, a vivid mass of white capped waves, Milly squealed with delight. The Jurassic coastline, ninety-six miles in all, was famous for its ancient rocks and prehistoric fossils. It was a place for discoveries. A place to go back in time. A place where the horrors of the last days would surely dissipate...

Sam had been concerned when Mother had removed herself to the countryside not long after Father had died. When the family house had sold quickly, Mother had simply upped sticks and left for good. It was hard to fathom how a Londoner, born and bred, would manage living in such an isolated place. But her artistic, bohemian spirit, had proved to be her saviour. She'd focused on her creativity, and her painter's eye had relished the entirely different scenery. 'You can visit me in paradise, whenever you like, darling…' she'd tried to reassure her daughter.

But Sam had felt bereft. It was as if she'd lost both her parents. Their marriage had been strong and supportive. Left behind in London it wasn't long before the problems in her own had become untenable. Only a year later, perhaps following her mother's example, Sam had made a similarly radical decision. Simon's acting career had taken a downward turn and he'd taken to drinking. Money had fallen short, and forced to sell their large house, one he loved more than her she'd discovered to her cost, he became physically violent.

It took a while to leave him and make a new beginning with little Milly. The chosen place was the quiet suburb of Wimbledon. It had offered life in the slow and the fast lane at the same time, with the common spanning out around them, and London only a stone's throw away. It was hard that someone had come along to spoil it. Now, just like her mother, Sam wanted to hide in the countryside.

Navigating the winding lanes to reach Mother's cottage was always a challenge. Sam usually took a few wrong turnings avoiding lethal potholes, or streams that had flooded, or errant sheep that escaped from the fields.

Milly loved to direct her. 'Not that way, Mummy! Or that way either. Nincompoop!' Peals of laughter.

Today was no different. It was a relief to arrive and find Mother waiting in the driveway. The moment the car came to a halt Milly leapt out and ran straight into her arms.

Milly's version of the terrible events spilled out. 'We've had to flee Granny. A bad man tried to hurt Mummy, but a good one saved her, and then journalists chased us out of London.' She sounded half excited, half terrified by the tale.

'Darling, you're safe with me,' comforted Stella Elliot.

'Is my bedroom just the same?'

'Of course, it is.'

Milly rushed inside to check.

Sam climbed out. Seeing her mother, tears sprang.

'Dear girl,' her mother held her until she'd stopped crying.

When Sam stepped back, her scarf shifted, and her mother saw the large dressing on her neck. 'Oh God, is that where...?'

Sam nodded.

'Will it heal?'

Sam fetched out her hanky and blew her nose. 'I may have a scar, but it doesn't seem to matter in the scale of things.' She pulled the scarf back into place.

'Are you hiding it from Milly?' asked her mother.

'Not just from her, but everyone, until it's healed ...I don't want their revulsion.'

'Mother led the way in. 'What matters is that your alive and well.' I have tea, and a freshly made chocolate cake to help take your mind off things. Whatever is the world coming to?'

Sam could see how living here had done wonders for her mother. That Dorset had been an inspired choice. Mother was everything a granny should be, as she fussed over Milly, and gave all the sympathy needed.

The cottage had a nautical charm about it. From the bedrooms, you could see the sea rolling across the channel. Hers was the smallest with a single bed, as though she was still a little girl. Milly's room was slightly bigger and full of games and play things, with the family bathroom next door. At the far end of the corridor lay the master, or rather the mistress's bedroom, with an ensuite.

Sam unpacked their few things, then freshened herself up, checked that the dressing was holding well, before joining Milly and her mother downstairs.

The cake was relished by then all, after which Milly performed cartwheels outside on the lawn until she was worn out. When it came to bedtime, the sea air rendered her asleep almost before her head hit the pillow.

Sam joined her mother outside. The evening air dusky from the smoke spiraling from a cigarette.

'I've become more of a bohemian without your father around to caution me,' said her mother.

Sam remembered how he'd been both entranced and annoyed by

Mother's free-spirited attitude to life. It must at times have seemed incomprehensible to a man who was prepared to give his own for the safety of others. Sam had been so proud of him being a soldier. But she'd also envied the freedom of her mother's work. How she could paint for hours, self-expression being all important.

Mother liked to reminisce about the past, and Sam needed the distraction. She sat listening as her mother recalled how fit Hugh Elliot had always been. 'Enough to run the London marathon year after year. He was very… physical.' Sam had to smile at her mother's need for her to know this. 'He saved so many lives dismantling landmines, and was in Angola when Princess Diana did her brave walk…' This was a story often told. 'It was a pity she married a prince who turned into a frog.' She leaned back and added rather naughtily. 'A bit like your husband.'

'You never liked Simon, did you?'

'He had great charm. But there was a lack of an inner core. And he seemed so angry about everything.' She paused. 'He didn't ever…?'

'I don't want to talk about it,' Sam brushed this away.

'Well, he seemed taken over by the characters he was playing.'

'A lot of actors are. I was taken over by mine too, sometimes.'

But you're not acting anymore, are you? Not pretending to be someone else.'

Sam shook her head. 'I've never felt more real in my life. But it's raw, and I'm on edge all the time.'

Her mother reached for her hand. 'A near death experience is devastating, your father often said. But he also felt it could be transforming. Working as he did with so much risk, life felt precious to him every single day.'

'Until it didn't.' Sam said this bitterly. Her father had lost his life when one of the mines he was dismantling inevitably blew up, his body scattered. 'Boom and I'll be dust!' he'd used to make a joke of the possibility of this. As a little girl it had made Sam giggle. She'd no understanding of what it really meant. Her father's absence for long periods had been disconcerting, but to have him never to return had been devastating, and the loss was still hard to bear

Her mind slipped back to Wimbledon the day of the attack, when the bomb disposal experts had arrived. How she'd trembled, fearing an explosion, knowing how close this was to how her father had died.

She changed the subject. 'Do you still have his philosophy books?'

'Of course.'

'They might help me make some sense of things.'

'They might indeed. Your father was always more introspective than me. I like to seize the moment - carpe diem.' She offered Sam a cigarette. 'Go on, you can seize it too, can't you?'

Sam had always felt more akin to her father with his thoughtful approach to life, his desire to be healthy in mind and body, and to search for meaning in everything. But feeling rebellious now, she took a cigarette, lit up, inhaled, and blew the smoke out in a long stream, and it did give some release.

Her mother reached out in the darkness to pat her hand. 'One day you'll find a good man just like your father, darling.'

'Hard to imagine when I fear each one I meet is going to attack me.' Sam stubbed out the cigarette, the taste of tobacco turning bitter.

'You must embrace the countryside, Sam. Nature really is the great healer. Look what it's done for me. There's no need to return to London until September when Milly starts proper school.'

'I haven't brought enough clothes to stay for long, and I have to start earning money.

'Well, don't think about that now. I can tide you over.'

'Thanks, but I want to do it myself, Mum,'

They sat in silence. Broken only by the sound of an owl hooting in the distance, and the continuous roll of the incoming tide.

9

A farm situated in the wilds of the countryside felt the perfect place to escape to. Jules hadn't been invited there in his soldier days. It had been Leo's private haven. Now his mate seemed eager to share it.

The chance to speed the Mercedes along a motorway was also relished. Jules felt that the 2009 SLK class convertible was the one good thing his father had ever given him. He recalled the shock he'd had when *Père* had made an unwelcome appearance at Mother's funeral. Having so abused her during their marriage it had felt hypocritical. It hadn't taken long to discover the real motive was not to mourn her, but to reclaim his prodigal son.

It was outside the crematorium that Henri Caron had made the offer of a partnership in his dubious business back in France. Stating it was a duty his one and only son owed to him. In a tense exchange Jules had explained he preferred to be on the right side of law, merci, that too many criminals frequented the casinos. His furious father was about to storm off, but at the last moment had made a confusing but conciliatory gesture. Having observed his son's interest in his impressive car, he'd gifted it. 'Prenez-le comme votre héritage. Vous n'aurez rien d'autre. Au revoir!'

Jules understood he could expect nothing more, as without a backward glance, Henri Caron had been driven away in a taxi, a cloud of dust left smouldering in the air.

The car was accepted as compensation for all the violent, drunken outbursts his Father couldn't control.

Jules drove faster as old hurts surfaced. His mother being brutally knocked to the ground. How, as a boy, he'd rushed to her aid only to be given a back hander. It had happened again and again. In the end his mother and he had fled to relatives in England. At fourteen, Jules had said adieu to the France he loved, and all his friends, just to get away from his wretched father. It made him angry just thinking about it.

As the wooded hills and hedge rowed fields of Berkshire came into view, Jules remembered how disappointed he'd been by the English countryside when he'd first arrived. How the Essex area around Colchester had seemed flat and featureless compared to the majesty of the French Alps, the backdrop to his home city of Nice.

Somebody blared their horn. He moved into the next lane, and at the first slip road, turned off. Then drove more slowly to have time to admire the gentle landscape around him.

It wasn't long before the panoramic vista of the Salisbury Plain appeared, with a majesty of its own. Almost hedge less, even tree less, with a wild, windswept beauty. Plateau chalk hills expanded for miles, and with fresh air blowing over him Jules began to breathe more easily. This was the England he could embrace. The sky was a deep summer blue and for the first time in days his anxiety started to ebb away.

When Stonehenge came into view, the monolithic stones glinting in the sunshine, drew his attention. He swerved off the road and into the car park. He loved this iconic place.

He tagged along behind a guide leading a group of tourists through a tunnel under the road. The Japanese visitors seemed more interested in taking photographs than listening to the older woman, who took her work to heart, and looked to Jules for approval. He alone learned Stonehenge went back to three thousand BC, and that there was bone data to prove this. He marvelled at the Sarsen standing stones, each one weighing around twenty-five tons. The inner circle of bluestones had been dragged, pulled, or rolled over logs to reach here, transported over a hundred miles from Wales, an unbelievable feat. The circular design was arranged like a celestial observatory, where predictions of eclipse and the equinox took place. Hundreds of visitors arrived every year to witness the summer and winter solstice.

Jules admired the structure of the smart visitors centre before he left. Grey glass, steel and timber structure with a sloping roof, made it merge into the landscape, seamlessly. He returned to the car in an inspired state of mind.

He drove on past the barbed wire fences, the sign the plain was also used for exercises on the hundred and fifty acres owned by the military. It was pleasing to see his old training ground was in good shape.

It took longer to find the narrow lane leading to the farm, with open grassland surrounding a sleepy looking stone house, a real homestead.

Jules disturbed the peace as he drove into the yard. Cackling geese and squawking hens flapped out of his way, and a sheep dog bounded out of the house to greet him. Followed by his giant of a friend, six feet five, Leo's weathered face was wreathed in smiles.

Jules climbed out of his car.

'I'm so glad to see you here,' Leo boomed out his welcome. 'Can't wait to show around my thousand acres of farmland.'

'A thousand? I'm impressed.' Jules knew his mate's decision to leave the army had not been without regret. That taking over the reins from his ageing father, had been done mainly, out of necessity.

'I saw barbed wire erected a little way back,' Jules added with a knowing nod.

'Well, the army's all around us. We rent the land from the MOD. They own it.' Leo explained. 'Tanks and trucks all over the bloody place when they do their war games.'

'And you thought you'd left soldiering behind.'

'Not entirely,' Leo chuckled.

Jules just managed to stretch his legs before Leo insisted on giving him a tour. Marching him around barns stacked to the roof with bales of hay and stacks of silage. And cowsheds stinking of manure with cattle lowing in the stalls. When they moved towards a smaller barn Leo gave a wink, though Jules didn't understand why until his friend flung back the doors.

Inside was an entirely different venture from farming. Instead, a professional gymnasium had been set up. First rate equipment, pummel bags, weights, exercise machines, chest and leg presses, along with skipping ropes, pumps, training shoes of all sizes, and boxing gloves laid out ready. Jules relished the large netted cage in the far corner, which he knew was for martial arts training. He hadn't visited his gym in Putney enough. His police work had taken up too much time. But he knew that exercise was always the best way to dispel his anger. 'This is just what I need, Leo.'

'I've formed a club,' his friend said proudly. 'I'm not short of members either. Army personnel are eager to practice combat routines.' Leo punched a pummel bag so it swung about. 'And,' he added with a broad smile. 'I've even got housewives signing up to learn how to defend themselves against men who should know better. Krav Maga is all the rage.'

Jules caught hold of the pummel bag. *Bam!* He punched it hard.

'In fact,' Leo continued. 'I've so many women wanting to train, it won't be long before I'll need a partner.' He gave Jules an intent look. 'I don't suppose you'd be interested?'

'You must be joking.'

'Seriously, I'm going to need someone and soon.'

'Well, I'm not planning on leaving the police,' he paused. 'Unless they give me the boot.'

Leo looked at him curiously, and led the way out of the barn. Jules wasn't sure when or even if he should tell his mate the real reason he was here, and drag him into it. But as they walked across the yard Leo started questioning him.

'I expect it's easier being on patrol in London than it was Afghanistan.'

'At least in Helmand you knew who the enemy was,' he answered. 'In London it can be anybody. An accountant, a lawyer, even a student can launch a sudden assault.' He fell silent still not ready to say more.

Leo, not understanding, gestured to the land. 'Well, with the MOD exercises on the plain, I feel I'm back in the throes of ambush and assault myself. Or at least the preparations for war. I've had to dodge real bullets at times, and repair electric fences that tanks knock down. If we want to move our animals to a different grazing area we must ask for permission. I had a hell of an argument with the Colonel about this only last week.'

'I'd like to have seen that.' Jules felt he should find some of Leo's spirit for himself.

Back in the yard, he pulled his bag from the boot of his car and they walked towards the house, a sheep or two grazing on the small lawn before it. 'Is it mainly sheep and cows?'

'Hardy ones, capable of giving birth unassisted, when I can't reach them.'

'It sounds like a huge responsibility.'

'It's also rewarding. I've had time to put down roots and get to know the locals.' He gave a sheepish grin. 'A farmer needs a wife, if you know what I mean.'

Jules shook his head in disbelief. In Helmand he and Leo had preferred to play the field with nurses from the local hospitals, all happy to have casual sex. It had suited when their lives could be lost in a moment, and any commitment seemed pointless.

Leo cleared his throat as though half embarrassed by his obvious change of heart. 'I met a woman recently, but she doesn't live around here. A friend she was visiting brought her along to watch one of my classes. They stayed for a drink and Veronica and I hit it off. She lives in the next county of Dorset, and I'm planning a hike along the coast to pay her a visit.'

They went into the house, where Leo kicked off his boots in the narrow corridor. 'You should come with me Jules. A hike would be like old times, and I'd like your opinion on whether she's suitable marriage material.'

'How on earth would I know, Leo?'

Leo smiled. 'Underneath that cool exterior lies a shrewd judge of character.' He poked Jules's arm.

'Mon Dieu.' He couldn't help liking that Leo appreciated his more serious side.

'Let's have a beer.' Leo led the way into the kitchen with its comfortable flag stone floors, cats lying on any vacant chair, and the sheep dog called Jock stretched out on the mat. In a rocking chair by the unlit fire an old man sat snoring. 'Dad will sleep through anything,' chuckled Leo.

They sat down drinking from the bottles. 'I stopped for a stroll around Stonehenge, incredible place,' said Jules.

'It's bonkers, if you ask me,' said Leo. 'People come to pay homage to death and rebirth. Revellers and pagans dance around the stone bedecked in garlands and flowers, chanting, and bowing to the gods. They think they see the faces of people long dead in the Sarsen stones. Dad loves the mystique, whereas I think it's a load of codswallop.'

Jules gave a wry smile. He was also skeptical about anything less than scientific. His interest was taken up by the construction of the site, more than in its fables.

They moved on to talk about their soldiering days. Not many people understood the sweat, the raw fear, and yet the glory of it. Leo's father, asleep in the corner didn't wake up even as they, in turn, recounted how many times they'd almost got killed, with Leo making explosive sounds to describe landmines blowing up. Or when insurgents shot back at them as they became exposed on the rooftops, like open targets. How they'd learned to run and leap from house to house like monkeys.

They recalled the amazing technology. Like the unmanned air vehicle called the Black Hornet, which buzzed ahead on patrols. Only ten centimeters long, it was like a large bee flying in and out of houses unnoticed, programmed to send back information about what was happening inside. Were insurgents gathered there? Was ammunition being stock piled? Were they about to launch an attack?

'Those hornets were straight out of sci-fi movies,' chuckled Leo, as he showed Jules up to the attic. Rickety stairs led to a large and welcoming room, a comfy bed and staggering views across the open plain.

'Do you miss the army?' asked Jules.

'Not much now the Americans have pulled out of Afghanistan.' He shook his head. 'How could they let the Taliban back into power? They've made a mockery of all our efforts, and the lives of Afghans a misery again.'

'Do you know what's happened to Salim and Abdul, our interpreter friends?' The pair had looked out for them when they were there.

Leo shook his head. 'They should be able to come and live here. But they'll need the right papers. I'm going to look into it.'

He left, and Jules threw the window open. He could only relish his own bit of freedom as he breathed in the animal scented air. Leo had told him they didn't use any fertilizer or pesticides on the farm, that there was nothing chemical, and it felt a clean and decent way of life.

His bag unpacked, he lay down on the bed, and dozed for a good hour. When he woke, he was being called down to supper.

Leo's father was already sitting at the table, a serviette stuffed under his chin, a plate of stew steaming before him. Old Tom had a friendly, if almost toothless smile. He obviously relished having his son back home. Leo's mother had died when he was a lad and the easy camaraderie between the two men made Jules a little envious. He'd never enjoyed this sort of repartee with his own father, as their relationship had been too unpredictable. Jules had always been ready to run if needed, a habit he'd found hard to lose.

'I hear you've had to escape from London,' said Old Tom. 'Girl trouble is it?' the old man's eyes twinkled.

Jules gave a nonchalant shrug. 'Kind of...' He'd left to escape the trauma of the attack, but also to avoid meeting the woman involved, Sam Elliot.

He waited until old Tom had retired to bed before he finally told Leo about why he'd really left London. They sat by the dying embers of a fire, Jules's tongue loosened with the help of some rum.

Leo, sworn to secrecy, went from disbelief to horror. 'I don't have time to listen to the news. But an attack in a sleepy suburb like Wimbledon is unbelievable.'

'I only had a split second to take the fatal shot or the woman would have died.'

'It was a hell of decision to make, and with you so new to the job.' Leo scratched his head. 'I can't see what else could you have done.'

'It's waiting for exoneration that's difficult. With all the press interest I worry someone might let slip my name.'

'No one in your unit would dare break the code of ethics, and I shan't tell anyone. Not even Dad. The fact is you saved a life and deserve praise for it.'

'Were we praised for what we did in Afghanistan?' Jules's medal set apart, the British public were less than enthusiastic. It was a salutary lesson to return home to find they had mixed views about soldiers, half admiring, half loathing them.

'If you need someone to speak up for you, count me in,' said Leo, with feeling.

'Thanks. It will mean a lot.'

They gave one another comradely smiles.

Leo leaned closer. 'Stay here until the enquiry is over. Immerse yourself in cow muck and sheep dung, and you won't have time to think about it.' He rose. 'Meanwhile you need a good night's sleep in preparation for the agony of working on my farm tomorrow.'

10

Sam woke to sunlight flooding into the small cottage bedroom. Comforted by the summer warmth, she dressed, looked inside her daughter's bedroom but found Milly was up already. She found her in the kitchen with Mother, eating a breakfast of freshly squeezed orange juice and toast, with homemade marmalade, laid out in style.

The radio was on and Sam listened while she ate. It wasn't long before the commentator brought up the attack, announcing that an independent police enquiry was being held. That the officers involved had been suspended from their units, pending the result, as they had questions to answer.

'I don't like their critical tone. I'd like to phone in and say they did what they had to,' said Sam.

'Phone who Mummy?' said Milly as she helped herself to cereals.

'The BBC. I don't like what they're saying,' said Sam.

'Well, don't listen to the radio then.' Milly repeated a warning often given to her about the television, as she added two teaspoons of sugar to her cocoa pops.

'Too much sugar, Milly.' Sam's scolding came too late.

'You can't phone in,' said her mother, more concerned about her daughter being discovered in Dorset. 'They could track you down. No one knows you're here, do they?'

'Only Andrea, and she won't tell.'

'You must keep it that way. I don't want to be under siege.'

Sam went upstairs. In the bathroom, she slipped off her scarf, and checked the dressing again. It was becoming a nervous habit. It was still in place and there was no blood leaking through. She didn't dare look underneath, but as the skin around it looked normal, it must be healing.

She looked in the cabinet to see if there were any new dressings, knowing she'd need to replace it soon. In her haste to leave she'd forgotten to bring the new ones given by the doctor. Here, there was only a pack of ordinary plasters and none were big enough. It was the same in Mother's ensuite. Catching sight of hair in the mirror, Sam was appalled to see how brazen her blonde streaks looked. Maybe, when she felt brave enough, she could venture into Bridport, buy some more dressings, and some hair colouring, too. She could return to her natural look and make it harder for anyone to recognize her. Then she might not have to hide away like a fugitive.

She left the bathroom in a more bouyant mood.

Jules woke in the middle of the night, his sleep broken by a hideous dream. *He took the fatal shot, but instead of hitting the attacker, the bullet struck Sam Elliot, and it was she who slumped down dead.* Drenched in sweat, he had to take a shower before returning to bed, and even then, he only slept fitfully.

The next morning, there was no chance to dwell on this night time delusion, as he was kept busy helping Leo with the harvest. He sat alongside his mate in the cab of a noisy combine harvester, as it cut the ripe and golden barley. Shaped into bales, the next task was to load the trailers, drive back to the farm, and build stacks in the haybarn. It took the whole day and was exhausting work. After a light supper, he went straight to bed, his mind and body too worn out to do anything but sleep.

The next day he worked hard again, until every muscle screamed, and when night time came, he slept through until the morning, his nightmare all but eliminated.

'I'll turn you into a farm worker, yet Jules,' teased Leo. 'Forget about being a bloody policeman.'

Suddenly, it didn't seem such a bad idea.

A few days later, before suppertime, a convoy of jeeps thundered into the yard and out jumped a group of cadets, dressed in camouflage gear. They marched into the converted barn eager for a training session in Leo's gym, sparring with one another before they'd got started, fighting already second nature.

Jules remembered how it had felt when he was at the start of his soldiering career, with the desire to be the best one could be. The SAS commandos had seemed like Gods as they'd put him through endless challenges. His mind and his body were pushed to the extreme. Some days he'd thought he'd go mad with the stress, others he was so exhilarated he'd felt like a God himself.

He went inside and changed into the tracksuit he'd brought, and went over to the gym. Leo was putting the recruits through their warm up moves, doing some heavy weight lifting. Jules knew there was nothing like feeling pumped up, muscles bulging, adrenalin rushing through the veins, head on fire. But it was all a game in here, not real warfare. These youths had yet to experience a life or death issue, which brought an intensity like no other, when the body and mind were focused on one thing, survival.

A pair of them started sparring inside the cage, enclosed by netting, so there was no escape. One was out to attack and the other to defend, punching, kick boxing, kneeing, karate chopping.

Jules stood to one side appraising them as they grappled. John, young and agile was quite balanced, whereas Connor kept toppling over. He was hit often as he was slow to dodge out of the way. His face was soon bloodied, his skin bruised. The trick of self defence was to use avoidance tactics and wait for the chance to hit back. Connor was not good at this.

Leo suggested he and Jules gave them a demonstration. He'd be the aggressor, Jules would defend himself. They started sparring, moving around the cage appraising one another for strengths and weaknesses. Leo knew Jules could move faster than a rodeo horse when it came to manoeuvring out of the way. That he'd need to make his attacks more complex to disable his mate. But Jules retaliated in kind, his ferocity and speed took Leo by surprise. A kick to the groin had him doubled over, a karate chop to his arm almost broke it, and a trip onto the floor allowed Jules to get on top and start punching without mercy.

Leo struggled to get away but was grabbed by the throat in a choke hold. Jules squeezed so he could hardly breathe. 'No need to bloody kill me, mate,' he growled.

Realising that he'd gone too far, Jules quickly pulled his hands away and looked at them in horror. What was happening to him? 'Mon

Dieu, Leo, I'm sorry.' He shoved them into his pockets, out of harm's way.

His mate ended the session with pointed words of caution to the men who'd been watching. 'Combat and self-defence techniques go hand in hand. You can't have one without the other. We train that others may walk in peace remember. That's the only motive justifies the carnage of war. Never forget it. We are not animals.' He gave Jules a glance. 'We are trained to defend people.'

The lads gave one another ironic looks. They'd rather enjoyed seeing one man beat the hell out of another.

They went to take showers and started fooling around. Then departed for a night out in the market town of Andover, sex, with local girls the next challenge.

'Be respectful,' Leo called after them, and shook his head.

As they showered Leo showed Jules the purple mark around his neck. 'What the hell came over you?'

'I'm more shaken up than I care to admit. I've had some bad dreams, and I'm still angry.'

'Well, lucky it was me being your punch bag. Someone else might not be so well disposed. You'd better get a hold of yourself.'

'I'll get my control back, don't worry.'

They dressed and returned to the house for a light supper. No more was said. But Leo kept a closer eye on his friend from then on.

As they ate, Leo's father took to telling stories about local folklore. By the time Jules retired to bed his mind was filled with tales about smugglers, Mummers plays, and Morris dancers. His own turmoil was eased by old Tom's warmth and humour. The different view of life was mystical and sleep making.

Another week went by with Jules proving to be a helpful pair of hands in the gym, as well as on the farm. He even joined in with a class for women and was the model of chivalry as he taught the principles of Krav Maga. He explained how every move should be clean and logical. That they should focus on self defence, stay on their feet, and keep moving, whilst always seeking the chance to escape. They should go for the attacker's weak points, the nose, the throat, the ankles, using palm strikes, and fingers to poke at the eyes. He showed them groin kicks and aggressive punches. His speed and technique proved so impressive that, much to Leo's amusement, some of the women asked for private lessons.

Jules was relieved to be back in his mate's good books. He'd always valued Leo's trust and didn't want to lose it. When he was asked again if he'd like to go on a hike along the Dorset coastline, it was hard to refuse. Particularly when he heard there was a music festival on in the town they were headed for.

'The first one to be held after the lockdowns,' his mate grinned. 'Everyone will be out to celebrate. There'll be country dancing, and later - *Latino.*'

Jules had spent his early youth enjoying doing the Salsa in the open squares in France, and the idea of dancing, appealed.

End of the week, Leo pulled out a map and planned the route. 'It'll be about twenty miles along the amazing Jurassic coastline, famous for fossils and antiquities from prehistoric times. You'll love it, my friend.' Jules smiled, feeling a real interest now. 'We'll head for Beer first, have a draft there, of course,' Leo grinned. 'Then go on to Lyme Regis.'

'Is that where your girlfriend lives?' asked Jules.

'No, but we should have a bite of lunch in a town famous for its maritime history before finishing up in Bridport.'

'What's Bridport famous for?'

'Rope.'

'*Rope?*'

'In the old days they used it to hang people with it. There's even a term that came from this - 'To be stabbed by a Bridport Dagger.'

'And you still want to end up there?' Jules teased.

'You I we do,' Leo chuckled. He'd arranged for lads from the village to help his father keep the farm ticking over. When Saturday morning arrived, dressed in their hiking gear, their backpacks packed with gum to chew, medical kits, pen knives, bottled water, sandwiches for lunch, and decent outfits for the evening, the pair climbed into Leo's Land Rover and set off for Dorset.

11

Two weeks had gone by and Sam felt it was now a necessity to venture into Bridport. She'd replaced the dressing on her wound with ordinary plasters but they weren't holding too well. She'd taken Milly to the beach and watched her swimming in the shallows whilst only paddling herself. Milly kept asking why she wouldn't join in and her reply, that the water wasn't warm enough, was starting to sound feeble. Sam knew she'd have to swim with her daughter soon.

Saturday morning and boldness was required. Milly was persuaded to stay behind with the promise that Sam would have a proper swim when she returned. She'd sneak into the town, find what she needed, and come straight home.

Still, she couldn't resist meandering along the coast. The sea was like silk, the sky above a vivid blue, and with her car hood rolled down, the air was humming with insects.

She stopped at West Bay to admire the small harbour. It was early, there were only a few people around, and she felt free to wander around the painted fishing boats, the nets laid out to dry on the shingle. Early morning kayakers were skimming back to the shore. And three small children, paddling, were throwing water at one another, and letting out shrieks of joy, a feeling Sam sorely missed.

She drove a little inland and reached the town of Bridport. There were more people about so she put on dark sunglasses and her floppy sunhat to hide herself, before stepping out of the car.

She headed into the narrow streets of quirky shops, cafes and pubs, saw the impressive clock tower, and the intriguing small museum. The windows were stocked with ancient fossils, intricate sea shells, and armour from Roman and Saxon times - a must-see place for Milly. Up an alley she spotted a sign for a chemist and went in. She found some adhesive dressings, just the right size, and added some large plasters. Then she moved on to the hair colourings. But seeing they were full of chemicals, she let out a tut.

Someone standing behind her also disapproved. 'You're right, they're rubbish.' The accent was a Dorset burr.

Sam turned to see a young woman with a long black hair, dressed in a flamboyant country style, check shirt, blue jeans, and even fringed cowboy boots.

The woman peered at her. 'Do you keep your hat and sunglasses on, even inside?'

Sam froze.

Luckily the woman let it go. 'My salon is just up the alley. I've a cancellation in about ten minutes. I could colour your hair with my handpicked products if you like.' And with a disarming smile the hairdresser disappeared.

Hard not to admire her gall. Sam lingered in the chemist, trying to stick to her plan, then headed into the alley. She couldn't help taking a small peak at the tiny salon tucked at the far end.

Inside, the hairdresser was at work blow drying a customer's short crop, nicely styled. A Cody Johnson song, 'Til You Can't,' was playing, and the lyrics, about not putting things off for too long, had an impact on Sam. Seizing the moment, she went inside.

'Welcome to the best hair stylist in this town,' called out the customer having her own finished.

The hairdresser smiled. 'Take a seat and I'll be with you shortly. My name's Chloe by the way. And this yer is June.'

June smiled through the mirror and Sam gave her a quick nod before sliding into a chair provided. She sat listening as Chloe chatted on to June about how depressing the news always was. How she only watched soaps on the TV.

'Me too,' agreed June.

No need to worry about being recognized. Sam took off her sunglasses and hat, and let loose her long hair. On the low table before her lay a pile of magazines. She scooped up, 'Hello.' Why not indulge in reading some gossip? Though celebrities were the last people she wanted to know about, except for the royals. As she peered at photographs of Kate Middleton, her hair a rich chestnut shade, it seemed to be such a good colour that when it came to her turn, she showed it to Chloe.

'I see, you'd like to resemble the future Queen of England for this evening's festivities,' teased the hairdresser.

'What festivities?' Mother hadn't mentioned this. But then she lived in her cottage like a recluse, most of the time.

'Our folk festival, of course. It's held every year towards the end of the summer. Last year was cancelled, so this one's going to be a riot. Even tourists are returning.'

Attending a riotous festival felt a step too far. Sam shook her head. 'I have to be home to put my daughter to bed.' Milly was always a good excuse. 'I'm a single mother.' She shrugged, then wished she hadn't given away this information.

Chloe immediately declared that being a single mother in this town was no handicap. It was almost the norm. 'Girls around here are often left holding the baby with so many army camps around, and soldiers coming and going. You can bring your daughter with you and do some line dancing with me.' Chloe did some steps kicking out her boots.

Sam and Milly had copied some of the moves on a video not long ago. Milly had loved stamping her feet and clapping her hands to the beat.

'I'm already wearing my outfit to advertise the event,' Chloe gestured to her clothes. 'There'll be a bit of Latino later when everyone gets pissed. It'll be worse this year now we have our freedom back.'

Sam sat wishing her freedom could come back too.

The hairdresser screwed up her eyes, and studied her customer through the mirror 'You don't need to go too dark. How about a russet colour? It will cover up these brassy bleached streaks. Who did them?'

'Someone in London.' Sam bit her lip. She'd shouldn't have let this slip either. Luckily Chloe was too intent on her hair to bother.

'Well, I have better ways to keep your sunny look.'

'My sunny look?'

'Oh yes, you radiate.'

Sam sat back liking the sound of this. And rather liking Chloe for saying it. 'Can you trim my hair as well?' she asked. Might as well have the full works now she was here in this one-woman hairdressing shop.

'Leave it to me.'

Chloe stayed quiet as she sent strands of Sam's hair to the floor, shaping it shorter. They lay looking forlorn. Sam felt her old life was being dismantled. When the job was finished she felt transformed. The russet brought out her greenish eyes, made her skin glow, and gave her the more natural look she desired. It was almost like being reborn.

The proud hair stylist stood back. 'Forget about resembling the future Queen, and be yourself.'

Chloe brought a mirror to show how the shorter hair swung about at the back, the style light and feathery, if a bit over curled. Thrilled, Sam paid in cash borrowed from her mother, and gave a handsome tip too.

'I don't even know your name,' said a grateful Chloe.

'Sam.'

'Sam who?'

To protect herself Sam used her married name. *Jones,'* she said.

'Right then Sam Jones, you can jolly well come along tonight,' the hairdresser urged. 'If only to promote my brilliant talent.'

Sam walked to the door, then looked back. 'I might just do that, Chloe.' Why shouldn't she break free?

Outside she spotted a charity shop displaying similar jeans to the ones her hairdresser had sported. A pair in the right size fitted perfectly. Rummaging about, Sam then found some old cowboy boots, a cowboy hat, a check shirt, and a silky green neckerchief. She added white cropped jeans for Milly and a matching T shirt. The whole lot acquired at a low price.

Back at the cottage, Mother approved of the transformation. 'The blonde look was never really you.'

Milly looked confused. 'I don't know who you are, Mummy.' Then she grinned. 'But I like the colour. Can we go for a swim, please?'

'Give your mother time to draw breath, Milly,' intervened Mother. 'She's only just got home.'

Sam escaped upstairs to change her dressing. She pealed back the silly plasters and saw to her relief that the wound was healing. The stiches had almost dissolved. She dabbed disinfectant on the scar that had formed, trying to ignore the ugly jagged edge. She covered it with the adhesive dressing, then placed an extra waterproof plaster on top so that it was well sealed. If any sea water did get in, the salt might do some good, anyway.

In a determined mood she went down to Milly. 'Ready for the beach?'

Equipped with buckets and spades, towels, sun creams, sun hats, and sunglasses, and decked out in swim suits, a cap lent by Mother to keep Sam's newly styled hair dry, the pair set off.

At the end of the lane they pushed into the path hidden away by overgrown bramble bushes, a path not many people knew about, that led to the more isolated East Bay.

By the time they'd scrambled down, they were hot and sticky. The beach almost empty, save for the seagulls strutting and squawking around as though they owned it.

Sam laid the towels out on the sloping shingle, and pulled on the somewhat quaint bathing cap, before she and Milly raced into the sea, squealing at the cold, Sam's scar stinging a little.

She watched Milly dive under and come up spewing water like a fish.

Relishing a bid for freedom of her own, Sam started crawling out to the deeper water, until her daughter shouted, 'Come back, Mummy!'

Sam returned, swooped Milly up and carried her onto the beach. They rubbed themselves down with the towels.

For the first time Milly saw at close hand the plaster on her Mother's neck. 'Why is that there?'

Sam opted to be honest but not graphic. 'To cover a mark left from the attack.'

Milly bit her lip.

'But it's almost healed.'

To her relief, Milly changed the subject, as children often do when they don't want to dwell on something. 'Can we build a sandcastle now?'

This was something they loved doing together, and they ran to where the sand was damp enough.

They'd become rather good at it. Sam had been happy to drive to

Bell Wharf in Essex, the nearest sandy beach to Wimbledon, where they'd learned, not only to sculpture towers and turrets, but to dig a moat, so that when the tide came in Milly could lie down and let the water run over her as she squealed about how all their hard work was being demolished!

They worked hard to finish it, and almost done, Sam left her daughter to carry on without her. She longed for a lie in the sun and lay down on her towel. And with her floppy sunhat covering her face, and the sun warm on her skin, she dozed.

Hiking along the Jurassic coast was more challenging than Jules had imagined it would be. The ancient cliffs were crumbling with age. There were arches, pinnacles, and stack rocks to maneuver around. The fear of landslides had them hiking where nature reserves had formed, the wild woods alive with birds. Rare greater and lesser spotted wood peckers, blue tits, marsh tits, long tailed tits, coal tits, flew about, whilst in the sky, buzzards circled. He and Leo came upon a grazing roe deer, and sent a fox skidding into his lair. Jules, invigorated by the salty sea air, became almost carefree.

They enjoyed a first beer at Beer, and, after another hike through muddy farmland, woods, clifftops, and down on the beach, they arrived at Lyme Regis in time for another.

The town was packed with tourists keen to explore its maritime history. Leo and Jules had to retreat to the sea front to eat their sandwiches. After this they ambled along the Cobb. When Jules learned that tons of sand needed to replenish the beaches was brought over from France, he felt an affinity with the place. Even more so when he remembered that a movie he'd seen was shot at the same location. 'It was called - The French Lieutenant's Woman,' he told Leo.

'Never heard of it.'

'Well, it's pretty old. One of Mother's relatives collected films from way back. When we first came to England he gave us private showings. This one was about falling in love and the risk it poses to your identity. How you can lose yourself in another.'

'Blimey. I'd better not do that with Veronica.'

'There were two parallel love affairs, one set in period times, the other was between the actors playing the parts.'

'Asking for trouble.'

'I remember an amazing shot of the woman in period dress as she walked along this same harbour wall, just like we are doing now. In the movie the wind was up and her cloak billowed about as she met her lover, The French Lieutenant. They had a passionate affair.'

'Sly buggers,' Leo chuckled.

'Lucky ones,' said Jules.

They left Lyme Regis, and marched up to the Golden Cap, where they stood gazing across the channel.

'Pity you can't see France from here,' said Jules.

'It's too wide at this point. You'd have to go to Dover for that. Come on, we've a way to go yet.' Leo marched on.

By the time they reached the small fishing harbour of West Bay, trudging along eight more miles of rugged landscape, they felt desperate for a swim. They wanted to avoid the hordes of tourists near to the main beach, and looked for a way down at the farthest end. They had to back track from the cliffs to find a path, half hidden by undergrowth, which they pushed through to scramble down.

12

They arrived to find it almost empty, save for a little girl building a
sandcastle, and a young woman sunbathing on the shingle.

They dropped their backpacks, stripped down to swimming
trunks, and strolled across the flattened pebbles. As they neared the
water's edge it became sandy, and the intricate design of the castle the
little girl was building, caught Jules's eye. It reminded him of ones he'd
built in his own childhood, the first sign of his interest in architecture.
He couldn't resist stopping to take a closer look. The battlement even
had indents, and the moat around it was flattened to give the solid base
required. 'That's really good,' he complimented the child.

Her expression was wary. She glanced over at the woman lying in
a bikini, a big floppy sun hat covering her face, a red ribbon tied around
the brim.

'Is that your mother?' asked Jules.

She nodded, then looked at him wide eyed, as he stood over her

He crouched down. 'We're just here for a swim,' he said.

She seemed glad to have this reassurance, particularly as Leo had
joined them, and a now dripping wet giant also towered over her.

'I need the moat to be deeper, but Mummy's gone to sleep.' She
rolled her eyes. Then gave Jules a pleading look. 'Could *you* help me?'

Jules looked at Leo and indicated to the dozing mother. Helping
the child might be taken the wrong way. 'I don't need any trouble.'

Leo gave a shrug. 'Oh, go ahead. Someone should be watching
over her. I've got to have a quick dip.' And off he went.

Jules was longing for a cool down himself, but the child handed
him her spade. 'You can use this.'

He bowed his head. *'Mon plaisir.'*

She giggled. 'You speak funny English.'

'That's because I'm half French. It's my pleasure to help you,' he
translated, and was rewarded with a toothy grin. 'What's your name?'
he asked her.

'Milly. What's yours?'

'Jules.'

'Dig deeper, Jules.' She bossed him about.

He worked fast as she fired out instructions. She knew her own mind, and chatted away. Jules soon discovered she lived in a cottage set behind the cliff tops, hidden away.

His work finished, he tamped down the base, and compressed it. Milly filled her bucket with more sea water and tipped it in, before she lay down herself, closed her eyes, and crossed her hands on her chest as if she was a mermaid. 'I shall wait for the waves to cover me,' she gave a serene smile.

'Well, don't drown yourself,' he warned.

Leo had returned, and he glanced over at the mother. She was sitting up and staring at them. He nudged Jules. 'I fear she's displeased.'

Jules looked, but couldn't see her face behind the hat and sunglasses. 'I'll leave her to you, Leo.' He gave Milly a wink and ran into the sea.

Sam had woken with a start. She only dozed off for a moment. When she saw that Milly was talking to complete strangers, she almost had a heart attack. They were formidable looking men. One was helping to dig the moat. She took breaths to calm herself. She knew Milly liked asking males for assistance. It was a way of filling the hole left by her absent father, even though Sam had assured her daughter *she* could do whatever was needed. If she didn't doze off... She felt a little guilty.

At that moment the two men turned and saw her. The one who'd been helping Milly, frowned, then threw down the spade and headed into the water. He dived into the waves, a dark agile form, whilst the other one stayed behind as though waiting for her.

Seeing a family walking along the beach towards them, and she was not alone anymore, Sam rose to her feet, ready to face the enormous man.

As she came up closer he had his back turned. She saw a large tattoo of a helicopter on his skin. He might be a soldier like her father was. This helped to embolden her. 'Milly, you know it's forbidden to speak to strangers,' she scolded.

67

Milly sat up.

The giant turned. 'I'm sorry, but we thought with the tide coming in she shouldn't be left on her own.'

Sam felt miniscule beside him, until she realised her feet were sinking into some wetter sand. She squelched out, stood on firmer spot, and drew to her own height of a hundred and seventy metres. 'I wasn't asleep, just dozing.'

'We were hiking up top and needed a swim. Found a path down to this more secluded part of the beach.'

'Not many people know of that route,' said Sam, a trite tartly.

'I expect you'd like to keep it that way.'

She nodded, embarrassed now.

He indicated to Milly. 'She asked my mate to help her and he didn't like to refuse. No harm was meant. Your daughter's a credit to you.' And the giant strolled into the water.

He'd been gracious, and she, crass. Sam watched him swim a slow methodical crawl to join his mate. They started to fool about, dunking one another. She had a sudden urge to join in and have some fun herself, not stand here like a man hater.

Milly lay back down in her moat. 'Look, the water's creeping over me, Mummy,' she cried, delighted. The waves were licking her tummy. She started laughing and shrieking at the cold.

The men began swimming back. Sam watched as they rose out of the water like Poseidon and Zeus. The one who'd helped Milly was not as tall as the other, he was dark haired, and uncannily familiar ... She looked away unnerved. 'I think we should go Milly.'

'But I'm enjoying myself.' The water was sweeping over her.

Sam, in flight mode now, ignored all protests, caught hold of daughter's hand and yanked her out of the moat. She wrapped a towel around her, gathered up the rest of their things, and, together they made a bolt for the path.

As they reached it Milly looked back to see the two men watching the incoming waves demolish the castle. 'Meanie Mummy, I've missed the best bit,' she cried.

'I'm sorry, but we can't just befriend two strangers like this.' Sam hurried her away.

Jules saw them disappearing. He gave a shrug, and walked on. Then down lay on his towel to dry off in the sun.

Leo joined him. 'Bright little girl,' said his mate.

'With a feisty attitude,' said Jules.

'Her mother was a bit uptight. I doubt she's a local.'

'She looked like a celebrity wearing that floppy sunhat with that flighty red ribbon attached.'

'She had the figure for it, too,' said Leo, and they both chuckled.

Back at the cottage, Milly was upset her beach time had ended prematurely. Sam felt sorry she'd reacted so badly. To make up for it she mentioned that a music festival was happening in the town that evening.

Milly leapt to her feet. 'Please, can we go, Mummy?'

'Depends how good you are for the rest of the afternoon.'

Milly behaved like an angel. Sam couldn't have backed out even if she'd wanted to.

Come early evening they were decked out in the clothes she'd bought especially. Milly was thrilled with her cropped jeans, cute white top, and dancing pumps. Sam, particularly liked her cowboy boots, and hat with the wide brim that she could pull down low. Around her neck she tied the silky neckerchief and was pleased it hid the scar so well.

Along with Granny, in her artistic, colourful kaftan, they all swanned out to the car.

Early evening, Leo and Jules entered the small market town of Bridport, bronzed from sunbathing on the beach. The pub they were staying in was oldie worldly, but the bedrooms were comfortable and modernized.

Jules was more than happy to laze in the ensuite jacuzzi and sooth his aching muscles. Lying in its warmth, he gazed out through the small window at the bustling town, and took in the festive atmosphere. Buntings were hung across the streets, and buskers were already playing music. Perhaps tonight he'd have the chance to let loose.

He dressed in his casual outfit, and a pair of white pumps for dancing, which he fully intended to do. If he could find the right partner. Then went downstairs to find Leo already knocking back the shots the barmaid was pouring out.

Jules knew this must be Leo's woman. She oozed physicality. Her fair hair was worn short and spiky, and she had a humming bird tattoo on one arm. Jules wasn't into tattoos himself, but Leo had a beauty of a Black hawk helicopter on his back. She was tall too, not much shorter than Jules, who at six foot two, still felt small beside his mate, Leo.

Leo was all smiles, and Jules's first impression was that this was a good match as he came to stand beside his friend to be formally introduced.

'Jules, meet Veronica.' Leo gave a broad smile.

A shot of shot of vodka for you, too?' Veronica started pouring one out.

'I'd prefer a glass of Burgundy. Have you a Pinot Noir?'

'Ooh, la, la! A sophisticated French man, are we?' She teased a smile from him. She found the right wine and poured a glass out. 'Now,' she smiled conspiratorially as she placed it down before him. 'Who shall I palm you off with tonight. Let me see. My friend Anita is just divorced and looking for a new man.' Jules shook his head quickly. 'Better still is my friend, Chloe, the favourite hairdresser in this town and a barrel of laughs.'

'I'm not keen on having dates fixed up for me,' Jules warned.

'Then you'll end up with nobody. The locals will pair off, and the tourists will keep to themselves.' Veronica smiled at Leo. 'And as you can see, *I'm* already spoken for.'

Hard not to join in the laughter at this remark. When Veronica's shift at the bar came to an end, the three of them set off for a night of celebration, in jovial mood.

13

The festival was already in full swing when they arrived. Torches blazed about the meadow. On a small stage, a band was thumping out country style music. People were lined up, stomping out routines, clapping their hands, and singing, 'Yippy I-O,' cowboy style. Some wore hats, some had spurs on their boots, some even had western style six shooters slung on their hip holsters. Mock ones, Jules and Leo could only hope.

Veronica bagged a table just vacated by a rowdy crowd, while Leo and Jules went to the bar tent. They returned with bottles of wine, beer, and a few glasses. The three of them then sat observing the dancers.

The atmosphere was one of camaraderie as people gyrated their hips to the, 'Cupid Shuffle, and the funky, 'Cha Cha Slide,' or so Veronica informed them.

'That's my friend, Chloe the hairdresser,' she pointed out the woman she'd considered as a possible date for Jules.

Not wishing to encourage this, he looked away.

'And what about the pair dancing beside her,' Veronica carried on regardless. 'A mother and daughter. That child can only be about five and look how she's keeping up.'

'The mother's a good mover,' said Leo.

Veronica poked his arm. 'I'm your date tonight, remember.' She glanced over to Jules. 'She'd suit him better.'

But Jules wasn't even looking. He was busy tying up a pump lace that had come loose.

Sam had started to relax and enjoy herself. Her hairdresser had seen her arrive and had come running up eager for her to join in with dancing. 'Take your hat off and let your hair hang loose,' Chloe had urged. 'Let your daughter join in, too.'

Sam had kept her hat on, but was determined to be friendly this evening. Unlike earlier in the day when she'd fled from those men somewhat rudely.

Leo screwed up his eyes for a closer look. 'Strike me down, if it isn't the pair from the beach.' He turned to his mate. 'What was the child's name, Jules?'

Jules roused himself to glance over. 'Oh, you mean, Milly.' He saw how she was kicking out her feet and stomping on the ground, still feisty. His eyes slid to the mother, who looked more laid-back tonight. Though she was sporting a cowboy hat worn so low it cast a shadow over her face. Only her hair could be seen, a tumble of brunette that caught the eye, along with a figure that moved with finesse.

The music came to a halt. The mother started chatting to the woman beside her, and Milly looked lost. She glanced about and spotted him. To his alarm she came running over.

'Hi. It's me again,' she gave a toothy grin.

Jules was taken aback. He tried to make light of it and high fived her. 'Bonjour, Milly.' At least she giggled. 'Won't your mother mind you running off like this?'

Leo intervened. 'Remember me, too? My name's Leo.'

She nodded.

'I think you'd better go before she misses you,' Jules urged.

Milly gave a conspiratorial smile. 'Only if you take me.'

Jules hesitated.

'Oh, go on,' said Leo. 'The child needs a chaperone in this crowd.'

Seeing the mother was looking worried now, Jules rose from his chair and did as he was told.

Sam had started to panic. Milly was there one minute and gone the next. She'd seen enough series on television where a child was snatched away in just such a situation for her heart to start racing. She turned to her hairdresser friend. 'Where is she, Chloe?'

What kind of mother loses sight of her daughter on a crowded dance floor? A nail in the coffin for single parenting.

It was nothing short of a miracle when a little hand grabbed hers, and a familiar voice piped up, 'Here I am, Mummy.'

Sam whirled around, gave a cry, crouched down, and pulled her daughter close, as feelings of relief mixed with fright swamped her. 'You must stay close to me,' she chastised. 'I thought I'd lost you.' So much for controlling the paranoia.

Milly started to tear up. 'I was safe with Jules, Mummy.'

'Jules?'

'The man from the beach,' Milly sniffed.

Sam saw only the white pumps of the stranger first, his feet planted on the ground before her. She tried to hide her dismay he was there at all, and that Milly saw him as a friend already.

She fished out her hanky, wiped Milly's eyes, and rose. She didn't want to run off like before, but didn't want to encourage this man either. She'd say a brisk, thank you for bringing my daughter back, before bidding him farewell. Instead, as they came face to face, she could only gasp - *You!*

She'd felt he was familiar this morning. Now, her mind raced back to Wimbledon, to the common, to her panic attack, and to this same man coming to her aid. Then he'd told her he was French a tourist. What was he doing in Bridport? She was taken over by doubt and suspicion. How could their paths cross twice in one day like this? First on the beach, and now here? Was he a journalist? She pulled Milly to her again.

Jules was stunned into silence. He didn't know what to make of Samantha Elliot being in the same town as he was either. Her indignant cry of *You!* was like a slap on the face. Her darker hair colour may have intended to confuse, but those eyes were unmistakable. They still had that - *save me,* look. Was her being here a mere coincidence or was there more to it? He should make a swift exit. But his curiosity wouldn't allow him to.

Milly had no idea what was going on. Except that the two adults she wanted to be friends seemed afraid of one another.

The music started again.

Chloe, relieved to see Milly safe, and curious about the handsome stranger, urged them all to get dancing.

Milly stood in between the pair and took hold of their hands. And not wanting to upset her, like robots, they started moving.

Sam took slow breaths, trying to calm herself. She took a furtive glance at the stranger, saw he was as confused as she was. When he glanced her way, their eyes met. She remembered how he was on the common. How calming he'd been, suggesting images of the sea. How

73

drawn to him she'd felt. His eyes so steady… She looked away. Beware of Frenchman it was often said. They were rude and arrogant and always cheated on their partners.

After a few mis-steps, Jules at least picked up the routine. He sneaked a glance at Sam. As their eyes met he felt a voltage strike through him. *Mon Dieu*. He could get into trouble with this woman. He focused on the dancing and picked up enough steps to make a decent show of it. He'd stick to the story that he was just a tourist passing through and get away as soon as possible.

The dance ended. Ignoring the protests, Sam sent Milly to sit with her mother, who thankfully hadn't seen her granddaughter's escapade.

Sam then turned to confront the Frenchman. 'You must admit that it's odd meeting you here as well as in Wimbledon.'

Jules thought it was odd as well. He'd hoped never to see her again, and here she was. Fate playing tricks. 'I'm staying with a mate in Salisbury,' he defended himself. 'He only brought me here to meet his girlfriend. No other reason.' He looked into her beguiling eyes. 'How about you?' he challenged. 'Why are you here?'

'*Me?*' Sam felt indignant to be asked. 'I'm with my mother.' She glanced over at her and Milly, chatting away. 'She lives here.'

Milly gave them a cheeky wave.

'Your daughter's… *formidable,*' said Jules, and he slipped a smile.

Sam softened a little. She liked the French pronunciation for formidable. She knew this was true of Milly. She'd often felt concerned about her daughter's forthright manner, but now she glanced over feeling a tenderness towards her. Milly hadn't meant any harm by running to the Frenchman, she was just being friendly.

Jules caught the tender look and felt moved. Such softness was a soldier's lot to lose. Too much pain, too much death, too much running…Under different circumstances he'd liked to have known Sam Elliot a whole lot better. Instead, he mumbled he'd be out of her way, and returned to his table, where he sat down and reached for the solace of his wine.

Sam returned to her own table, where she reached for hers. Took a sip to steady her nerves.

She received a questioning look from her mother. 'Who was that man?'

'Oh, just someone Milly met on the beach earlier. A tourist. Here today gone tomorrow.' Sam tried to dismiss him.

She bought a pizza from a nearby stand, and some chips, which thrilled Milly. After which they did more dancing until Milly became sleepy.

'You stay on, Sam,' said her mother. I'll get us a taxi home.' Stella Elliot gave an encouraging smile. 'You should dance.'

Sam felt she should go with them, but the music changed to Latino, and the sultry rhythm seeped into her bones. As her mother and daughter slipped away she stayed, tapping her fingers on the table. It was hard watching other people struggling with the Salsa, a dance she'd learnt to do with Simon. The one good thing they'd done together.

Jules looked over and saw the Granny slipping away with Milly. The music had changed to Latino and people were making an *oreille de cochon* - a pig's arse, of the salsa. He had a crazy urge to walk over and ask Sam Elliot to dance with him. But knew he couldn't risk another encounter. He stayed where he was, finished his glass, and poured another.

'Steady on,' said Leo.

Jules couldn't explain to his, *happy as could be mate*, with one arm flung around his woman, that his own situation had escalated to another level, and warning lights were flashing. He was about to make excuses for an early exit when Veronica added a further complication. She called over the woman who'd just danced alongside him and Sam.

'As I told you before, Chloe is the best hairdresser in our town, as well as the best mover and shaker.'

He thought he'd made it clear he'd pick a partner for himself, *merci*, but this was ignored.

'People tell her all their secrets,' Veronica added with a wink.

He wouldn't be telling Chloe his. He clammed up as she came and sat down beside him in a waft of hair spray that had turning away. It didn't put her off. It seemed nothing could put Chloe off as she flirted.

75

'A Frenchie, are you?'

He winced at the term. 'Originally I came from France.'

'You remind me of that film star.'

'Who might that be?'

'Alain Delon.'

Jules feigned insult. 'He's eighty, or even dead!'

'Well, I had a poster of him on my wall as a teenager, from that film, 'Once a Thief.' He was young, then.'

'When he played an ex-con?' She nodded. 'Is that how you see me?' It was a touch too close to how Jules was feeling in his present situation, as though he was already a criminal.

She gave an infectious laugh. 'Don't mind me. I enjoy teasing people.'

Jules knew a lot of men would enjoy her effervescent company, and that he was being evasive.

'You on holiday?'

She asked too many questions. 'Maybe.' His eyes wandered over to Sam Elliot, who was sitting at her table alone.

Chloe followed his gaze. 'Oh, I see. She's from London. Name's Sam Jones.'

He knew it was really Elliot. He surmised another name was being used for protection.

'She came to my salon this morning and I changed her hair colour.' Chloe rose from her chair. 'Go and chat *her* up if you prefer. I'm obviously wasting my time.' And in a huff, she walked off.

'I didn't mean to be rude.' Jules called after her. He was about to go after her, but a local man beat him to it, and Chloe was whisked onto the dance floor.

14

Jules watched as the red-faced, beery nosed man shuffled the hairdresser around the dance area like *à l'aveuglette* - a pig in a poke.' He was about to go and rescue her when she threw her hands into the air and walked off, the farmer left red faced. Men were not pleasing Chloe tonight. Jules expected she'd head back to his table, but instead she went over to Sam Elliot, and started, what appeared to be, a heated conversation.

Jules focused on his wine. The festival was becoming more raucous. Drunken lads were singing along to the music. Girls were kicking up their heels trying to perform the salsa and failing. Leo and Veronica had joined in and were tripping over themselves, but still having fun. He should be having some too, instead of thinking of leaving. He couldn't resist another glance at Sam Elliot.

Chloe caught his eye and returned a challenging look. He watched in trepidation as Sam Elliot rose from her chair. Then, encouraged by Chloe, she walked over and sat down at his table.

The latter's revenge was sweet as she match-made. 'Sam is longing to do the salsa, *Jules*. I told her that being French an' all, you'd be the perfect partner.' And on the pretext of returning to her own hopeless one, Chloe left them, alone.

Sam felt awkward being there. Persuaded against her better judgement. Why did she feel drawn to him?

Jules felt caught in a bind. He felt he shouldn't dance with her even if he wanted to. They sat in a charged silence. It was a relief when Leo and Veronica returned and caused a distraction.

'Try as we will we can't get the steps right,' said Veronica.

'That salsa's too damn difficult,' said Leo.

Sam, gave them a smile of sympathy.

'Well, well,' chuckled Leo. 'It's the lady from the beach.' He held out his hand. 'We never introduced ourselves. Names Leo Henshaw.'

'Sam Jones.' They shook hands.

He introduced her to Veronica and the pair started chatting.

Leo looked at Jules. 'I thought the Salsa was a must for you.' Before Jules could stop him, Leo interrupted the women. 'My mate's not a bad mover for a soldier, you should dance with him, Sam.' And he winked at her.

She looked at Jules in confusion. 'I thought you were a tourist.'

He couldn't answer.

Leo did it for him. 'We served together in the army. I hope you don't object like some folk do.' He indicated to some lads standing not far off, glowering at them. 'See. They can spot us a mile off.'

Sam remembered the tattoo of a helicopter on his back when they were on the beach. She couldn't help being curious. 'Where did you tour?'

'Afghanistan.'

'My father was a soldier. I know how they can get pilloried.' She saw the two men exchange glances. 'He was a bomb disposal expert in Iraq and Angola. He was there when Princess Diana walked across a minefield.'

'Lucky man,' said Leo.

'A brave one too,' said Jules, his eyes kinder.

'Maybe he was too brave,' said Sam. 'He....' She hesitated, the memory of how he'd died still too painful to reveal to strangers. She took a breath. 'I think we owe soldiers a debt of gratitude.'

Her pride in her father was touching. Jules could see there was more, but upset now, she reached for her bag and stood up. 'I should leave.'

Sam started to walk away. She should never have come over.

Jules watched as she pushed her way through the crowds.

'You going to just let her go?' said Leo.

A drunken lad leered at her. When the lout grabbed her arm and pulled her up against him, Jules saw her freeze in the way she had once before and in moments he was up and running over. One punch and he'd sent the drunk sprawling to the ground. He then took Sam's hand and led her into the throng. The decision of whether to dance or not, made for them.

The youth shouted after him about how bloody soldiers thought they could steal all the girls, until Leo came and towered over him, and the lad saw there was more sense in slinking away.

Sam made no protest as Jules started dancing. She was glad to be safe. All she had to do was follow his lead, focus on the steps, and forget about everything else.

The music dictated they should come closer to one another. One two, one two, sideways, forwards, backwards and repeat. At times they were almost cheek to cheek. He could feel the slender shape of her. She could feel his energy. Flashes of scent and aftershave mingled. Her skin smelt sweet, his, spicy.

Last time Jules had held this woman she'd fainted, her body limp, and not responsive as it was now. Dancing together was an entirely different experience. For Jules it felt both right and wrong at the same time, an exciting, and illicit encounter. He twisted her under his arm, she twirled quick footed. She was the perfect partner.

When the music stopped they slowed to a halt and stood staring at one another. Jules struggled with a desire to kiss her. Sam struggled with the wish that he would. When the band started playing again she wanted to carry on.

He did too, but his mind said different. He'd allowed things go too far already. He should leave this woman alone. Get too close and she could unravel who he really was.

He wrenched his eyes away. 'Best not spoil a perfect dance,' he said, and stepped away.

Sam, caught up in the warmth of being close, was hurt by his sudden distancing. But not wanting to show this she managed a casual shrug. 'If you wish.'

Jules felt a heel as he left her alone and made a bolt for his table.

Sam watched him go, his body no longer fluid, his shoulders held back and rigid, like he was on an army manouveur. She returned to her own table feeling discarded.

She'd leave immediately. She collected her things, and headed for the car park.

Jules saw her go, but sat hardening his heart against her.

Leo didn't make it easy. 'We were spellbound watching the pair of you.'

'It was like, 'Dancing with the Stars,' said Veronica, hand on her heart.

'Why did you walk away?' said Leo.

Jules shook his head impatient for a change of change subject.

But Veronica wouldn't let it go. 'You liked her, didn't you?'

'She's too fragile for my taste,' he countered.

'She'd soon toughen up if she came to my gym,' said Leo.

Jules knew she probably would, and that it could be the best thing for her. But the idea of her coming near the farm appalled him. He almost lost it when Veronica snuggled up to Leo and showed interest. 'Maybe you should give special classes for us women?' she purred.

'Classes in what?' Chloe had returned, her hopeless partner abandoned again.

'Self defence,' said Veronica. 'Leo's the best teacher there is.'

'Blimey. I've just had trouble explaining to my farmer friend that no really means *no*. I had to slap his face in the end.'

'Dangerous,' said Leo. 'I have better moves. Ones that would prevent any chance of retaliation.'

'Now, I am intrigued,' said Chloe.

'We could come for a weekend.' Veronica gave Leo a kiss on the cheek.'

'It'd be a laugh,' said Chloe.

'A laugh?' Leo was indignant. 'It's bloody hard work. You'd need to take it seriously to make it worthwhile.' He looked at Jules. 'What do you think?'

Jules wanted the whole idea dismissed. 'I think it'd be a waste of time.'

'Thanks for the vote of confidence,' said Chloe. 'I bet you'd be nicer about it if Sam Jones was coming.' She pouted.

'He thinks the Londoner's too fragile,' said Veronica.

'Then she'd benefit the most,' said Chloe. 'We could ask her to join us, Jules.'

It was getting out of hand. 'Please don't.' He banged his glass down, and stood up. 'It's been a long day. I'm turning in.'

To their surprise, he strode off.

'He's a strange one.' Chloe was miffed.

'He doesn't want anyone getting too close to him, right now,' said Leo. 'He has his reasons.'

'And what are those?' she asked, but Leo wouldn't answer.

Jules walked off towards the town berating himself for ever coming to Bridport. He'd only succeeded in letting his guard down. Last thing he needed was Sam Elliot attending Leo's classes. He couldn't have her there, couldn't trust himself to be anywhere near her again.

He entered the lane outside the car park and was annoyed when a golf convertible zoomed out with its headlights full on. *'Idiot!'* He shook his fist, as it had to swerve to avoid hitting him.

Sam had reached her car to find it hemmed in by farm trucks. She scraped the bumper getting it out, and furious, she'd belted into the lane. When a man appeared in her headlights she had to swerve to avoid him. Only when she passed by did she see it was Jules, outlined in her headlights, his fist raised in protest.

She drove on praying he hadn't seen it was she. Men like him were best avoided. Maybe she should have knocked him into the bloody ditch!

Inside the pub, Jules went straight to his room, showered and climbed into bed. Falling asleep was another matter. He felt heady from too much wine, and his brain kept reliving the dance with Sam. When Leo and Veronica later returned to make exuberant love, they encouraged all the wrong notions. He tossed and turned all night, and bashed his pillow in frustration.

15

The next morning, after a light breakfast, both suffering from the excesses of the night before, Jules and Leo packed their backpacks, ready for the hike back.

Veronica took her time saying goodbye to Leo. The idea of self defence training had taken hold. 'Chloe and I would like to come the weekend after next,' she told him.

Jules was relieved to hear Sam was not included, and went ahead to give them privacy.

When Leo joined him, no more was said, and they set off for West Bay, in rhythmic strides.

When they reached the clifftops, Leo broke into a song from their days in Afghanistan, 'Still a Soldier.' A song that usually helped to rally the spirits, and Jules joined in. Once, the song was over, however, Leo started asking questions.

'What's the real story about last night, Jules? Sam seemed lovely to me. I know you don't want to be involved with anyone, but you were so good together. It was like all the lights blazed on.'

Jules strode on faster. He didn't need to be told this. They were still blazing inside him.

His mate caught up. 'You'll end up an unhappy old man if you miss such opportunities.'

'Some of us aren't made for happiness,' Jules fired back.

'Some of us don't give it a chance,' rebuked Leo. 'Veronica and Chloe are keen to come to the farm. If they brought Sam along, you could give it another go.'

'No, I couldn't. It's not that simple.' Jules would say no more.

The pair hiked with only a few words between them. Stopping off for a quick lunch in Lyme Regis, before setting off again at a faster pace.

When they finally reached the Land Rover, Leo had a last try at confronting his friend.

'We never had secrets in Afghanistan. Don't hold back on me

now.'

'*Merde!*' Jules stared out at the darkening skies, a storm gathering, never mind the one erupting inside him. He turned to his mate. 'It's vital this stays between us.'

'That's a given. Spit it out for fuck's sake.'

'I've already told you about the attack in London.' Leo nodded. 'About shooting someone dead to save a woman.' Jules paused. 'Well,' he hesitated, still not quite believing it himself. 'It was Sam I saved.'

Silence. Leo was unable to take it in. 'The woman from the beach?' he repeated. 'The woman you danced with? Are you sure it's the same person?'

'How could I forget her?'

Leo was shocked now. 'Bloody hell!'

'I also met her by chance the very next day. I came across her on Wimbledon common. She was distressed so I offered some assistance, praying she couldn't know who I really was. When the attack took place, I wore a balaclava to be anonymous.'

'Of course, you did.'

'On the common I told her I was a French tourist, and she believed me. But last night you blurted I'd also been a soldier. She could start wondering who I really am. I need to keep my distance.'

'Jesus. And I pushed you into dancing with her.'

'That's why I was reluctant. But, it wasn't your fault, Leo. I wanted to. I really like her. That's the problem. I feel this connection between us because of what we went through. She won't understand it, but I do.' He shook his head. 'It's fucked up anyway. She'll be angry with me now.' He looked at Leo. 'You know she was blonde in London. It was Chloe who changed the colour.'

'Bloody hell.'

'And her surname is not Jones, it's Elliot.'

'Bloody hell.'

'I wish you'd stop saying that.'

'Sorry, but it's all the subterfuge. Hair colour changed, a different name, she's as much a mystery as you are. Who is the real Sam?'

'Well, she's an actress.' Jules shrugged, then felt unkind, when Leo responded by saying he should stay away from her for that reason alone. That actors spent their lives pretending to be other people, that for them nothing was real. 'What's she doing in Dorset, anyway?'

'Staying with her mother. I think media attention might have driven her out of London.'

Leo gave Jules a sorry look. 'Both of you running. I hate what these attacks do.' He grabbed Jules by the arm. 'What do we do if Veronica and Chloe persuade her to come to the farm?'

'I'd have to run like hell,' said Jules. 'Leave.'

'I'm not having any woman come between us,' growled Leo. He switched on the engine. It was hard to express the love he felt for Jules, but it was there all the same, a brotherhood 'You're not going anywhere. I'll put the classes off.'

'You sure Leo? Mon Dieu, I'd appreciate that.'

They drove back to Salisbury, relief flooding through Jules, that he'd avoided another meeting with Sam Elliot.

Sam also took a run on the clifftops, that morning. She caught a glimpse of the two men hiking over the next hill and disappearing. 'Good riddance,' she muttered to herself. Her ear phones on, she was propelled forwards by Cyndie Lauper, singing, 'Girls Just Want To Have Fun.' Having only recently rescued herself from a bad marriage the last thing she needed was to fall for some errant tourist, or soldier, whoever he was. All she'd wanted last night was to have some fun anyway. She ran faster through the golden grasses. It was time to take stock, find a way forwards, and not look back.

At the cottage she took solace in her father's philosophy books, searching for ideas that might inspire a new direction. In her teenage years, being an actress was all she'd ever wanted. As an only child, she'd loved dressing up and pretending to be different characters, partly to keep herself company. But the profession required you to be an extrovert and she was no longer sure this suited her. She felt drawn to the introspective, and wanted a more private life.

She picked up a pen and a small notebook and started writing her thoughts down. Maybe she could write a book. One that would not only aid her own recovery, but could also help others. Self-help books were popular now as people had turned to writing in the lockdowns.

Her mobile bleeped.

It was Chloe. 'How about meeting for a coffee? Veronica and I want to talk to you about something.'

Sam was into her work, and didn't feel like going out. But Chloe made it hard to refuse. 'Don't you want to spend more time with us?' Her tone was hurt.

Leaving Milly cartwheeling in the garden, under Mother's watchful eye, Sam put her work aside, and set off for the town.

She loved driving along the winding coastal road. The Dorset hills undulating on the one side, and the sea capped ocean rolling in on the other, gave both a gentleness that felt containing, and a wildness that invigorated.

When she reached Bridport, however, it felt more like a graveyard compared to the exuberance of the night before. The festival had left both locals and tourists with hangovers. The few that were up about walked around like zombies. It was a pity that *having fun* seemed to exact such a price.

There was only one café open. Chloe was sitting beside Veronica as they sipped large black coffees, looking bedraggled.

'How do you manage to look so fresh when we look like shit,' grumbled Chloe.

'I went home early. Had more time for my beauty sleep, I suppose,' she teased.

'I didn't get the chance for any sleep at all, thanks to Leo's activities.' Veronica groaned. 'I'll get cystitis if I don't call a halt.'

This had Chloe and Sam snorting.

Chloe turned to her new friend. 'Veronica tells me Jules abandoned you last night.'

Sam tried to dismiss this with some school girl French. 'C'est la vie,' she shrugged.

'You never know what lies beneath that Gallic charm,' agreed Chloe.

Sam's Cappuccino had arrived, but it was lukewarm. She sent it back and asked for an extra hot one. They'd never be so lax in Wimbledon and she felt a sudden urge to return. But her country friends had another idea for her.

'We're thinking of attending some self defence classes and wondered if you'd like to join in,' said Veronica.

'Why? Do you think I need them?' Sam felt defensive at first.

'Well, you had to be rescued from a drunk, didn't you?' said Chloe.

'At least Jules did something right,' said Veronica.

Sam didn't relish having to feel grateful to him. It made her look weak. 'I left my marriage when my husband became aggressive. I'm not an idiot.'

Chloe and Veronica exchanged glances.

'We didn't know about that,' said Chloe. 'Is that why you're on edge with men?'

'Maybe.'

'Well, you're not the only one. I also had trouble last night with my farmer friend. He became, shall I say, over enthusiastic. It'd be good to learn how to defend myself so that men like him think twice about taking advantage.'

Sam could see Chloe and Veronica were serious about this. 'Where would these classes be held?' she asked.

'Leo's farm,' said Veronica, with a sly smile.

'*Leo's* the trainer?'

Veronica grinned. 'Chloe and I plan to go for a weekend, as he lives a long way from here.'

Sam stirred her coffee. 'When would that be?'

'The weekend after next. Could you make it?'

Sam knew her mother would take care of Milly. But she was worried about her neck wound. Physical exercise might affect the healing process.

An even bigger problem stood in the way. 'I can't go if the Frenchman's there,' she said. 'He'll think I'm chasing him.'

'Arrogant pig,' said Chloe.

'I can tell Leo to keep him out of the way,' said Veronica.

'Is that a promise?'

Veronica nodded. 'You can't let him stop you.'

'No, you can't,' said Chloe.

Sam could see that it was also an opportunity to get to know these two women better. Something she wanted to do. She wrestled for a moment longer and then gave in. 'I could drive us there in my convertible,' she offered.

Chloe downed the last swig of her black coffee. 'That'd be a blast.'

Veronica took the last swig of hers, and beamed at them both. 'I'll call Leo and get it fixed up.'

The men arrived back at the farm in darkness. As they entered the house the landline was ringing. With Old Tom already in bed Leo just managed to reach it in time. He broke into a smile when he discovered Veronica was calling. 'Missing me already?' he chuckled

Jules went to the sink and filled a glass of cold water. He stood listening as he sipped it. Heard the conversation, which was warm at first, turn into an argument about the trip to the farm.

Leo banged down the phone. 'Bloody hell. She was all geared up to come the weekend after next, Chloe and Sam included. Upset that I've refused, doesn't cut it.'

Jules put down his water. 'Look, I don't want to cause a rift between you. I'll go back to London early.'

Leo scratched his head. 'There must be another way.'

Jules had a thought he should have had sooner. 'I suppose I could go for a hike on my own.'

Leo, perked up. 'Why the hell not? But not around here, too many army exercises. You could go to Exmoor this time, a hundred miles away,' he grinned. 'You can take my ordinance map, and have some peace exploring it on your own.'

'I could disappear for the whole weekend and return when the women have left.' Jules felt almost gleeful.

The problem solved, they both tramped up to bed.

16

Jules enjoyed helping his mate around the farm. He hardly thought about Sam Elliot. Once or twice the memory of dancing with her did break through, and stirred his loins. He had to focus on shifting more bales, until it passed.

He found pleasure working the land. He liked striding across the uneven ground to the far horizon. The open fields were golden with late summer wheat, and in the greener part, frisky young lambs tore around in mobs.

One day he arrived to find one of the mysterious crop-circles had been formed. Strange, complex shapes in the middle of the barley, like the vortex swirl found in seashells or galaxies. Beautiful to look at, but hard to gage, as to how or why they'd suddenly appeared.

'Wiltshire's famous for them.' Leo told him when he returned to the house. 'People say folk around here are responsible, but no one catches anyone in the act.'

Later, over supper, the discussion intensified, with Leo suggesting the circles came from dying comets arriving from outer space in a ball of fire. 'I mean how else can you explain the mathematical quorums, geometric or abstract shapes left behind, except they come from some extraordinary outside force?'

'No burnt earth to prove it's a comet,' his father argued. 'It's more mystical than that.'

'Perhaps the comets expire before they hit the earth,' offered Jules. 'They might skim over the surface leaving shapes in their wake.'

Old Tom knew better. 'Locals say witchery is involved. The devil's mowing some call it.'

This evoked laughter from Leo and Jules, who both thought a scientific explanation more credible. Though Jules understood this part of England was full of unanswered questions with its sacred sites, mythical stones, and pagan rites. To some it might seem a spooky place, but he was finding it stimulating. His architectural interest was always aroused by how things were formed, shaped, and built, and what meaning this could hold for people.

Time passed pleasantly enough. When the planned weekend for the women arrived, Jules had intended to set off early to avoid any chance of seeing them. But come the day, old Tom was unwell, and Leo needed help feeding the animals.

'It won't take long,' he reassured Jules. 'Then you can go straight off.'

But by the time hay had been delivered to the cows out in the wilds, and all the water troughs checked, Saturday morning had almost gone.

Luckily, Jules had packed his things the night before. He fetched his sandwiches from the fridge, and tried to say a quick goodbye to Leo and his father.

But the old man held him up even more, intent on telling him about all the things he should look out for on Exmoor – 'Red deer, wild ponies, kites and hawks, and all kinds of different trees and grasses… I'd come with you if I wasn't so weak, damn getting old.'

Jules finally reached his car. He was looking forward to being out in the open, where he could walk until he was too tired to think anymore. He'd become anxious in the last days as there'd been no news about the police enquiry and the torment in his mind had started to reignite.

He switched on the engine, and sped out into the lane, determined to make up for lost time.

Sam had just entered from the other end, having made the journey from Dorset faster than she'd anticipated. Milly was in the care of her mother, and there was a freedom from responsibility, except for the driving, of course.

The hood was down. Mid-summer and it was hot, the landscape golden. They could see lads on trailers way out in the fields bringing the last of the harvest in, and wolf whistles echoed in their ears.

'Men aren't supposed to do that anymore,' said Sam in her PC London voice. 'It's not correct, you know.'

'Well, *woke* isn't popular around here,' said Chloe. 'We don't mind men flirting with us.'

'Not even the amorous farmer who got out of hand at the festival?' said Sam.

'Well, maybe not him, but a wolf whistle is harmless. It's the way men let us know they think they're attractive. We don't want them to be so inhibited they won't come near us, do we?'

Veronica gave a saucy look. 'Not my Leo, certainly.'

Laughing at this, Sam picked some music for them all to enjoy. 'We Are The Champions.' Queen's signature song blared out. 'This will pump us up for what lies ahead,' she said, enjoying the growing friendship.

She slowed for the pot holes in the lane. They had time to marvel at the farmland. Cows and sheep were dotted about the grassy fields, and there were few hedges to curtail the acres of golden wheat.

Chloe's attention was caught by something unique. 'Turn the music off and stop,' she commanded Sam, who thinking something was wrong, came to a sudden halt.

But Chloe undid her seat belt, knelt up on the back seat, and pointed in glee. 'Look at that crop circle. The patterns are fucking amazing!'

Sam turned to look, the swirls and geometrical shapes so impressive she ignored the fact she was stationary in the middle of the lane. It wasn't until she heard another car coming around the corner that she turned back and saw it hurtling straight for them. The driver had to slam on his brakes and wrench the steering wheel to avoid a head on collision. The silver Mercedes then skidded onto the grass verge and ended up headfirst in the ditch, where its engine cut out, and its wheels were left spinning.

The three women watched in a horrified silence as the driver opened the car door and struggled out. *'Merde!'* swore Jules.

'Shit!' Seeing it was him Sam slumped down in her seat. She hissed at Veronica. 'You promised he wouldn't be here.'

'I didn't think he would.'

'Look out, here he comes,' said Chloe, back in her seat, she belted up again, as Jules stormed over.

'Putain d'idiot! You could have killed us all,' he lambasted Sam. 'What were you thinking?' He remembered how she'd cut in front of him outside Wimbledon police station not so long ago, after she'd given her statement in. Not that he could mention it. Or how he'd followed her home. In a car she was a liability.

Sam mustered her courage to defend herself. 'It was just as much your fault, you were speeding.' It was what she was here for after all.

'I was in a hurry to leave,' he fired back.

His rudeness took her breath away. All she could do was glare at him.

'Don't blame, Sam.' Chloe butted in. 'Blame those crop circles.' She pointed over. 'We had to look.'

Jules shook his head in despair. 'Crop circles?' He looked back at his car. How could he get out of here if his car was wrecked? 'God knows what it's going to cost to repair,' he mumbled in despair, more to himself, than to them.

'If you need me to pay for any damage, I will,' said Sam, feeling guilty now.

Veronica was more reproachful. 'You shouldn't be here, Jules. Leo said you'd be gone.'

'I was delayed. Old Tom was unwell, and my help was needed.'

Silence, save for sudden breeze that ruffled Sam's hair.

Jules felt his anger dissipate. She looked lovely with strands blown awry. He knew that he shouldn't blame her entirely. He put his hands up. 'Ok, I was going too fast,' he admitted. 'I'll deal with any damage.' He looked at Veronica. 'Ask Leo to call a breakdown truck from the village, will you. Then I'll be out of your way.' And with a last shake of his head, he returned to his beloved Mercedes.

Sam watched him retreat to his car, and felt regretful. She could a see it was his pride and joy. She should have pulled over to the side of the lane.

Chloe felt otherwise. 'A man who loves his motor than anything else deserves everything he gets.'

Sam drove on and reached the yard to find an agitated Leo, who leaned his hands on the bonnet of her car. 'What the hell's happened?

91

I heard the screeching of tyres. Are you all alright?'

'Only just,' replied Veronica.

'Jules had to avoid us. His car ended up in the ditch.' Chloe couldn't resist a smirk.

'Christ.'

'He wants you to call the breakdown truck to help him out,' said Veronica. 'You said he wouldn't be here,' she added with a glower.

Leo ignored this. He pulled out his phone and started talking to the local garage. Then he ran up the lane to join his mate.

Sam parked, scattering the hens and geese about the yard. The whole place was a menagerie for animals. A few stray sheep were grazing on a side lawn. A sheep dog on a long lead barked. All around was land, as far as the eye could see, boundless acres of it.

'Leo must like open spaces,' said Chloe, as the three climbed out.

'Fortunately, so do I,' responded Veronica.

Sam was feeling too upset by the latest encounter with Jules to respond to anything. Why did he bother her so? She hardly knew the man, and yet at some level, she felt she knew him all too well.

The other two nosed around, and she followed them through a large barn filled with cows, who looked at her big eyed. When she entered the smaller barn beyond, she saw a fully equipped gymnasium, with weights, rowing machines, and pummel bags.

'Leo takes this very seriously,' warned Veronica.

'It looks daunting,' said Chloe, who pointed at a netted cage in the corner. 'Look at that contraption. Are we supposed to work inside it?' She backed away ready to forget the whole thing.

Sam thought it looked impressive. 'I expect it makes you really focus on the moves.'

Veronica hustled them both out. 'Leo will want to show you this himself. I shouldn't be giving you a preview.'

As they reached the yard, he came marching back.

'Is the car okay?' Sam couldn't help asking.

'It will be. And once it's fixed up, Jules will be away again.'

'Good.' Sam flicked back hair to show she didn't care, even though this wasn't entirely true.

17

Leo led them into the house. He seemed eager to impress Veronica with the countrified kitchen, oak table and chairs, and soft cushions on which numerous cats lolled. 'I hope you like cats?' He looked worried for a moment.

'Of course, I do.' Veronica set about stroking them, one by one.

Chloe on the other hand started sneezing. 'I might be allergic to so many at once.'

'I'll send them outside if you'd prefer,' said Leo.

Chloe assumed a gallant air. 'No, I'll be okay.' Sneeze.

They were taken upstairs. Sam and Chloe were given a bedroom each. Veronica, with a wink at the others, went into Leo's.

There was an attic floor above. Sam suspected Jules had been sleeping there. He'd have the same view as she had from her window. She walked over, opened it, and took deep breaths. The air was fresh, the wide open plain like an escape route to freedom.

She unpacked, changed into black leggings, a fitting top and her trainers. And with her neckerchief tied firmly around her neck, she went downstairs.

'You look ready for action,' said Chloe, who was dressed in a loose blue leisure suit. Veronica was in a similar outfit in grey.

The three of them made their way out to the barn.

Leo was indeed proud of his gym. He showed off the equipment, and the mighty circular cage enclosed in wire netting, explaining it was used by soldiers for martial arts training.

'I've heard that can be brutal,' said Chloe.

'The military is stationed all around here. Cadets attend classes on weekdays. The cage helps to concentrate their minds.' He gave the three women a challenging look. 'I expect we'll get around to using it for you three before the weekend's over.'

'I might scream blue murder to get out of it,' said Veronica.

'I might refuse to go in at all,' said Chloe.

Leo raised his eyes to the heavens and sat them down for a prep-talk.

'Krav Maga is about self-defence. You learn moves to deflect a violent assault. It's about de-escalating situations rather than enflaming them as you would in combat techniques, where you're out to inflict maximum pain, or even to kill someone.'

'*Kill?*' Chloe had another fit of sneezing. 'It's not just cats. It happens when I get nervous, too,' she explained.

Leo had to wait until she'd recovered before he could continue. 'It's about using moves that will disable someone. Take-downs and take-counters. Are you ready?'

They weren't sure they were but all three nodded their agreement.

Leo clapped his hands together. 'Right then. Let's get warmed up.' He had them jogging on the spot. Then marching for five minutes. Doing arm swings. Lunges. Squats. 'Next, we have to get your muscles pumped up.'

He moved them onto the dumb bells for bicep curls. Then took them to the pummel bags, where he kitted them out with boxing gloves, and fired out specific instructions. 'Stand square to the bag. Palms down, knuckles swinging at it hard. *Bam!*'

'I didn't know it would be this sweaty,' complained Chloe.

'I've broken three of my nails,' complained Veronica.

'Stop whining,' said Leo.

He moved them in closer, their heads almost touching the bags, as they learnt how to throw hooks, knuckles flat, hitting left and right, their heads moving from side to side.

'Okay, now we'll make it a moving target.' Leo swung the bag at them so they had to dodge around it and pummel from either side. Chloe got hit in the face a couple of times.

'These bags ought to come with a health warning,' she complained.

'Well,' warned Leo. 'Assailants will give you none. Hitting back hard is the only way to defeat them.

He came up to Sam, who was moving around in a willowy manner. 'No good just being graceful, Sam. You've got to be committed to take charge of the situation. Put your whole body behind every punch.'

'What if I hurt someone?'

94

'God give me strength,' said Leo.

Sam's knuckles had started to feel sore even with gloves on. But she kept going as she didn't like failing. Sweat started to pour from her. The scarf hiding her scar was soon soaked. It was easy to imagine Jules was the bag each time she hit, her frustration with him finding an outlet.

Seeing her becoming fiercer, Leo encouraged her. 'That's it. Make men fear you.'

He told all three they should also use their voices against a potential attacker 'Yell, shout, if anyone ever comes near,' he urged.

All three women were soon hitting and shouting at the same time.

They practiced evasive body movements, dodging around, twisting and turning, never leaving their backs exposed. By the end of the morning Leo was praising all three. 'You deserve a reward. A bowl of soup cooked by my old man.' And he led the way back to the house.

The light chicken broth with homemade bread was delicious. Leo's father was a dear old man, whose dedication to the farm was etched in his gnarled hands as well as the lines on his face. 'Been tending the land all my life,' he told them. 'Couldn't do anything other. It's in the blood.'

Leo sent the three women to their rooms afterwards, to rest. 'Only for an hour, and then it's back to the gym.'

'And I thought this would be a lark,' said Chloe as they went upstairs.

In her room, Sam lay down on her bed and fell instantly asleep.

It was a pity she dreamt about Jules and his car almost crashing into hers. Waking an hour later, she took a shower to wash the memory away.

In a clean leotard and top, she then headed for the barn. The other two were already at work. Leo had stepped up the pace and was showing them how weaponize their hands, their arms, their legs, even their feet. Sam would never be as strong as they were, but she joined in, and moved like lightening.

'You should take up kick boxing. Jules is the expert,' Leo said without thinking, and saw her grimace. She'd no need to worry, his mate was on his way to Exmoor by now, and far away.

The women gathered the women around him, Leo asked what

they'd learned so far.

'How to punch a man where it hurts,' said Chloe, with cheeky grin.

'How to surprise an attacker when he's least expecting it,' said Veronica.

'How never to turn your back,' said Sam. 'How to shout and yell.'

'Good, good, good.' responded Leo. 'Assailants bank on you being afraid of them. It fuels the power they have over you. Take that away and you've turned the tables. You should go for their weak points.' He pointed to his groin, his arms, his throat, his nose, and finally the eyes. 'Stick your fingers into their sockets, like this.' He stabbed at his own.

'Ugh!' All three balked at this.

But Sam couldn't help wondering what might have happened if she'd done it to her attacker. Would it have stopped his onslaught? She felt a little faint, thinking of this.

Leo looked at her in concern. 'You okay, Sam?'

She took a breath. 'If someone grabbed you by your hair, jerked your head against them, and put a knife to your throat, what should you do?'

Leo immediately guessed she was referring to the attack. 'Did someone take hold of you like that, Sam?' he asked gently.

For a moment she looked as though she was about to tell him everything, but then she pulled back.

'No, but they might.'

He didn't press her. He just called the others over. 'What would you two do if someone came at you with a knife?' he challenged.

'A karate chop on the arm to make him drop it,' said Veronica.

'Kick him in the balls,' said Chloe relishing the idea a bit too much.

Leo told them this was fighting talk. Then showed them what would work better. He placed a fake knife in Veronica 's hand, and made her raise her arm ready to strike. In a swift move he grabbed hold of her wrist, pulled it down, twisted it around so that the blade pointed at her not him, then made stabbing movements towards her stomach. 'See, I've turned it on you.'

'You moved so fast, I had no chance,' said an impressed Veronica.

Leo made them all have a go. All three became quite competent at the disarmament move, and encouraged by their progress, he brought the day to an early end.

Supper, with steaming hot beef stew, baked potatoes, and leeks grown in the vegetable garden, was a lively affair. Leo's father told tales about life in the old times in the wildest parts of Wiltshire. About smugglers known as Moonrakers, who hid contraband in the rivers and lakes. And ghosts of deceased felons, murderers, lords and ladies, and even priests, who tourists swore to have seen on nightly ghost walks held in the city of Salisbury.

The women were so enriched by folklore and visions, that, along with exhaustion from the gym, they went to bed and slept like phantoms themselves.

18

Jules only calmed down when his car had been lifted onto the breakdown truck and taken to the village garage. He'd get it fixed soon as possible and be on his way.

It was a pity the mechanic seemed out of his depth with a continental Mercedes. It took the man an age to fathom why the engine had seized up. How one of the catalytic converters was fucked, and that Jules would need a new one.

'I'll have to drive to Andover to buy it, which will take time. The car won't be ready before this evening, I'm afraid.' The man gave a sorry shrug.

Jules's hike across Exmoor would have to be delayed until tomorrow. He had no choice but to find one locally. But in the opposite direction to Leo's farm. The mechanic told him of a route that would bring him back to the village in a round trip, but warned him to look out for military. 'They might have war games going on.'

Jules gave a rueful smile. They were not such a problem for him, except for spoiling his peace. He removed his gear from the boot and set off on the advised track at a steady pace.

It was good to walk in the vast expanse of open land stretching for miles around. There were occasional clumps of beech trees, but for the most it was grassland, short cropped. Being late summer there was an abundance of insects, humming bees, and butterflies, burgundy and blue, that rose like confetti. Jules tramped along not thinking too much. He ignored the areas cordoned off for military exercises and focused on the natural environment.

Lunchtime, he felt hungry. Seeing an old evacuated hamlet on the other side of some barbed wire, he climbed over. He took a risk there'd be no war games, sat down on some tumbledown stone ruins, and ate his sandwiches.

A skylark started singing above him, a few rabbits scampered out of the undergrowth, and once his food was devoured, he bunkered down on the ground, closed his eyes, and dozed.

He woke to a shuddering hum. He sat up and peered into the distance to see a dot coming closer. The Apache helicopter swooped low over the hamlet and kicked up dust as it flew over him.

He waited suspecting it was just doing a reconnaissance. When it didn't come back he gathered his things and went into the open. He was about to head back to the hiking trail when he saw a group of transport carriers rolling across the land towards him. A gully lay nearby, so he slid in to take cover.

The carriers halted. He sneaked a look and saw infantry soldiers piling out. They took up positions in the hamlet, hiding behind walls, and in other gullies, not far from the one he was in.

The plain came alive when three Challenger 2 Warriors, rumbled across the plain, guns protruding. The Apache helicopter returned and dropped mock explosions. The Warriors joined in blasting shells through the air. The ground all around exploded, and the sky smoked, as the infantry soldiers battled to defend themselves, firing back with high velocity guns.

To a layman it might have looked like chaos, but for Jules it was orderly enough. Mock warfare was not always executed with precision, as it was only a practice. It was hard not to ponder, as he lay there, fighting raging all around him, whether war was justified anymore, with politicians making such terrible decisions. The only thing that kept a soldier going was the sense it was in a noble cause.

When the skirmish finally ended, the heavy armoury driven away, and the infantry was left to recover, he ventured from his hiding place to join them.

They were taken aback as he strolled up. One knew who he was.

'Good God, Caron, are you trying to get yourself killed? They're not all dummy bullets.' Archie MacLean was an ex-commando. He'd fought alongside Jules, and Leo on numerous occasions. 'What are you doing around here?'

'Taking a hike,' said Jules. 'I took the risk you wouldn't be exercising, today.'

'More fool you,' Archie chuckled. 'I'd heard you'd joined the police.' He raised his eyebrows.

Others eyed Jules with curiosity.

'That's right, but I'm on leave, staying with Leo on his farm.'

'Leo's got a good outfit there,' said Archie. 'The lads like working out with him.' There were murmurs of agreement.

'Don't you miss the blood and thunder of the army?' asked an eager looked recruit.

Jules didn't answer. Didn't say that the army didn't feel right for him anymore, or the police force. That the idea of settling down on a farm like Leo's seemed more appealing, living a life of peace not war.

Archie scratched his head. 'Maybe you got out at the right time, Jules. I'm not sure how much longer I can stick it. I mean we've left medieval tyrants in charge of Afghanistan. The people will have no more freedom, and no more democracy. What was the sacrifice of British soldiers, for?' He spat onto the ground.

Jules knew soldiers had immense focus, discipline, determination, and not least the courage to serve and die for their country. He agreed it should mean something. 'It's the politicians who are to blame for making the wrong calls,' he said. 'Not soldiers.'

The men gathered their things muttering their agreement, before heading for the carriers that had returned to pick them up.

Jules carried on with his hike, his mind soothed by the steady walking over a flat terrain.

He was late returning to the village, and in need of a shower. He didn't feel up to driving to Exmoor that evening. He'd wait until the morning and have a good night's sleep first. But when he tried to book a room he found they were all taken.

'A group of journalists have come from London to report on the army manouvers,' the Publican told him. The man gave a resigned shrug. 'After a posh dinner in the officer's mess they'll return here drunk and disorderly, I fear.'

Last thing Jules needed was to be surrounded by volatile reporters. He had an early supper of a steak and salad, and left before any press arrived.

He could only hope his car was ready, and he could drive on and find somewhere else to stay the night. But he found the garage was closed. He had to knock up the mechanic who lived in the house next door. When the man appeared, he was apologetic.

'Your car won't be fixed until Monday, I'm sorry,' he said.

'*Monday?*' Jules saw his plan to hike across Exmoor evaporate into the night air.

'I can give you a lift back to the farm, later,' said the mechanic. 'But I've a football match to finish first. Want to come inside and join us?'

Jules ended up watching Manchester City playing Manchester United with the man and his three excitable sons. They supported different sides, and when, for two of them, the wrong team won, there was almost a punch up.

He was exhausted by the time he was finally driven to the farm. He asked to be dropped in the lane so he could sneak across the yard and enter the house, unseen. Hopefully in the morning, he could rise early, and leave in the same way.

19

In his attic bedroom, Jules showered quietly, then fell into bed, assured no one knew he was there. He could do another hike tomorrow and still avoid seeing Sam Elliot.

He wasn't to know that a barn door banging in the middle of the night would wake them both.

They each tried to return to sleep, hoping that Leo would deal with it, but nothing happened. The noise carried on until they could ignore it no more.

Sam was the first to make a move. She pulled on her nightie and slippers, crept downstairs, and braved the wind that was blowing outside. She'd forgotten her phone and had to battle across the yard with only flickers of moonlight to show the way. The noise was coming from a barn that reeked of silo. She found the cross bar on the door was hanging lose. Covering her nose with one hand, she tried to push it back into place with the other. But it fell out again, hit her finger, and a splinter pierced into her skin. *'Ouch!'*

Jules had climbed out of bed and come outside. He too had battled the wind. He saw a figure in the darkness. As he came up close, he heard the exclamation, and beamed the light forwards. *'Merde!'* He couldn't believe it was her, after all his effort. No way he could ignore her now.

Sam couldn't believe it was him either. Half of her was relieved he was there, the other half wanted him gone. In a daze she moved aside to let him solve the problem.

She watched as he placed the bar back with sublime ease. Noted how everything he did had an intense focus. Just like when he'd danced with her.

Her finger was throbbing. She tried to suck out the splinter, but tasted the blood now dripping down her skin, crimson red, warm and sticky. She felt a rush to her head, and in a repeat of what had happened the first time they met, she gave a defeated moan, and passed out.

Jules caught her before she hit the ground. He held her steady. It was like *deja vous* as he swept her up and carried her back inside. A silken nightie clinging to her slender form.

In the kitchen, he eased her into old Tom's rocking chair, and patted her cheeks to bring her around. 'Sam...?'

She opened her eyes. 'What happened?'

'You fainted.' He fetched her a glass of water. 'Stay there. I'll be back in a moment.'

He went up to the attic and fetched his hiker's medical kit, always useful at such times, and returned to sit beside her.

Sam felt mortified. 'Sorry, but I'm not good with blood.'

He couldn't help glancing at the plaster on her neck.

Sam who'd discarded her scarf for the night, felt a white lie was necessary. 'I had a mole removed.' Best she could do.

He nodded, but said nothing. He focused on her finger. Told her to look the other way as he pulled the embedded splinter out with tweezers, and dabbed on disinfectant.

She bit her lip as it stung. He deftly put on a plaster, and when it was fixed, she sneaked a look, saw how neat and tidy it was. No blood anywhere. 'Thank you.' She smiled at him.

He stared into the now grateful eyes, the lashes soft on her skin, and felt that invisible thread drawing him closer. It was an effort to pick up his medical kit. 'You should get to bed.'

He rose to leave but she placed a restraining hand on his arm.

'Why are you still here, Jules?'

'My car got trashed, remember.'

She bit her lip. 'I seem to only cause trouble.'

He changed the subject. 'How was the class with Leo?'

'I learned a lot.'

'Such as?'

'How to pack a punch.' She aimed one at him.

He ducked, chuckled, and then escaped to the door.

'Running away again, Jules?'

He hesitated, his hand on the knob, his back kept to her. 'There's things you don't know about me, Sam,' he said quietly.

103

She was about to tell him he didn't know things about her either, but she held back, and kept the focus on him. She came over and whispered. 'You're not just a French tourist, you're also a soldier, what else might you be? Why can't you tell me, *Jules?*'

His name was said so softly he felt himself weakening. Her breath was warm on his ear, and the fragrance of her skin was like a drug. 'None of this is your fault,' he whispered back. 'You're near perfect.' His lips were almost on hers. He should stop this and run for the hills, but he could feel the heat of her, feel the heat of himself. His day spent watching soldiers in battle, the sweat, the physicality, had stayed with him, and desire overcame any restraint.

Sam too felt aroused. After a day punching pummel bags, pushing her body beyond its limits, she could not resist their lips meeting in a kiss, one that thrilled them both.

Any idea of stopping felt impossible. Jules pushed her back into the kitchen as they continued kissing while undressing one another. Her nightie shimmered to the floor, his dressing gown followed. He laid her down beneath him on the fireplace rug, as all the pent-up feelings of the last weeks begged for release.

Tongues teased, hands stroked. They found the hidden spots that sent ripples of pleasure through them. Jules felt a tenderness he thought he'd lost as he sank into her. They moved in rhythm like one person, rising and falling, slower then faster, until the intensity built to an almost unbearable level as they reached a shared and shattering climax.

They lay together in silence. They were stunned by how good it had been. Both felt vulnerable. Both felt lost and yet found.

It was a while before Jules gently removed himself.

Sam pulled on her nightie. He, his dressing gown. Nothing needed to be said as he led her back upstairs. Only when they reached her bedroom door did he pause in sudden concern. 'We can keep this a secret, can't we?'

She looked at him, understanding he needed this without being asked why. 'On one condition,' she replied. 'That you'll join in with the classes and not run from me anymore.'

He nodded. It was fair enough. Besides he badly wanted to be with her.

She placed a soft kiss on his cheek, told him they both needed to sleep, before she went inside her room, and closed the door.

He went up to his attic bedroom, opened his windows and stood looking out at the starlit sky, the moon never brighter. He wanted to shout to the world he'd just found the woman of his dreams. He felt no regret. Any doubts he banished from his mind. Nothing should spoil the joyous feeling of being so close to her.

Sam climbed back into bed and listened as he padded across the floor above. Heard the creak of his bed creak as he climbed in. Then all was quiet, save for her own satiated breathing, and the beating of her rekindled heart.

20

Jules overslept. He woke to light filtering in through the curtains, and with a start remembered what had happened the night before.

He rose and took a shower as he tried to reason there was nothing wrong with his becoming involved with Sam. Or for making a promise to join in with the classes. She still didn't know who he was, so where was the harm? He'd keep his identity a secret until the enquiry results were through, then, when all was well, he could tell her the truth.

He dried himself, and reached for his mobile. Maybe Ted Rowlands had news.

He woke his partner up. On holiday with his family in Brighton, Ted was having a lie in, and Jules heard the irritated grunt. Then sounds of a bed creaking, and a door opening and closing.

'You disturbed the wife up as well as me, Jules,' Ted grumbled. 'I've had to come out onto the balcony.'

'Sorry, but I'm impatient for news.'

Ted sighed. 'Look, I don't think you have anything to worry about. I spoke with the commander yesterday. He said he'd told the enquiry we were commanded to use protocol. That no one could dispute we'd followed due process, or at least tried to. That they will have to exonerate us.'

'Well let's hope they do,' said a relieved Jules.

When Ted started complaining that Brighton was too full of bloody tourists and he couldn't wait to return to London, Jules said goodbye and switched off. The idea of returning to London was not on his agenda right now. He liked being here too much.

He dressed ready for the gym, slipped into the bathroom and slapped on some *Sauvage* aftershave. The spicy smell always made him feel like celebrating.

He could hear animated chatting coming from the kitchen as he went downstairs. But when he opened the door and walked in they all fell silent.

'My God, Jules, what are you doing here?' said Leo.

'My car won't be ready until Monday. I had to change my plans.'

Veronica, sitting next to Leo, looked at Sam, sitting with her head down at the far end of the table, in concern.

Chloe looked at Jules in indignation.

He owed an explanation. 'There was a barn door banging in the night. I got up to fix it but found Sam was there before me.'

Sam held up her finger. 'Unfortunately, I got a splinter. But Jules sorted everything out.' She smiled. 'And it led to us calling a truce.'

'A truce?' mocked a surprised Veronica.

'Bloody hell,' said Leo.

'More fool you,' said Chloe. 'Ill met by moonlight, was it?'

Jules ignored her jibe. He was relieved Sam had put things so succinctly, without saying more than was wise.

Leo scratched his head. 'Not like me to leave a barn door unlatched. Too otherwise involved I am.' He winked at Veronica.

She blushed.

'I can't keep up with any of you,' said Chloe, looking a bit left out.

'Well, I hope you're going to join in with the classes, Jules,' said Leo.

'Maybe, I will.' Jules gave Sam a quick smile, before he sat down, and helped himself to some breakfast.

Leo rose from his chair. 'Time for the rest of us to get started. Chop, chop ladies.' And he led the way to the barn.

Veronica and Chloe gave Jules wary glances, before following. But Sam came over to give him a shy kiss.

'How's your finger?' he asked.

'Well taken care of. Don't be long.' And she went after her friends.

He cleared away the breakfast things first. He arrived to see her pummelling one of the bags. He suggested she threw punches at a real person, and held a pad against his chest.

She was cautious to start with. He could see she didn't want to hurt him. But as he stood firm her confidence grew, until with each hit she seemed to lay claim on him. He didn't mind. He liked that she wanted to do this.

He taught her some kick boxing. Real stand up fighting, striking at his torso, kicking high and low at his ankles, and elbows, not easy to implement. She fell over to start with, but picked herself up, dusted herself down, and found her balance again. When she gave him a blow in the ribs he doubled over, feigning injury.

She ran to him. 'Are you okay?'

He nearly kissed her there and then, but Leo was looking over suspiciously.

'Just fooling around,' Jules whispered, and gave her a push that sent her tumbling to the ground.

Leo called him over, and took him aside. 'Go easy on her, will you.'

'Me go easy on her?' It was laughable. The change in the woman whose life he'd saved was palpable. She was no longer fearful.

Leo glanced over at Sam who was now punching thin air, and whirling around kicking out. 'Her body will soon be a lethal weapon,' he gave Jules a questioning look, 'if it isn't already.'

Jules did his best to remain impassive.

'Tell you what,' said Leo. 'Why don't you and I give a demonstration of how it all comes together.'

Moments later they were inside the cage, the three women watching from the side, as the two men encircled one another like sparring animals. Leo had taken the aggressive role this time leaving Jules to defend himself.

He soon showed the women how to escape from a choke hold. How to twist under an arm, how to throw a kick at his mate's groin, and avoid an assault from behind. How to show fake compliance and then make a surprise fight back. How to trip Leo up.

Caught off guard, his mate crashed to the floor. 'You're a sly bugger,' Leo chuckled.

He rose and offered the three women a challenge. 'If you can take down Jules using the counter moves we've just shown you, I'll give each of you a bottle of Dad's homemade ginger beer to take away.'

Veronica tried first, but failed to make a mark, even with nails striking like talons. Jules just ducked and dodged and she ended up scratching her own arm. 'Dammit.'

Chloe did her best to knock him down but ended up on the floor herself. 'You're like a block of granite, Jules,' she complained.

Last one to try was Sam. She came up close, breathed in his aftershave, sniffed in the spicy freshness of it, and stared at him with those luminous eyes. He was lost, and taking advantage of his moment of weakness she kicked his leg from under him and felled him in one go.

Laid out on the floor he looked up as she stood over him, her hand punching the air, and Chloe and Veronica cheering as though she'd won a boxing match. Instinctively, he retaliated, grabbed her ankle and pulled her down on top of him, every contour of her body pressed into his. He knew the trouble this could bring and in a quick defensive move he reversed the position so she was under him, his arm holding her down. 'Get out of that if you can,' he challenged.

All she did was raise her head and with mischief in her eyes she kissed him full on the mouth. He couldn't help but respond, their secret out, as the others watched in a stunned silence.

'I bloody knew it,' said Leo.

Jules didn't care. All restraint went. Only a bleep from his mobile interrupted them, the relentless vibration causing him to answer it.

He felt his hopes rising when he heard his commander's voice. Everything would be well he was sure. He extricated himself from Sam, stood up, and walked from the cage, leaving Sam to deal with her astounded friends.

'What the hell's going on?' asked Veronica.

'Have you gone mad?' Chloe sounded a little jealous all the same. 'He dumped you last time, remember.'

Sam, flushed in the throes of love, just smiled at them. Nothing could worry her. Not even Jules marching out of the barn. He needed to recover just as she did.

Out in the fresh air however, Jules felt his stomach plummet. The information coming down the line was not what he wanted to hear. He had to lean on the farm gate for support as the commander informed him that even though the police conduct authority had indeed exonerated him, there was a new development. That new evidence had been brought forward, and the family of his attacker were now threatening a civil action against him.

'Whatever for?' he asked. 'What's the new evidence?'

His commander wouldn't say. He just gave him orders. 'You need to come back to London. I'm talking to lawyers. We need to stop this before it goes any further.'

Jules felt fearful not daring to think what he could be accused of. The call over, he didn't return to the barn. Instead he went inside the house and turned on the radio. Heard what the commander had said being repeated by a news reporter. How the officers involved in the recent terror attack had questions to answer. That phone footage by a dutiful teenager now shed doubt on their claims that due process was followed. *As a result,* the reporter finished on a dramatic note - *The family of Ahmed Aziz, the student attacker, were accusing the officer of manslaughter or even, murder!*

Jules sank down at the table and put his head in his hands. 'Mon Dieu.'

He heard the exuberance in the commentator's voice at the chance to relay this damaging turn of events against the police. He feared he'd be subjected to a media scrum, one that might not stop until they'd found out who he really was. Found out everything they could about him, including his involvement with Sam.

He went up to his attic bedroom and stood at the window trying to counter the hopelessness he felt. He looked at the miles and miles of open space before him, had an image of Sam and him running freely…Instead of which, their bid for happiness had to be over before it had hardly started. That the only way he could keep her safe was to end it.

He slumped down on the bed feeling defeated by this cruel twist of fate.

He was roused by voices in the bedrooms beneath. The women were packing. He sat bolt upright. He knew he should go down and face Sam, who'd be expecting him to advance things further, not sever the tie between them.

Leo's voice boomed up the stairs. 'Jules, the women are leaving.'

The three were standing by Sam's car as he followed Leo into the yard. He gave a nod to Chloe and Veronica. Sam, standing a little apart gave him a questioning smile.

The one he gave back was a grimace through gritted teeth. He hated having to do this. He knew she wouldn't forgive this second rejection.

She stood waiting for him to go over. He attempted light heartedness as he stayed where he was, and called out, 'Drive carefully, or an idiot might come around a corner - *Bam!*' He gave a jokey grin.

She was not amused. Her expression changed from confusion to anger, when he didn't go to her.

It was not helped by Chloe and Veronica loudly stating their disapproval.

'The bastard,' said Chloe.

'He's got a bloody nerve,' said Veronica.

Sam's eyes filled with tears.

He knew there was nothing he could do, no comfort he could give her. He allowed the lad inside to take over - *le moins courir* – the one with little heart, who knew how to bid adieu with eyes cold and excluding. He could be harsh when he needed to be. He would break the invisible thread between them before it ruined her life as well as his. He stared coldly until she felt forced to look away.

Sam was bewildered by this cruel dismissal so soon after their intimacy. And in front of everyone. It was humiliating. Far worse than the rejection of before. He stood to attention like the soldier he had once been, his expression implacable, as he crushed any chance for love under his feet, without any explanation, his behavior, brutish.

She turned to the gentle giant for an answer. 'Why is he doing this, Leo?'

Leo gave a helpless shrug. 'I'm as baffled as you are, Sam.'

She swallowed, then steeled herself. She couldn't give Jules the satisfaction of seeing her crumble. She kept her focus on Leo. 'Thanks for the classes. You're a great teacher,' she said loud enough for Jules to hear. 'I'll know just how to defend myself from unscrupulous men in future.' Her tone was bitter.

Leo wanted to be helpful. 'I could find a good gym near to you in

London, Sam. To keep up what you've learnt.'

She nodded, but couldn't resist one last glance at Jules. When she saw him shove his hands into his pockets and look down at the ground not wanting to even look at her anymore, she knew it was all over.

She climbed into the car with her friends, switched on the engine, and drove away, not looking back once.

Soon as her car had disappeared, Leo strode over to his mate. 'What the devil are you playing at?'

Jules raised his hands in despair. 'It's all turned bad again. Just when I thought I was a free man, there's new evidence. The family of the man I killed are threatening to take out an action against me. I could be accused of manslaughter or worse murder. The press will try to find out who I am. If they discover I have any association with Sam they'll drag her into it. I have no choice but to end it. Forget about any foolish *amour.*'

Jules turned on his heel and strode indoors.

21

Sam drove along the lane in a wounded silence. Her heart felt squeezed so tight it could hardly beat, the blood sucked out of it. This would teach her for behaving like a love-struck teenager who'd half thrown herself at a man. Hope had soared only to plummet to earth again.

'You shouldn't waste any more time on him,' said Chloe. 'He blows hot and cold like a Christmas turkey.'

'He's too complicated,' Veronica chipped in.

Sam didn't want them to know how sad she felt. That the glimmer of light that had glowed inside her had been all but extinguished. That she was about to be enveloped in darkness again.

She strove to use bravado in front of her new friends. 'I've probably had a lucky escape.'

'I should say so,' said Chloe.

'He has no feelings,' said Veronica.

Sam half envied the way Jules could shut them down when hers were so exposed and easy to read.

As she drove on she softened a little. She wanted to understand him if she could. Not turn him into a horrible person too hastily. She knew how soldiers could suffer from post traumatic stress, and wondered if this might explain his erratic behavior. He'd said there were things she didn't know, and her mind filled with questions needing answers. 'Has Leo told you where Jules lives?' she dared ask Veronica.

'In London like you, Sam. But I don't know where. Leo was cagey. A soldier's loyalty to his mates is unquestionable as you must know.'

'Why did they leave the army?'

'Leo came home to work on his father's farm, the old man was too frail to do it alone.'

This seemed a healthy reason. 'What about Jules?'

'He had to take compassionate leave to nurse his mother. When she died, he didn't return.'

This showed Jules in a kinder light, and Sam felt encouraged.

'What does he do for work?'

'Leo's cagey about that, too,' said Veronica.

Chloe let her imagination run loose. 'I can see him in MI5, as a — *spy!*

She and Veronica shared a chuckle.

Sam kept quiet. She knew how enigmatic men could intrigue. That it was part of the fatal attraction. But she couldn't engage with the idea Jules was working for the security service, it felt too James Bondish.

Her mind drifted back to their first meeting on Wimbledon common, when he'd come to her aid. How kind he had been. It would be hard to return to London knowing he was there but not knowing where, or what he was doing.

She tried to focus on her driving, as her two friends dozed beside her, safe in their rural lives, untouched by horror as hers had been.... She'd let the car slip too near the verge. She had to straighten up. The jolt woke Veronica.

'What the heck, Sam?'

'Good job we have our seat belts on,' said a flustered Chloe.

'I lost my concentration, sorry.'

'I hope you weren't falling asleep,' said Veronica.

'No. I was recalling something...'

Veronica leaned closer. 'Something that upset you?'

Sam didn't answer.

'Look, we know about you divorcing your husband. But is there something else you'd like to get off your chest?' said Chloe.

'You seem on edge a lot of the time,' added Veronica.

Sam wrestled with herself. She knew these two women were her friends now, and that maybe it was time to trust them more. When the next layby appeared she drove into it, switched off the engine, took a deep breath, and told them why she'd fled London for the safety of Dorset.

They listened in a horrified silence. When she slipped off her scarf and showed the plaster, they gasped. 'He sliced into my neck.' She touched the spot.

'I wondered why you always wore a scarf,' said Veronica.

Chloe leaned forwards and placed her hands onto Sam's shoulders. 'I can't imagine how awful it must have been.'

'Nor I,' said Veronica. 'No wonder you were scared by that drunk at the festival.'

'Well, I'd felt safe here, and he threatened that.' She turned to Chloe. 'I asked you to change my hair because I didn't want anyone to recognize me. Journalists had hounded me out of London. and I didn't want them finding me here.'

'I heard about some attack in a London suburb,' said Chloe. 'But it never crossed my mind you were involved.' She looked at her. 'You poor darlin'.'

'I don't want to be pitied. You've helped already taking me to Leo's classes, and I feel stronger already. Please don't tell anyone what I've told you. I need to keep Dorset as my bolt hole.'

'Mum's the word,' said Veronica.

'Girl Guide's honour,' said Chloe. 'Though I never was one.'

It was good to share a chuckle. Sam felt relieved she'd told them. The pair didn't dig any deeper. But they stayed awake for the rest of the journey to keep a watchful eye on her.

When they reached Bridport, Chloe let out a sigh of relief. 'Home safe.'

It made Sam think of her own home in London, and she felt a sudden urge to be there. 'I'll have to go back soon,' she said. 'Face it again.'

'Well, no hurry is there,' said Chloe.

'We must do another weekend at Leo's, first,' said Veronica.

But Sam didn't want to return to the farm and be reminded of Jules and the way they'd parted.

'Well, don't disappear without saying goodbye, will you,' said Chloe.

'Thursday's are karaoke night at the pub,' said Veronica. 'Just come and join in.'

The two women climbed out, and after a last concerned look at her, they walked off together.

When she arrived back at the cottage, Milly ran out to greet her.

115

'Can we go to the beach tomorrow, Mummy?' Her daughter begged.

'We'll go every day this week, if you like.' She swung Milly around until she squealed.

'I love it here Mummy.'

Sam put her down. 'But you miss London too, don't you?'

Milly's eyes teared over. 'I'm scared about starting proper school,'

Sam crouched down beside her. 'You'll be fine. You're *formidable.*' She used Jules's word without thinking.

Upstairs in the bathroom, she removed the plaster, and was dismayed to see the skin around the wound had become inflamed. The exercise with Leo must have affected it. She dabbed disinfectant on frantically, and put a larger plaster on. It was another reason to return to London and have it checked out.

Later, when her daughter was tucked into bed, she went into the sitting room and found her mother watching the news. 'Sam, you should listen to this.'

The commentator had breaking news about the police enquiry into the Wimbledon terror attack, and how it had - *exonerated the two officers involved.*

'That's fantastic.' Sam was relieved for the firearms officer.

'Let's have a celebratory glass of wine.' Her mother went off to the kitchen to fetch some.

Sam was about to switch off when the commentator made another announcement which all but cancelled out the other one.

The family of the attacker Ahmed Aziz have denounced the police conduct enquiry as a white wash. They claim to have new evidence which shows the officer who shot their son did not follow due process. They are consulting lawyers about bringing a High Court civil action.

Sam was horrified. When her mother arrived with the glasses of Shiraz, she no longer felt like celebrating.

'What can this new evidence be?' said her mother, also dismayed.

'I'm not sure. But if it goes ahead I'll be called as a witness. I don't think I can bear to go through it all again.' She looked at her mother. 'Can I refuse?'

Stella Elliot took hold of her daughter's hands. 'And not help the poor officer. Think what your father would say. He believed in standing up for what was right. 'Remember, *The battle for good and evil runs through the heart of every man.' Solzhenitsyn*

It was a quote Sam's had father often used. She'd been brought up with his soldier's code of ethics, about loyalty, respect, and doing one's duty.

But it was hard to help a stranger. One, whose identity was hidden behind a balaclava.

She went to bed and had the strangest of dreams. She was dancing with a man wearing a mask like the one in the musical, 'Phantom of the Opera.' She was whirled around as if taking part in some macabre ritual. One that kept her in the dark about who he was.

In the morning she called Andrea, wanting to find out how things were in London. 'I expect you've heard the Aziz family are threatening to take out a private prosecution.'

'Yes, and it's stirred everything up again,' Andrea warned her. 'Flowers are being placed at the spot where the attacker died. Some people want them removed, but others are defending the right to leave them there. The different cultures are antagonized.'

Sam had feared this.

'Everyone's been wondering where you are, but I've not said of course.'

'I was thinking of returning.'

'Well, journalists aren't loitering around your house anymore. They're more interested in badgering the Aziz family.'

Sam felt no sympathy. 'They shouldn't be taking the officer to court,' she said sharply. 'I feel so sorry for him.'

'You should come back.' Andrea tried to encourage. 'You'll need to settle Milly here before she goes to primary school.' Sam knew this was true. 'I could send my cleaner around to give your house a dust over, not that I'm trying to influence you. But I've missed having you around.'

Sam felt heartened by this. She didn't want to leave her house empty for long either. She took a deep breath to steady herself. 'I'll be there Saturday afternoon. I'll call you when I've arrived.'

Jules had to wait for his car to be fully roadworthy before the mechanic would hand it over. Not until Friday could he head back to London.

Leo drove his mate into the village to retrieve the finally operative car. He understood his friend's return to London was imperative now. 'I can give your lawyer a character testimony, if you need one,' he said.

'I may hold you to that, Leo.'

Jules removed his bags from the jeep, placed them into the boot of his car, and pushed down the lid.

'I shall miss having you around,' said Leo. 'With Dad getting frailer you've been a real help.' He gave Jules a soldierly hug, one meant to banish all fear, a fierce grip, and a hearty slap on the back, before Jules climbed into his car. 'Don't forget to keep up martial arts in London,' urged his friend. 'You'll likely need it. And keep in touch by phone.'

Jules nodded. He climbed into his car and left the giant figure of his friend standing by his jeep, his big feet rooted to the ground. Not for the first time Jules wished he could have a similar sense of permanence in his life, instead of feeling he had to keep running.

At least he could enjoy driving the Mercedes again. Feel its power. Two new tyres, a replaced converter, a new back light, which he should have replaced earlier, as well as new windscreen wipers, which batted away the light drizzle as he cruised along. He passed though villages with grand Manor houses, and cricket pitches.

He remembered when he'd first arrived in England how ridiculous the game had seemed. How he'd always refused to be roped in to play it outside his home in Colchester. It reminded him how he'd always felt different. How at school he'd been bullied for his French reserve. It was only when he'd befriended cadets at the local military base where he'd idled around, that his life in Colchester had improved. It was they who had introduced him to martial arts which had led to the bullies at school backing down. He'd left with better results than expected and had immediately enrolled as a cadet himself. Instead of being fearful, he was the one to be feared as he was turned into a fighting soldier. Aged nineteen, he'd gone on his first tour of Afghanistan. This had been another initiation into life's brutalities. He'd watched mates being blown up, bones in fragments, blood spurting like fountains as they cried out. But in the rugged Afghan landscape, jagged mountains, deep valleys, and the bluest of skies, he'd felt closer to people than at any other time in his life.

His mind drifted to Sam and how close he'd felt to her. It had evoked a feeling of belonging. A feeling that he could at last stop running, which made it all the harder to have the chance taken away.

He pressed his foot on the accelerator and raced towards London.

Sam was determined to enjoy the rest of her week in Dorset. She took Milly down to the beach to build more sandcastles. They collected fossils and seashells; ammonites of insects, fishes in crystal limestone; whirly cone shaped shells, and glass from broken bottles, sculpted by the pounding waves.

In the cottage garden she showed off some of the kickboxing moves that Leo and Jules had taught her. Milly copied, and became almost as fierce as she was. Eyes dark with anger, her daughter kicked out her legs and punched the air with her small fists. Sam felt both admiring and a little concerned it had come to this, that even her little girl was afraid of men.

In the evenings she poured over her father's philosophy books, looking for the answer to the hurt she was feeling. She soon understood it lay within herself. That only she could make a difference. She started making more notes for the self-help book she'd envisaged. Creativity became a way of overcoming the darkness she felt inside.

Thursday evening, she met up with Chloe and Veronica in the Harbour Pub, but didn't feel up to the karaoke singalong. She asked them to sit with her in a quiet corner where she told them of the new development in London. 'There will probably be a trial. I'll have to testify, and I'm dreading it. I keep having this dream about dancing with a mask wearing stranger. It feels a bit crazy...'

Veronica took hold one of her hands, and Chloe, the other.

'You're a warrior woman, now,' Veronica gave her a stern look.

'You can stand up to anyone,' said Chloe.

When she left, they gave her strong, farewell hugs.

'Keep in touch,' said Chloe.

'Come back here if it gets too much,' said Veronica.

'I will be here for Christmas, by which time it should all be over.'

Sam drove back to the cottage feeling bolstered by her country friends.

When Milly was tucked into bed she joined her mother in the garden, and together they watched the sun setting for one last time, the sea turning crimson, and the hills around touched by an umber glow. 'I shall miss this,' said Sam, as the vibrancy started dimming.

'And I shall miss sharing it with you,' her mother responded. 'Winter will arrive all too quickly, and I'll be cut off, and alone.'

Sam knew the roads would ice up or worse be drifted in snow. She reached out and took her mother's hand. 'Will you be alright without us?'

'Luckily, I appreciate solitude in my older years. Don't worry about me.'

'You were there when I needed you, Mum. I'm so grateful.'

'Dear girl. I only hope it's made up for the past. I was often too preoccupied. Being married to a soldier was both wonderful and difficult. Full of partings and meetings and the fear of loss. Your father always carried a letter with him ready to be sent in the event he didn't make it home. That was my reality.'

Sam stared out into the silent darkness pondering this. She'd do her best to forget about Jules and focus on the firearms officer. It was to him she owed her loyalty, not to some feckless Frenchman. Jules had probably forgotten her already. She felt ashamed she'd given herself to him so easily, love was for idiots.

The weekend arrived, and with Milly fighting back tears saying goodbye to granny, they set off for London. The slight drizzle made it easier to leave the beach, the sea, and the hills of Dorset behind. As the windscreen wipers swiped back and forth, like a confirmation summer was over, Sam felt a new resolve. Ahead lay the bleak winter, the threat of a trial, and her chance to stand up and be counted. Didn't they say that the truth shall set you free?

Something had to.

PART TWO

22

'London'

It was dusk by the time Jules reached his flat in Putney. He unpacked, and ordered a takeaway pizza. He opened a bottle of burgundy, put on his headphones, and lay on his sofa listening to 'Black Ops, 'Call of Duty.' The music suited the kind of cold war he was now having to face. He must fight back instead of softening into feelings that weakened him. He would not think about Sam from now on.

Saturday morning, he missed the silence of the countryside as he was woken to the sounds of the city. Barges hooted on the river, car horns blared on the streets, buses rumbled along. He almost missed the bleep from his mobile just listening to it.

He had to rally himself to answer. But when he saw it was his commander calling, he sat up. 'Yes, sir?'

'You're back, Jules.' Evans cleared his throat. 'I'm afraid that the Aziz family are pressing ahead with their civil action. It's going to the High Court. The Director of Prosecutions have taken it on.'

Jules felt gutted at the unfairness of this. He'd hoped that the new evidence could be exposed for the sham it was, and the case dropped. But with the DPP involved there was no chance for this. He swallowed down the bile. 'Is Ted also being charged?'

'Not in the same way. His is more about negligence. He'll insist he gave fair warning and that you were left with no choice but to shoot.'

Jules hated hearing that word now. 'When will the trial be?'

'We're pushing for before Christmas. We can't have the bad publicity going on and on.'

It would still be three months away. Jules quelled a rising panic. How could he wait that long?

'We'll do our best to make it happen soon, lad. We've an excellent legal firm ready to defend you,' continued Evans. 'My secretary will email you the details, as they'll want a meeting.'

Jules took a breath. 'Right, sir.'

Evans then gave him more bad news. That he had to start a new job come Monday morning. That a placement had been arranged at Putney Police station, near to where he lived.

Jules was grateful for it being near, but not happy to hear his task was about handling complaints from the public. Or, that he'd be working alongside others who'd also been demoted, for some misdemeanor or other. The commander told him not to reveal much about himself to any of them, before switching off.

The bloody war had started. Nothing for it but to get ready for battle. Jules went into soldierly mode. He flung back his covers, showered and dressed in his running outfit. He needed to clear his head and loosen up his limbs.

He headed for his nearby gym, a neat little outfit. The instructors were pleased to see him returning, and already knew he liked to be discreet. They gave him the usual access to a more private back room, where he worked out on the machines until his feelings had calmed down.

It was still early in the morning, and there were not many people around. The riverside was quiet as he pounded his way back to the apartment. The sight of the sun glinting across the water at least lifted his spirits.

He had a light breakfast and called Ted. His partner was also aghast about the coming trial.

'I return from Brighton to hear we're being hauled into court, and you accused of manslaughter or for God's sake ...*murder?*' Ted fumed.

'The commander's organizing good lawyers,' said Jules.

'I should bloody well hope so. Meanwhile we've been demoted to shite desk jobs. I'm a Duty officer at Wimbledon Police, starting eight sharp Monday morning. What about you?'

'I'm in Putney, fielding phone calls about complaints against the police.'

'Blimey. Let's meet on a regularly basis to commiserate, shall we? I promise to have your back from now on.'

Relieved to hear this Jules switched off, determined to enjoy the rest of a free weekend.

He took a ferry boat ride along the river, mingled with a few tourists, and enjoyed the cooler September sunshine. He visited his local pub for a few pints. Then ate a hot curry at a nearby Indian restaurant, before returning to his apartment for an evening alone.

He needed something stimulating to take his mind off the boring job he was about to begin. Architecture was his passion and he had a wealth of knowledge already, but wanted to increase this. He looked up courses on the subject, online.

He knew the basic building blocks, the concepts of force, compression and tension, but needed to up his Mathematics, his Algebra, his Calculus, and his Trigonometry. Scrolling down he saw he could work towards obtaining an actual qualification. And if he applied for an internship in a real practice, he could eventually become a professional.

He sat back. If he worked hard enough something that had only been a dream in his youth could become a reality. With his career in the police now under scrutiny it could become an obvious alternative, as well as a lifeline in his present circumstances.

Sam arrived back in Wimbledon on Saturday afternoon. When she saw people happily strolling on the common in the sunshine it reminded her of why she'd chosen to live here. To walk on the open heathland as a free person. She must remember this.

Entering her house, she saw Andrea's cleaner had already visited. Everything was tidy, the rooms dusted, the beds newly made, and the mail piled up on the kitchen table.

Milly claimed her home back by rushing around checking everything was as they'd left it. Then she went into the garden and jumped onto the swing.

Sam followed her out and was pleased to see the lawn had been mowed, probably by Jeremy, Andrea's husband. She felt lucky to have such London friends.

She carried in the cases and unpacked them. She gave Milly some juice to drink, and allowed her to watch some television in the sitting room. 'Elinor Wonders Why,' intrigued Milly. She liked being taught about nature by a clever rabbit.

Leaving her contented, Sam returned to the kitchen to deal with the mail. It was mostly junk and the inevitable bills. She was about to bin the rubbish, when an envelope slipped to the floor.

She picked it up, and opened it.

The letter inside was dated shortly after the attack had occurred. It was hand written. The writing was italic, artistic and insistent. When she saw the signature at the bottom Sam felt anxious. She had an image of Muslim mothers standing apart at the school gates on the day of the attack. How they'd received hostile glances from the other mothers. How she had been too traumatized to try and ease the situation.

She felt impelled to read the letter.

'Dear Sam Elliot, I speak as a woman from the Muslim faith who was ashamed of the attack on the high street. Islam should never be used as a political weapon. But I too, am suffering the consequences, if only by association. I have tried to explain I only went to school with Ahmed. That I had nothing to do with his actions that day. But still the mothers shun me because I am of the Muslim faith. I am asking for your help in changing their attitude. My daughter shouldn't have to suffer by also being ignored. The children treat her as if she were a leper. I am desperate. 'Wassalaam.' Aisha Hamdi.

Sam felt thrown back into the fray. She remembered how high emotions were then. How everyone had felt fearful and untrusting. She also knew how hard it was to be ostracized, how isolated it made one feel. It was how she'd been treated when she'd arrived in Wimbledon as a single parent. She slipped the letter into her pocket, determined to speak to Aisha at the first opportunity.

Milly, now bored with television, wanted something they could do together. They started a jigsaw puzzle. Sam felt the weight of looking after her daughter on her own again, with no granny to share the responsibility. It would be good when there was a school routine.

Later that evening, she called Andrea and thanked her for the loan of her cleaner, as well as for her husband's efforts with the lawn.

126

Andrea said it had been no trouble at all. That the cleaner could come again if she'd like her too.

Sam promptly accepted the offer. Then moved onto the more difficult topic of Aisha's letter. 'Is what she says true?' she asked. '

'She said things we didn't like, so yes, we ignored her. It was on your behalf.'

'What sort of things did she say?'

'Things like - the police were too hasty. That the attacker shouldn't have been shot.'

'But then I'd have died.'

'Exactly.'

Sam went quiet.

'Look, don't worry about it now. We'll deal with it when school starts.' Andrea changed the subject. 'Why don't we go shopping together on Monday? Polly needs a larger uniform, and Milly, a new one. I could pick you up in the morning.'

The problem of Aisha was put aside at the thought of an outing in Wimbledon. Sam felt relieved she'd have Andrea's company.

The weekend was spent easing back into home life. Sam sorted out a leak under the kitchen sink, and cleaned all the windows. She couldn't afford to pay for someone else to do such tasks.

She also made a visit to the hospital to have her scar checked out. She saw a different doctor from the one she'd seen after the attack. It was a woman who scolded her for not coming in sooner. She was told to be more vigilant in the future, or otherwise the wound might never heal.

23

Monday, and Jules set off for his new assignment at Putney Police station. It was useful he could walk there from his apartment. The air was nippy as he hurried along in his drab grey suit, bought specially for a dull desk job. His only rebellion was the azure cashmere scarf he'd wrapped around his neck, a stylish item from France.

Inside Jubilee House, he found a queue already waiting at the information counter. He stood listening to tales of lost wallets, lost pets, even lost people. He felt lost himself as he stood waiting to be greeted by the robust Duty Officer.

'Caron, you've come to work with us?' Jules nodded. 'I'm Braithwaite. I ask only that you follow the rules, be friendly and cheerful at all times, as we're a community here.' Being called by his surname made Jules feel he was back in the army again, being regimented, and he wondered if Braithwaite had also served.

He checked himself from asking and becoming too pally, as he'd been told not to reveal much. He found himself standing to attention as Braithwaite barked out the duties required in military style.

'Coffee is served at ten. Lunch is at noon, and the day ends at six. The job is about taking complaints from the public, you understand?' Jules nodded. Braithwaite pointed at a door. 'You'll find others in there, go join them.'

Jules took a breath, and walked in.

Dotted about the room were desks with screens around them, ones he thought must be sound proofed, as people spoke into landlines. A man looked up and indicated for him to sit at the only free space. Jules found the desk piled up with forms. There was also a set of head phones.

The man finished his call and swiveled his chair around to him. 'New here?'

When nervous, Jules always answered in his native tongue. *'Qui.'*

'French?'

'Half English, too.' Jules said this to put himself in a better light.

He feared his French accent would make the job more difficult. 'Name's Jules Caron.'

'I'm Billy Brown from Manchester.'

Billy made no apology for his robust Northern accent. He offered his hand to shake in a friendly manner, and Jules took hold, if a little tentatively.

'We're the first port of call for locals.' Billy informed him. 'The genuine complaints go on to the Main Complaints Commission. People fill in these forms first. He lifted a pile up as if they weighed a ton. 'There's a backlog. You'll need to sift through carefully. Call back the ones that seem genuine to confirm they still want to go on...' He looked contrite. 'What you need for this job is some French *patience.*'

Billy's pronunciation was so poor it made Jules wince. But he soon discovered that the need for *patience* was all too accurate. The forms were often badly written up, and hardly made sense. When he did call someone, he was immediately asked what had taken him so long to respond, and bombarded with abuse. His accent led to rude comments, such as, didn't he know Brexit had happened? Why didn't he go back to where he came from? That there were too many foreigners in the police anyway. Others just cursed him and cut him off. By coffee time, he felt battered.

He opted for a black expresso from the machine, and went outside to a small walled yard to find some peace. But found two women already there, smoking cigarettes. One of them offered him one. His days for smoking Gauloise were over, but he accepted a Marlboro Gold hoping to drift in a corner and be left alone. Last thing he needed was an involvement with any women. Sam had been warning enough.

But these two weren't going to let him off lightly. The one with the blonde hair, who he put at around forty, looked a bit jaded with life. The younger one was more eager and inquisitive.

'You're not the usual male type sent to work here,' she said.

'What is the usual type?' he couldn't help asking.

'Not French for one thing. Not boring is the other.'

'How do you know I'm not boring?'

'By that stylish scarf your wearing, and the spicy after shave.' She

129

sniffed. 'That lot in there wouldn't have a clue what *Sauvage by Dior* smelt like. Unlike me.' She winked. 'I worked in a men's store before I joined the police where I studied the full male range. The one you're wearing is – *crisp bergamot with spicy pepper top notes, enhanced flora, amber, vanilla, and cedar for a well-rounded strong, finish, which lasts all day.*'

Hard not to smile at this.

'I'm Kisi by the way.'

He stifled a chuckle. 'Kisi?'

'It means a child born on a Sunday, and not what you're thinking, cheeky,' she pouted. 'Church is a must where I come from.'

'And where is that?'

'Ghana, but I've lived in London for years. My papa's still lives there but my mum's English.'

'So, you're torn between two cultures like I am.' He felt better finding someone with a similar issue. 'Do you also get abuse from the callers?'

'Tell me about it.'

'I've already been told to return to gay Paree. Any tips for how to know which calls are worth bothering with?' He looked from one to the other.

'Well, not the abusive ones,' said the older one.

'It's the women who say they've been assaulted by an officer you need to listen to carefully,' said Kisi. 'They are usually scared they won't be believed.'

Jules felt defensive. 'Maybe some of them shouldn't be.'

Kisi looked at him in dismay. 'When it's taken all their courage to make a complaint in the first place, you cannot *victim blame.*' She glowered at him.

His police training for antiterrorism hadn't covered any terms like this. Jules returned to his desk feeling out of his depth.

He was a man of action anyway. Sitting down all day, listening to irate callers, was an anathema to him. Men vented their fury abut perceived police incompetence. Women about their believed bias against them. Some sobbed so much it was impossible to hear what they said. At the end of the day he felt obliterated.

Back in his apartment he collapsed on his sofa. It was lucky Leo called to ask how his day had gone, otherwise there would have been a struggle to return in the morning. 'It's the worst job on the planet,' Jules raged. 'I have to listen to angry people all day. I'm trapped like an animal.'

'Like my sheepdog penned up and barking to be free,' said his mate.

'Too right.' Jules calmed down thinking of the farm. 'Truth is, I can hardly bear to hear women claiming they've been assaulted or even raped by policemen, who took advantage of their vulnerability. Men seem to cause women nothing but misery.'

'Well,' said Leo. 'Women are less afraid to speak up since the 'Me Too,' movement.' He paused. 'I remember how you sent Sam Elliot packing. It was pretty brutal.'

'I was making sure she'd keep away from me for her own good, that's all.'

'Well, you should have been more considerate about it, my friend,' Leo still chastised him.

Jules felt it was too late to do anything about it now. He'd clamped down on his feelings for Sam. And he had worse things to worry about. 'I can't go soft,' he told Leo. 'The DPP have endorsed the civil action taken out by the family of the attacker. The trial is going ahead.'

'Jesus.' Leo was sorry to hear this. He urged his mate to keep a cool head, and to soldier on. Not to give up hope that things would turn out well in the end.

Monday morning, Andrea arrived to take Sam and Milly for the planned shopping trip. She drove down to lower Wimbledon using the back streets, knowing her friend wasn't ready to return to the scene of the attack.

Sam was also nervous someone might recognize her, with the newspapers doing more reporting of late. She stayed close to Andrea when they reached the Centre Court shopping Mall, as it was packed with other mothers also eager to buy school uniforms. It took a while to find the clothes they needed, and to reach the front of the queue to pay. By the time they did, to her dismay, Sam's wallet was missing.

'It must have dropped out on the way in,' she told the assistant, who shook her head.

'More likely, it's been nicked.' The woman looked at Sam more closely. 'Don't I know you?'

Sam fled before this went any further.

She searched for her wallet but couldn't find it anywhere. Andrea had to pay the bill, and they all congregated outside the shopping mall not sure what to do.

Andrea pointed out Wimbledon Police Station which was just along the street. 'Maybe someone's handed it in.'

Last time Sam had visited she'd given in her statement, and she felt anxious at the idea of returning.

'I'll go and ask for you,' offered Andrea.

Sam didn't want to appear feeble. 'No, I should go myself.' Leaving Milly in her friend's care, she walked towards it.

The station entrance was thankfully empty, except for the officer busy on the phone. He wasn't the elderly man she'd seen the last time she was here, who'd been so kind to her. This man took his time finishing a conversation, and when he did, he looked dismayed to see anyone was there. As though he wanted to do as little work as possible.

The truth was more complex. Ted Rowlands was on his first day of his new placement. He was doing his best to hide his shock at seeing who was standing before him. The hair was darker, but the face was all too familiar, the victim from the attack was impossible to forget. He stammered out his words. 'H...how can I help you?'

'I've lost my wallet.'

In moments like this at least one could retreat to bureaucracy. Ted reached for a form. 'I'm sorry to hear that.' He wanted to be respectful.

'Maybe someone's handed it in?' said Sam, hopeful they had.

Ted wished it were so. 'A good Samaritan, you mean? Pity they're so rare. I'm afraid it's probably been nicked.' He saw her face fall and could have kicked himself. If there was ever a good Samaritan it was she. Her honest statement, given to main command, had helped his partner and he. She'd didn't need to have her wallet stolen and suffer more indignity. He felt sorry enough to take a risk. 'I think I recognize you. Samantha Elliot, isn't it? You were involved in the terror attack.' She didn't answer. 'You did a real service giving in your statement.' He found it hard to stop now. 'I hope you can do it again for the trial.'

She looked at him with frightened eyes. 'Is it really going to court?' He nodded, but wasn't sure he should have told her, particularly when she leaned closer and whispered words he didn't want to hear.

'Is there any way I could find out who he is? I'd like to meet him and thank him for what he did. It's hard having to defend a stranger.'

Ted recoiled, knowing he'd said too much. That he must shut down this line of questioning. He retreated into formality again. 'I'm afraid no one can know that. It would put him at risk from reprisals.'

'I wouldn't tell anyone.'

Ted shook his head, and said firmly. 'It's - *impossible.*'

He focused on her missing wallet. Asked for a description - brown leather with a credit card inside. Took her contact number, and told her that if it turned up she'd be informed. Then he filed the information away.

Sam, mortified at asking for the impossible, made a hurried exit, berating herself. Of course, no one would give her the officer's name. She was being ridiculous. She should do her best to defend him and leave well alone. It was the fault of the dream she kept having about dancing with a stranger. It was making her crazy.

Ted returned to his computer feeling spooked. He'd have to warn his partner about this encounter when they next met. Last thing Jules needed was Samantha Elliot hunting him down.

Sam returned to Andrea, but said nothing about the conversation. She didn't want her friend thinking she was an idiot. Instead she busied herself on her mobile, cancelling her bank card, and ordering a new one.

Thieves never thought about the ripple effect in stealing things, the chaos it brought. She'd wanted to arrange some fun events for Milly before school began in earnest. Without a card she couldn't. Cash was hardly accepted anymore.

24

The credit card arrived a few days later, and Sam felt enabled to give Milly some fun before school started. She forgot about her foolish conversation with the duty officer, and spent the rest of the week organizing treats. A picnic on the common, swimming lessons at the local pool, and even a trip to the now reopened London zoo.

Her daughter loved the new Pigmy enclosure and the Tiger territory, but found the wild dogs scary. As they drove home, her anxiety about starting Primary school, returned. 'I don't have a friend of my own,' she said, forlornly. 'I'll be alone.'

Over the summer preschool activities, Milly had felt left out of the group. Sam feared that, due to the divorce, her daughter had grown up faster than the other children, who sensing this, may have retreated.

Back home, Milly took solace in the fossils and seashells they'd found on the Dorset beach, which gave Sam an idea. 'Maybe, you could pick some out to share with the children,' she suggested. Ancient and unique to the area they'd surely attract interest, and friendships might evolve from a spirit of generosity. Milly spent the weekend deciding which ones she could bear to part with, and which ones she simply had to keep.

Sam was in two minds about her daughter being absent for a full day. She'd miss her company. But it would also give free time for work and earning money. The capitol, left over from the half sale of the marital home, was fast dwindling. Being an actor, Simon's income was irregular, and his alimony payments were often lost to tax in Canada.

Sam sat at her desk and flicked through the notes she'd made in Dorset for a self-help book. She doubted it alone could be the answer to her financial woes, as getting it published would be nigh impossible. But a few paragraphs about Leo's self defence training caught her eye. A shining example of how to stand up for oneself. Maybe if she started with some Krav Maga moves it would grab the reader's attention and give it a kick start…

Unbidden an image of Jules came into her mind doing kickboxing, lithe and swift. It was hard not to wonder where he might be in living in London. She'd first met him on the common, and it made her suspect it wasn't far from here. What would she do if she came upon the him?

Run, if she had any sense. Even if she would like to know why he'd ended things so brutally.

On Sunday evening, her school uniform laid out ready, Milly punched her way around the bedroom to bolster herself, before worn out, she settled down for bed.

She relaxed as Sam read aloud from – 'I Don't Want to go to School' – The escapades of a dinosaur and a mouse had Milly giggling, and she went off to sleep without further ado.

Next morning, she rose eager to put on her new uniform.

Sam took photos, which she forwarded to Granny in Dorset, who facetimed back immediately.

'You look so grown up,' said Stella Elliot. 'This is a momentous day in your life, Milly. I'm so proud of you.'

Sam walked her daughter along the few streets that led to the school. A colder September had brought the first scents of autumn. The aroma of wood smoke mingled with the sweet musky smell of decaying leaves.

When they arrived, other children stood holding tight to their mother's hands, reluctant to go through the gates until the very last moment.

Sam felt better when she was welcomed back. Olivia, the model, told her how much better she looked. Barbara, the psychologist, reminded Milly she could come on a playdate whenever she wanted to.

Emboldened by this, Milly brought out her fossils and shells, and was soon surrounded by both mothers and children. It gave Sam the chance to look around and spot two people standing apart, as though still being excluded, a Muslim woman and her child.

Olivia saw her too. 'We've tried to engage, but she's not like us.'

'How do you mean not like us?' Sam felt defensive on the woman's behalf.

'Well,' Olivia flushed. 'She's not on our side. She said things we didn't appreciate.'

'I think she wrote to me,' said Sam. 'She's upset. I should speak to her.'

'I'm not sure that's wise.' Olivia looked concerned.

At that moment the woman gave Sam a challenging look, and determined to sort this out, she walked over.

She was given a cool reception. The woman seemed haughty and defensive, and her child hid behind her. Sam pulled the letter from her pocket. 'Are you Aisha? Did you send me this?'

The woman glanced at the letter, and then dismissed it. 'I wrote that a while ago, but you didn't answer.'

'I had to flee to the country to escape from journalists.'

A flicker of sympathy in her eyes, before Aisha glanced over at Olivia and the other mothers. 'Well, they're blaming me for someone else's actions. Just because I knew Ahmed Aziz, doesn't mean I'm like him.'

'You knew the attacker?' Sam was dismayed.

'We were at school together. He was a gentle person then, and from a good family.'

Sam found this hard to hear. It made him sound more human, a classmate, a friend, even someone's son. She shivered.

Unabashed, Aisha carried on. 'You do know there's new evidence.'

'You've seen this *evidence?*'

'No. But the Inman from the mosque has. He said it's a phone video that shows no warnings were given.'

Sam had to gather herself. 'Well, I heard them clearly.'

'It'll be you against the witness.'

'I shall tell the truth.'

Aisha went quiet for a moment before gathering herself. 'I have the right to question what really happened without being punished for it.' Her child poked her head forwards. 'And my daughter deserves to be made welcome on her first day of school.' She glanced over at Milly who was still surrounded by children, 'as much as yours.' She coaxed her daughter to stand in front of her. 'Don't be shy, Noor.'

The child gazed up at Sam with tears in her eyes. It was hard to see how anxious she looked.

Sam slipped her a smile. 'Hello Noor, I'm Sam.' She offered her hand. But the child lowered her head and stared at the ground.

'In Arabic, Noor means brightness,' said Aisha, trying to rouse her daughter.

Sam tried humour. 'My daughter's called Milly. I don't know what it means Noor, except perhaps – *trouble.*'

The child looked up and gave a faint smile. Then lowered her head again.

Sam remembered how lonely it had felt when she and Milly had been ostrasised.

She turned to Aisha. 'When I first came to this school Milly and I were also ignored. I'm divorced and a single mother. I think the other mothers feared I'd steal their husbands. I wouldn't of course. But people react badly when they feel threatened.'

Aisha looked at her more sympathetically. Sam glanced over at Milly, who caught her eye, and came running over.

The two children stood staring at one another in silence. Aisha started stroking Noor's hair and the gold bracelet dangling from her wrist caught Milly's eye. Aisha held it closer to her. 'The writing's is Arabic - *Sabr* and *Salah,* which means patience and prayer in English.' She flicked her wrist, the gold caught the light, and glittered. 'I made it.'

'Are you a jeweller?' asked Sam.

Aisha nodded.

Sam glanced back at the mothers, saw the chance of bringing them together. 'I'm sure they'd like to see your work.' Too late she saw Aisha was insulted.

'I don't need their approval,' she bristled. 'I need their acceptance of me as a person with equal rights.'

'I'm sorry, that was clumsy of me. I was trying to overcome the impasse.'

'It's up to them to do that by apologizing.'

The two children fidgeted at the rising tension between the two mothers. Instinctively, Milly held a somewhat cherished fossil to Noor.

There was a pause before the child took hold. But she looked happier when Milly told her she could keep it.

The school bell rang. Noor took fright again, and clung to her mother.

In turn, Milly stepped closer to Sam, who gave her a last hug and whispered, 'Maybe you and Noor could help one another?' Milly reached her hand out to Noor, who after a moment's hesitation, took hold, and together she and Milly walked into the playground. They didn't look back until they reached the school doors. A last glance at Sam and Aisha, who frantically waved, before the two small children disappeared inside the building.

Others followed until the playground was empty, mother's left aimless at the gates in a silence, like the one after the last post.

Aisha reached for her hanky. 'We have lost our Baba's.'

'Life's going by too fast.' Sam reached for hers. They both wiped their eyes. 'Look at us, sissies,' sniffed Sam.

'Not entirely,' said Aisha. 'You did come and speak to me. It can't have been an easy thing to do. I only hope the other mothers will follow your example.'

With a warmer smile she walked away, and a group of women from her own community crowded around her. Sam saw how popular she was.

Her own group of mothers were too preoccupied by the loss of their children to ask any questions. She could only speak with Andrea about the issue with Aisha, as they walked home.

She told her friend that now that the trial was certain to happen, it could make things even more divisive. That they needed to make amends with the Muslim mother's at school.

Andrea responded well. Saying that with the term now started everyone should pull together for the sake of the children. And if an apology was needed she'd see one was given.

The mood lightened and Andrea changed the subject. 'I like your new hair colour. It's not as glamorous as being a blonde, of course.'

'I've no wish to be glamorous. I want to be ordinary.'

'Well I'm ordinary and it's boring.'

They both laughed. Sam knew that with her skittish nature Andrea could never boring, anyway.

Sam touched her hair. 'I had it coloured in Dorset. The hairdresser became a friend.'

They'd reached Andrea's home. 'You haven't said how you spent your time there,' she fished for her key.

'It was quiet and peaceful at first, but later it became quite exciting.' Sam couldn't help a secretive smile.

'Well then, I think we need a girl's night out at the 'Rose and Crown pub,' so I can hear all about it,' said Andrea, as she opened her front door.

Sam clutched onto the gate. 'I'm not sure I'm ready to face the high street.'

Her friend turned back. 'I know,' she said gently. 'But you'll have to try soon. We could go together. Have a quiet coffee and get back some normality, first.' And Andrea, the solver of all problems, went inside.

Sam had the more pressing problem of how to earn money. She arrived home determined to resolve this. The idea of returning to acting didn't feel right and she had a better idea. When her marriage had ended, and she was alone with Milly, she'd studied in the evenings to gain qualifications as a drama teacher. Now, she was determined to make use of this and she decided to call her agent with a proposition.

Sid Roper was more than happy to hear from her. He launched in with ideas of his own. 'Everyone's been asking about you after that monstrous attack. I could get you on the Graham Norton show. You'd get so much sympathy that offers for acting would come flooding in.'

Sam was appalled. 'Sid, you can't be serious. I could never talk about what I went through on a chat show.' Her agent went silent. 'I'm not going back to acting. I'm calling to offer coaching for actors on your books. I'm a qualified drama teacher and could help brush up their audition videos, and boost their confidence.' She didn't add she hoped it might also boost her own. 'I want to work from home.'

Sid complained she was selling herself and him short, before coming around to the idea. 'I do have some novice actors who could do with improving their diction. They mumble their lines these days. I'll suggest it to them and see what happens.'

Encouraged by this, Sam went to her computer and put in a more general advertisement offering classes in public speaking. And used her old married name of *Jones* for the email address, as a protection.

25

Jules tried harder with the complaint calls. But he couldn't help interrupting when things became hard to bear. He asked Kisi for more advice and she told him to imagine himself in the same position of powerlessness as the women he was listening to. That he needed to be more empathetic.

It shouldn't have been difficult. He already knew about powerlessness from his childhood. It wasn't only women who suffered in this way. But having spent his adult years trying to suppress any feelings of helplessness, he found listening to others in distress was challenging his own way of coping. Namely never to weaken, to fight, and be strong. That failing - to run in the opposite direction.

The complainants bandied labels about for their conditions like, PTSD. ADHD. OCD. He preferred to use simpler language to describe what was happening to him. How he was losing himself as a man set apart. A man who walked alone. He had a lawyer to meet any day to discuss the coming trial and a show of strength was what he needed, not empathy. He didn't want to become a puny version of himself when he needed to be taken seriously.

Sam felt the need to be fitter for her return to work. She remembered Leo had offered to find a gym near to where she lived. She'd call him and ask for the details.

It still took a few days to pluck up the courage to call. The last time they'd met was when Jules had ended things badly in front of his mate, humiliating her. She felt caught off balance when Leo answered straight away. 'I thought I'd have to leave a message, that you'd be busy outside,' she said, flustered.

'Well, I do have a cow calving so this will have to be quick.' There was a pause. 'Are you okay?'

'Yes. But I wanted to pick your brains about finding a gym near to where I live. To keep up the good work.' She told him it was in Wimbledon, and waited as he rummaged about, paper rustling.

'I suppose Brixton's too far?'

'A bit.'

'How about Wandsworth? I know one run by an ex-soldier mate.'

'Is he as good as you and Jules?' The name was out before she knew it.

'I'd have thought Jules was a person non-gratis for you, Sam.'

'He left questions I deserve answers to,' she said acidly.

Leo fell silent, then cleared his throat. 'I'd get yourself strong Sam, and forget about him.' She was given the contact website for the gym. 'Mention my name to Adam and Tim.' He lowered his voice. 'I wish you all the best, you know that, don't you, Sam?' And the gentle giant ended the call.

She felt he was rooting for her but couldn't say so. She didn't waste any time googling the gym. When she discovered it operated an open-door policy, and that she could drop in at any time, she seized the opportunity, changed into her outfit, and drove straight over.

The gym was located on the southside of Wandsworth common. London had more greenery than any other city in the world.

On arrival at the basement room, full of the usual equipment, she was made welcome. The instructors were impressed that Leo Henshaw had sent her, and more than eager to assist. Tim had a group to deal with. But she did an hour long Krav Maga work out with Adam. After which, she was ready for a cool down drink.

Adam joined her and started talking about his soldiering days in Afghanistan.

'I felt safe with Leo on the rooftops as a sniper. He hardly ever missed, him and his partner.'

Sam felt her pulse quicken. 'You must mean Jules Caron.'

'Didn't know his name. He was more elusive.'

'Jules was at Leo's farm. He taught me kickboxing moves.'

'Well, you better show me.'

Adam made her work out for longer.

Before she went, she let her curiosity get the better of her, and told him that Jules lived in London but that she had no idea where.

Adam said he didn't either, but added that some of his ex-soldier mates, might. That they often held reunions.

He picked up her now empty bottle. 'You'll be coming here again, won't you?'

'I will.'

Well, if I hear anything, I'll tell you then.'

Sam left the building feeling brave but also stupid for asking. If Adam did find anything out how could she go looking for Jules when he'd made it clear he wanted nothing to do with her. She drove home feeling agitated.

It was fortunate that Andrea chose this day to improve the atmosphere at the school gates. It revived Sam.

Her friend had persuaded Olivia and Barbara and the other mothers that that with the trial going ahead it was time to make a bridge with the Muslim mothers. That for the benefit of good relations between the different cultures an apology should be made to Aisha.

It was done by the gates so that everyone could hear. Aisha accepted with grace. Sam saw she was not one to hold grudges. All the mothers mingled together after this, trying to be friendly.

Divisions started to heal as the normal pressures of school life stook over. Children fell over, fell out, but quickly made up again, as they strived to become what the headmistress desired - *One big happy family.*

Milly and Noor became firm friends, which brought Sam and Aisha closer. After school they took to walking on the common to allow their children to unwind. It wasn't long before they were discussing how to ease the tensions in the wider community. Sam told her new friend she still hadn't been able to return to the high street. That she hated the idea of seeing flowers left for her attacker.

'They're not all for him,' Aisha tried to reassure her. 'I left white roses as a symbol of peace for everyone involved.'

Sam was moved by this. When she returned home she called Andrea. 'It's time I faced the high street. Can I take up your offer to accompany me?'

Andrea said she'd like nothing better, and it was arranged for Thursday at noon.

26

Thursday was also the day that a commiserating lunch had been arranged between Ted Rowlands and Jules. One where they could unburden themselves about their new placements.

Jules used the back streets to reach lower Wimbledon, still wanting to avoid the high street in case bad memories were stirred.

His partner was waiting at the assigned café, with British bacon butties, and steaming mugs of coffee. Jules would have preferred a lunch of a Caesar salad and a glass of wine, but he set about eating as much as he could stomach. After an obligatory first bite, he asked Ted how being a duty officer was going.

'Bloody boring. I sit at a computer most of the time studying crime statistics, waiting for a member of the public to appear and harass me,' his partner grumbled. 'How's yours?'

'Dealing with complaints is like dodging bullets.'

'I'll bet.' Ted leaned forwards. 'Mind you, I had a shock on my first day.'

Oh?' Jules took another bite of his buttie, but found it was no better than the first.

'I was behind the counter and in walked the actress whose life you saved - *Samantha Elliot.*'

Jules choked himself.

Ted leaned back and folded his arms. 'Her hair colour had changed, but it was still her. She'd lost her wallet, or worse, it had been nicked. She came in to ask if anyone had handed it in.'

Jules let air out through his teeth.

'Don't worry, she'd no idea who I was.' Ted paused. 'However, I told her that I knew who she was.'

'Why did you do that?' Jules felt worried now.

'I felt sorry for her. I asked if she knew the trial was happening, and she was shocked. She said it would be hard to defend a stranger. She wanted to know who he really was so she could thank him in person for saving her.'

'Mon Dieu.'

'She was fishing for you, Jules.'

'I hope you put her off.'

'Most definitely. I told her it wasn't possible. That there could be reprisals if anyone knew his identity, and she left shortly after.' He leaned closer. 'You do know she'll be the most important witness for the defence. I have her details. If her wallet turns up, maybe I should deliver it in person, and encourage her not to lose her nerve.'

'I don't think that's a good idea.' Jules could see Ted was on a mission. His religious faith sometimes made him intervene when he shouldn't. 'It could look like coercion.'

Ted looked worried now.

'You think we should leave her alone?'

Jules nodded and changed the subject. 'I'll be meeting with the lawyers soon. I promise to keep you in the loop.' And he made a hasty exit.

Mid-day, Sam and Andrea set off for the high street with determined steps. The dull skies fitted their sombre mood as they walked along arm in arm.

When they arrived, they found the street was jammed with traffic. Cars were bumper to bumper, engines idled, and fumes of petrol left a stench in the air.

'Time people they were forced to buy electric cars,' complained Andrea, who already had one herself. 'Do you want to come back another day?'

Sam shook her head. 'I can't avoid this any longer.' And on they went.

Jules was annoyed to find his route blocked by an accident. He was sent on a diversion up the hill and could only go through the high street, the very place he'd wanted to circumvent. The situation was made worse when he found himself snarled up in traffic. He had to sit bumper to bumper with other cars, his Merc half straddled over a pedestrian crossing. To his dismay, he was near to where the attack had happened

145

and gruesome images pushed into his mind - people running, blood on the pavements, Ahmed holding a knife to Sam's throat...

He hit the radio button, leaned his head back, closed his eyes, and allowed Pavarotti's rendering of, 'Nessun Dorma,' to obliterate horror from his mind. He was grateful such a voice could transcend anything.

Andrea took umbrage when she saw some idiot had his car half blocking the pedestrian crossing. The volume of music coming from inside was far too loud. The driver had his head laid back, and his eyes closed, as if he was in a trance. She shouted at him, 'Turn it down!' But nothing penetrated his reverie.

Sam was too focused on crossing the street to worry about any of this. Pavarotti's voice only served to spur her on, and she pulled Andrea away.

Barbara, the psychologist, had given the advice that to avoid panicking Sam should concentrate on the people here today. Ones who were drinking coffee, and sitting at café tables. How the convivial atmosphere they created would help counter any bad memories. Then the heart palpitations, the sweating palms, and shaking lips that might render her helpless, would dissipate. But when Sam saw flowers placed on the ground where the attacker had lain dead, not the white roses that Aisha had once left, but blood red ones, she was bombarded by sickening images. The attacker's knife at her throat, his sweat dripping onto her skin, the bullet hole between his eyes...

Unable to continue she backed away. 'I can't do this. It's no good.'

Andrea placed an arm around her. 'Breathe, breathe,' she urged. 'You can't give up now you've come this far.'

A quote from her father's books came to Sam's aid. *Keep your face always towards the sunshine, and shadows will fall behind you.* She lifted hers to the noon sun's rays, felt it warming her, as she and Andrea stood close together. The fun and laughter of the day soon filtered in. The hellish images dissipated, and Sam returned to the present.

'How about a that cup of coffee?' she said to her friend.

'Expresso, black?'

'A Latte would suit better.'

Her step lighter, Sam followed her friend to an empty outside table, where she sank down, relieved the ordeal was over.

The traffic started moving again. Jules came out of his reverie and turned off the music. In his haste to leave he jerked the Merc forwards, and it stalled. The crunching noise of clutch failing drew the attention of two women at a nearby café table. One turned to glare at him. But it was the other who arrested his attention. Her tumble of hair reminded him of Sam, who'd already been brought back into his mind, by Ted.

For a moment he allowed himself to imagine it really was her. That he could roll down his car window and call out, 'Sorry, you lost your wallet. Sorry, I left you the way I did. Sorry, for everything,' like any normal guy might. But he was anything but a normal guy. He was a man about to be sent to trial. He couldn't call out even if he wanted to. And with her head down, as she sipped her coffee, he couldn't really be sure it was she. People started honking their horns from behind him, impatient for him to move, and his gears released, he revved away at full throttle.

The noise had Andrea glowering after him. 'He would be driving a bloody Merc.'

'A Merc?' Sam raised her head, but only saw a flash of silver disappearing.

She reached for her coffee, content for once to sit back and watch the world go by, the good life on the high street, restored.

27

Jules had on his crispest white shirt, and the slim French suit he'd recently acquired, for his meeting with the lawyers.

He took the district line to Waterloo. From there he walked over the bridge and headed to Fleet street on his way to Lincoln Inn Fields. On the way he passed two courts, 'The Royal Courts of Justice,' an ornate Victorian Gothic structure with several towers, and over a thousand inner rooms, like a fairy tale building. And the more intimidating, 'Old Bailey'. The gilded Lady of Justice rising above it on a globe of the world, her sword and balancing scales held high as a warning to all those contemplating doing any wrong.

His step grew brisker. He'd brought along a dossier of information he'd collected about how fanatics operated. How they built a false story to hide their real purpose and could even fool their own families before they reached the point of no return. He wanted to show how they had real intent to do harm.

He arrived at Lincoln Inn Fields and passed through the warren of passages, history in the very walls, even Shakespeare had walked these streets. He found the firm he was looking for in one of the historic buildings situated in an area known as, 'The Chambers of Barristers.'

He went inside the elegant Georgian building to find chandeliers hanging from ceilings, plush carpets under his feet, and ornate cornices. Hard not to feel intimidated by the grandeur.

A clerk walked him along numerous corridors where office doors were left open and he could see barristers at work with files and papers piled high on their desks and people coming and going. There was so much activity Jules wondered if any of them would have time for him. When he was shown into a large room with no files around as though it was only used for interviews, and offered a seat at an empty desk near to a bay window, he stared at the small park outside, wishing he was there instead of waiting in this bleak room for his lawyer to arrive.

Hearing footsteps, he turned, expecting to see an experienced, elderly man, one who'd reached the lofty position of being a senior silk.

Instead, a woman entered.

He tried to hide his disappointment as she walked towards him, her high heels clicking on the mahogany floor. She was wearing a loose black trouser suit, held a laptop under her arm, and looked in her early forties.

He didn't want to appear chauvinistic. Kisi had lectured him on this. It was the lawyers age that disturbed him. He'd read the firm's blurb. It took twenty years to reach the status of senior silk. His concern must have showed.

'Don't worry I *am* a senior silk.' She held out a hand. 'I'm Tanya Osborne. And you are - Officer Y.'

It felt hard to be reduced to a letter. He hesitated before he took hold. Her skin was cool, her manner impatient, as though she was eager to get started.

She moved behind the desk, sat down, opened a desk drawer and pulled out a piece of paper, which she pushed across the table. 'Your case has gone through the committal proceedings. The trial should take place in a few months, time. I need you to sign this.'

He looked down and saw an agreement declaring she had the right to act for him.

'I need you to use a new signature for anonymity.'

'Won't Officer Y do?''

She shook her head. 'It has to be a proper name for documents.'

Jules was getting used to being invisible, but for a moment he was flummoxed as to what he could use. Then he remembered a dead architect he'd once admired, who'd had the same mixed heritage as him. 'Will *Jean Bailey*, do?'

'There's a good English ring to Bailey.'

'You think the English side is more important?' He couldn't help the sarcasm in his voice. He didn't sign the form either. He wasn't sure she was right for him.

She frowned. 'You can't afford to become riled this easily, *Jean.*'

'I've a lot to be riled about. How can phone footage that must have been tampered with be used as evidence? My partner gave three clear warnings. They must have been wiped off.'

She leaned forwards. 'I will subpoena the lad to hand the video over and have it checked independently.'

Jules felt encouraged, but still didn't sign the form.

She leaned back. 'I called your partner earlier.'

Jules wondered how Ted had reacted to her.

'It's a pity his camcorder jammed and we have to rely on his verbal testimony only. Are you sure he gave due warnings?'

'Of course, he did.' This was crucial.

'He'll speak for your good character, which will help.' She paused. 'Is there anyone else who could do the same?'

For a moment Jules fell silent remembering his father's damning attitude towards him. But he swiftly recovered. 'My unit commander will speak for me. Evans. And a mate who fought alongside me in Afghanistan, Leo Henshaw.'

'Good, we won't use their real names. Nothing must be traced back to you.' She leaned forwards. 'By some accounts you're a hero. By others you acted recklessly. The prosecution claims you're a hot head and trigger happy, which is it?'

He felt indignant. 'Neither. You need to be cold as ice to take a shot. Heat doesn't come into it.' Tanya Osborne's cheeks flushed, as though she was a little hot herself. 'I'm not a hero either,' he added. 'I just did my job.'

She nodded. 'Fine. That's good.'

At this affirmation, Jules fished inside his briefcase, and pulled out one of the files he'd brought along. He explained it contained information about the assailant. 'Ahmed was under our surveillance. I was worried he was building up to something before the attack.'

'You mean had you acted earlier, what happened could have been prevented?' She looked shocked as she read on. Jules stayed quiet. 'Shouldn't bells should have been ringing?'

They had been for him. 'Ted thought I was rushing to the wrong conclusions.'

'Sounds like your partner made the wrong call.'

'I don't want him vilified on my account. He's a good man.'

150

'I'll do whatever it takes,' said Miss Osborne.

Who was it said - *a man is no greater than his ambitions?* Jules observed the eyeliner accentuating her dark eyes. The light sheen of lipstick on her lips. Better to have Tanya Osborne on one's side than as an adversary. He signed the form and pushed it over to her.

She nodded, and then started scrolling down her laptop, her expression business like. 'It's reported that the police federation are dropping the policy of *shoot to kill,* under pressure from politicians. Were you informed of this before the attack?'

'No. I was not.'

'Are the police being supportive?'

'Some are.' Ted had told him the unit was behind him, but that others in the force were more divided.

'You've not been with them for long.' She looked sympathetic. 'This must have been a hard initiation.'

'I got used to those in Afghanistan.'

'I see you were awarded a medal for bravery. That's another plus.' She was firing out the information she had on him. 'It's your father who is French, I see.'

He nodded. It was tiring explaining this. 'But we are estranged. I came to live in England with my mother when I was fourteen, after which they divorced.'

'The prosecution will probe how a dysfunctional family might have affected you.'

Jules felt perspiration break out on his brow. He reached for his hanky and wiped it away. He felt like damaged goods. 'How can I stay anonymous if they examine my past and expose where I've come from?' He was worried that his father's connection with casinos and criminals would be revealed.

'We'll keep France out of it.'

'How?' His accent would give him away.

'The trial will be heard in a closed court for safety reasons. You'll appear by video link with the screen darkened and your voice disguised. I will do everything I can to protect you. I've not lost a case in a while, and I don't intend to lose this one either.'

151

She opened her desk drawer and pulled out a burner phone. 'Use this for any communication with me, in your new name.' She tapped in her own number and handed it to him.

She closed her computer and stood up. 'That's enough for now. Keep any contacts of a personal kind to a minimum. And keep out of trouble.'

Jules left only hoping he could. Much longer at his desk job in Putney, and he'd explode.

28

A couple of weeks passed before Sam returned to the gym in Wandsworth. She'd pushed the idea she might find out more about Jules to the back of her mind and was taken by surprise when Adam had news.

'One of my ex-soldier mates ran into Caron in a quiet pub in Putney and the Frenchman let slip that he lived nearby.'

'Putney?' This was a suburb right next to Wimbledon. Jules had been close, all the time.

After another hour of exercise, Sam returned home not knowing what to do with this new information. It was a relief to be distracted by a call from her agent.

'I have four actors on my books interested in being coached by you,' announced Sid.

'That's fantastic.'

'I'll see they contact you soon. When you've had enough of being a teacher maybe you'll come back to acting.'

She laughed at this, thanked him for his effort, and ended the call.

She went to her computer to check whether anyone had answered her advert. And found an email from a businessman who wanted help with a stammer. She wasn't sure she could do anything about this, but emailed him back offering a date for a preliminary meeting in a week's time.

He replied instantly, and it was fixed in the calendar. Ben Miller's stammer might be a challenge, but she had her first client.

She felt a desire to celebrate, and on impulse called Andrea. 'How about that girl's night out? My work is taking off and I feel the need to break out of a boring routine.'

'So, do I.' Andrea was happy to oblige. 'Jeremy owes me some babysitting. How about this Saturday? You could bring Milly over to ours for a sleep over with Polly, and we can sneak off to the Rose and Crown.'

Sam allowed herself a more risqué idea. 'Maybe we should go

further afield. How about Putney? We could visit a quiet pub where we could talk more privately, and I can tell you about my time in Dorset.'

Sam wasn't sure she should tell her friend about her secret lover. Or that she was hoping to see him there, if only for one last time.

It all sounded innocent to Andrea. 'Great idea. 'We can let our hair down later. Go and dance the night away at - 'The Half Moon.'

Sam had heard of this famous pub, but had never been. She knew it had live bands playing, and sounded fun.

Usually, after work Jules had a quiet drink in his local, but come the weekend he liked to break out of the monotonous routine and head for something different. Saturday evening, he walked over Putney Bridge heading for the vibrant sound of music coming from a pub famous for its tribute bands.

'The Half Moon,' was as usual packed to the brim. Jules had to push his way through a mob to reach the one vacant bar stool left.

The French barman was always glad to see a fellow countryman. Maurice poured out a large glass of burgundy for Jules and smiled conspiratorially. 'Ça va être une nuit folle! Le groupe Elvis Presley joue. Vous devriez descendre et participer.'

Jules rarely joined in with anything these days. But, as he sat sipping his wine, Elvis Presley's, 'All Shook Up' pounded up from the cellar. The sound mingled with the chatter of the London classes, as, the working week over, they drank champagne, and swayed to the beat without a care. He found himself drumming his fingers on the bar, a bit *sans souci*, himself. Emboldened he looked around for someone to dance with. Maybe *Maurice* was right and he should join in. What harm would there be if he jived the night away? At least he'd forget his troubles.

Andrea drove them to Putney, her electric car gliding along the high street in an eerie silence. Sam was worried they'd run some poor person over who didn't hear them coming.

They parked in a side street and headed for the river. Andrea was pulled towards the sound of loud music and Sam had a job to persuade her to visit a quieter pub first.

'It'll be too noisy in there to talk. You said you wanted to hear about my time in Dorset, remember?'

'Sorry Sam, I'm getting carried away by our night of freedom.'

The first pub was quiet because it was almost empty. There was no Jules to be seen. A lone old man sat listening as Sam filled Andrea in about her time in Dorset.

Her friend was happy enough to sip her gin and tonic and hear Sam recall her jogs along the cliff tops, with the spectacular views of the sea in all weathers. How she'd made two new friends in the local seaside town. Chloe, with her sharp tongue, and Veronica, with her desire for robust sex with an ex-soldier. How Leo had run courses in self defence, which the three of them had attended. How they'd driven to his farm on the Salisbury Plain, where he had a gym set up in a barn. And how they'd learned the amazing, Krav Maga.' Sam ended with a flourish.

Andrea hadn't a clue what she meant. 'Krav...*what?*'

'Krav Maga. It's a form of contact combat. A martial arts training in self defence. I'm still doing it here.'

'Good grief.'

I won't need your rape alarm anymore, Andrea. I can take care of myself. I can kickbox and punch hard. And, it's great exercise.'

'When it comes to exercise this will do nicely, thank you.' Andrea lifted her gin and tonic up with a sweep of her arm, took a good gulp, and plonked the glass down again. 'How's that for movement?'

Sam couldn't help laughing. She felt a little light headed after her own martini. She glanced at the door on the faint chance Jules might just appear. She was on the brink of telling Andrea about him when her friend suddenly stood up. 'This place is as dead as a dodo. Let's go.'

The moment had passed. Sam thought it was probably a good thing she hadn't said anything about Jules. There was no sign of him anyway. She pushed her head inside two other pubs on the way down the street hoping to see him, but of course she didn't. Only then did she give up all hope it could happen. That she was wasting her time.

They had reached the river. Lights rippled across the water as ferry boats carried their evening passengers. Passing barges honked out warnings, their large cargos, piles of wood and concrete, loomed out of the darkness.

People were streaming towards the sound of music and Sam started to feel something she hadn't felt since her return from Dorset – excitement. She should enjoy the night out, embrace the feeling of celebration, and forget about her wayward lover.

She was glad of her coat in the late October air. Underneath she had on a sleek fitting velvet dress. The V neck might be a little too low, but at least the velvet choker around her neck, hid her scar.

They entered, 'The Half Moon,' to find it packed with revellers, who they had to squeeze past. Any seating on the upper floor was taken, so they went down to the cellar, the music growing louder with every stone step they took.

They walked in see a dance area, with a stage at one end, where a middle-aged male band was belting out, 'Rock Around The Clock.' The lead singer had greased back hair, and a glittery outfit, and was doing a good imitation of Elvis Presley. People were jiving like mad. Men lifted their partners up and swung them around as if they were made of rubber. The smell of perfume and sweat was so overwhelming Sam wanted to go back upstairs. But two guys came sauntering up. One had a smooth smile, and his hair slicked back.

'Fancy a dance?' he crooned to Andrea.

'Why not?' Determined to enjoy herself she followed him onto the floor.

Sam had little choice but to allow the other guy to take her, too.

Jimmy proved to be a keen dancer. A bit too keen. Sam was twisted and twirled around to - 'Blue Suede Shoes.' And, 'All Shook Up,' as they followed in rapid succession. Turned out Jimmy was a die-hard Elvis fan, who sang along to each song. She did her best to match his enthusiasm but found his moves more a test of stamina than of dancing. It was so unlike the physical zing she'd experienced with Jules back in the summer. When the music changed to, 'Love me Tender,' and Jimmy moved in for a smooch, she ducked under his arm. Andrea was left to deal with her own increasingly amorous partner alone, as

Sam fled upstairs.

She retreated to the ladies, looked in the mirror and saw her disheveled appearance. Hot and steamy to no avail. She cooled her face with cold water, gave her hair a good brush, and put on some lipstick, before venturing forth. The evening was not turning out as she'd hoped and a glass of sparkling wine was the only answer.

Her chance of ordering one, however, turned out to be impossible. As a single woman she was ignored. Men waving wads of cash, ordered multiple glasses and pushed her back. Spotting a lone guy sitting on a bar stool, she edged up behind him.

As he commandeered the bartender with a careless snap of his fingers, she tapped him on the shoulder. 'Can you order a sparkling wine for me, otherwise, I'll be waiting all night.'

Instead of doing as she asked, the man twisted around to face her. Silence.

29

They were both too shocked to speak.

Sam had given up on this happening.

Jules had convinced himself it shouldn't.

Now, they were so close they were almost touching.

Jules couldn't help noting how lovely she looked. Her hair shining, her cheeks aglow, her eyes pale and lucid.

Sam couldn't help noting how striking he was. His hair cropped, the same strong features, only the eyes were a little duller, as though he needed someone to brighten them up. Half of her wished she could do this. The other wanted to give him a good slap for hurting her.

Jules found his voice first. 'What are you doing here, Sam?'

'I'm on a girl's night out. How about you?'

'Having a quiet drink.'

'In a noisy pub like this?'

Jules felt caught. At least if he had to let her down this time he'd do it kindlier. He slid off his stool. 'Look, I know you're mad at me. And I deserve no better. But I have to go.' He indicated to his seat. 'Take my place and enjoy your evening.' He turned to leave.

She couldn't let him do this to her again. His glass was still half full. She could smell the fruitiness of the Burgundy, redolent of cherries. 'Why can't you finish your drink?' She kept her eyes on him as she sat down on the stool. 'Explain why you treated me so badly.'

He asked the bartender to bring her the wine, and with a grin Maurice threw in a bag of nuts for free.

Sam raised her glass, hoping Jules would join her. Instead, he pulled his scarf, a stylish azure blue, tighter around his neck, and turned away again.

She felt a kind of fury, and with her free hand she reached out to stop him. She'd almost caught hold, when, from nowhere, Andrea appeared and barged in between them, blocking him out.

'Sam, how could you abandon me?' she chastised. 'What are you doing here, all alone?'

'I'm not alone. Look…' Sam edged her aside. But to her dismay Jules had gone, slipped away by stealth. 'He was right in front of me!' she cried.

'Who was?'

'I was going to make him explain.'

'Explain what?'

Sam slipped off the stool. 'Take my place Andrea. Enjoy the drinks. I'm going after him.' And leaving her baffled friend behind, she rushed away.

Jules walked briskly back over the bridge, now crowded with people who he dodged around, taking quick glances over his shoulder to check Sam wasn't following. He didn't think she'd been there by accident this time. Somehow, she'd found out that he lived here.

Sam ran out of the pub only to be held up by revellers, strolling by the riverside. She scanned the embankment for Jules, and looked along the bridge but could see only a mass of people. She almost gave up until she spotted the flash of his blue scarf, under the light of a lamp post.

She had to sprint to keep up as he vanished down a pathway at the other side of the bridge. She sneaked after him, saw him enter an old converted warehouse, once a storage facility, but now a block of apartments.

Reaching the building, she studied the numerous bells and saw this name at the very top. She felt a shiver of anticipation, but hesitated. If she rang would he allow her in? She doubted it. Best to wait for someone to come out and hope they'd allow her to slip inside without giving Jules any warning.

It was an agonizing five minutes before a woman appeared. She looked at Sam suspiciously. 'Who are you looking for?'

'Jules Caron. I think something's wrong with the intercom.'

'Really? They were tested only recently. Pity he plays his music so loud he can't hear anything else.' The woman took pity and held the door open. 'Here. Take the lift.'

Sam stepped inside. Moments later she was on her way up to the top floor.

Jules was about to make a coffee when he heard the knock. He turned the music down thinking it was his neighbour coming to complain. He opened the door. When he saw it was Sam he let out a groan and tried to close it again. But she put her foot in the way and he was forced to allow her in.

Like a warm breeze she walked past him. He closed the door and watched as her eyes skimmed around the room. She took in the kitchen, the beamed ceiling, the open plan sitting room, and the plate glass window overlooking the river...

'Oh, this is fantastic,' she said.

He tried to stifle the ridiculous pleasure he felt at her approval. He stood at a distance from her, but could feel the invisible thread pulling him to her. His heart was thumping. He was sure hers was too. He needed to slow things down. It was obvious she had no intention of leaving and it seemed churlish not to offer her some of the coffee he'd just made. 'How about a black Expresso?' he said, with feeling.

'Perfect.'

Their eyes met. He had to tear his away.

'Do you work locally as well as live here?'

She was going to ask her questions come what may. He nodded and poured out the coffee.

'You only pretended to be a tourist. What is it you really do?'

He placed her cup down on the table. 'I handle complaints.'

'I'm not the only person finds you difficult then,' she scolded, and let slip a smile.

He shook his head, and indicated for her to sit at one end of the large sofa, whilst he went to the other, keeping the distance between them still.

'Chloe had a mad idea you were working for MI5.'

'Chloe would.'

'Who are the complaints against?'

'The police.' It was out before he could stop himself. 'But only at a desk job.'

'You must hear about all sorts of crimes.'

Jules sipped his coffee.

Sam knew if she was going to find out anything now was her chance. 'You must have heard about the terrorist attack on Wimbledon high street, back in the summer.' She waited, but he said nothing. She had to take it further. 'One that I was involved in….'

She saw him flinch. He put his cup down with a clatter, and went to stand at the window, where he stared out at the river.

She rose and went to stand by him. They watched the same the ripple of lights on the water, heard the same chugging sound from passing boats, saw life going on without them.

Jules chose his words carefully. 'Code of ethics won't allow me to talk about it, Sam.'

'Not even with a trial coming? One in which I have to be a witness for a total stranger.' Her voice was rising. 'It's hard not knowing who he really is. I keep dreaming about a masked man, one who does a weird dance with me. It's driving me crazy.' A sob escaped.

Jules pressed his hands against the window. There was no way out. Somewhere on the river a tug boat hooted, the haunting sound like a signal that the *fight de resistance* should be over. As she stood this close he wished it could be. That he could reach out and take hold of her like he wanted to.

Best he could do was to place his hand on her shoulder in a show of solidarity, and keep it there.

His touch sent a warm glow searing through her. He was near enough for her to smell his spicy aftershave. A scent she'd known before…before…before? The memory of standing beside the firearms officer on the fateful day came rushing back, when the same spicy aroma had drifted over her…

The truth hit like a vortex, overwhelming, irresistible. She could only speak in a shocked whisper. 'It was *you* who saved me, Jules. *You!*'

Unable to hold back any longer he tried to take hold of her. But to his dismay she pulled away, a look of horror on her face.

'You must have known this all along. On the common when we first met. In Dorset when we danced. In Leo's classes? Even when we made love?' She bit her lip. 'Was it only pity you felt for me?'

'No. It wasn't like that.'

161

But she raised her hands. 'Don't say any more.' She retreated to the sofa, and picked up her bag. 'I must go.'

'Sam, let me explain.'

But she was at the door. 'Don't worry, your secret is safe. I'll do my best for you in court.' She opened it, then turned back. 'Thank you for saving my life, but you're right, we shouldn't be seeing one another at all.' She fled into the corridor.

He heard the lift doors open and close, the machinery whizzing. More than anything he wanted her to stay. For him the running was over.

Determined to catch her he took the back stairs. Rushed outside to find no one there. 'Sam! Sam!' he yelled. But the echo vanished into the darkness. He'd found and lost her in a moment.

30

Outside, the air had turned colder as Sam fled back over the bridge. The lights on the river looked more like spikes than ripples. And the barges sliding across the water seemed ghostly. That Jules was the firearms officer was both believable and unbelievable at the same time. Something she'd known all along, but also hadn't. The truth had lain dormant inside her and had now exploded.

In the pub she found Andrea slumped on the bar stool looking tipsy, as well as rejected. Her friend pointed at the two empty glasses. 'I drank both. You'll have to drive me home. Where did you go?'

Sam couldn't tell her. 'It doesn't matter anymore. I couldn't find him.'

She helped her friend out of the pub and back to where the car was parked. She helped Andrea into the passenger seat and took her place beside her. Her hands were shaking as she switched on the engine. She drove on auto pilot, her mind scattered. She hardly registered whether the traffic lights were red or green, before she reached Andrea's home, by some miracle, safely.

Jeremy was cross at the sight of his inebriated wife. 'She never gets drunk. What's been going on?'

Sam couldn't explain. 'Should I take Milly home with me?' she asked him.

'And wake the child up? Sam, you're not thinking straight. Leave her here. Go and get a good night's sleep. Come for her in the morning.'

Like a scolded child herself, Sam did as she was told.

Once home however, she sank down onto the cool tiles of the hall, put her hands around her knees and rocked back and forth. The truth shall set you free rang hollow now she knew the price was so high. That the man she loved was also the man who'd saved her. The man she owed her life too.

She went to bed, but sleep evaded her for most of the night.

Jules also hardly slept a wink. He woke to light filtering in through the blinds. For a moment he thought Sam's shape lay under the sheet, and he thought she'd stayed with him. But when he pulled it back all he found was an empty space. It was she who'd run away this time and he who couldn't bear it.

He rose, went to the windows, lowered the blinds, and let the fingers of the dawn light in, knowing that everything had changed. For the first time in his life a woman had power over him and he didn't mind. All he wanted was to see her again.

Sunday, and all was quiet as he went down to the garage where his car was parked. He drove out of the apartment block and coasted through an almost empty Putney on his way to Wimbledon. He knew where Sam lived having tailed her there once. Her house was at the end of the street with an ash tree overhanging it.

He arrived and sat for a moment wondering whether he should go straight to her front door and demand to be allowed in. He was about to step out of his car when he saw her come running out. She went across the road not far ahead of him, and powered her way down the street.

He locked the car and went after her.

Sam was also up at the first light. Pent up with emotion she'd pulled on her track suit. A run was what she needed. She'd jog around the park next to Milly's school and free her mind of thoughts about the man she shouldn't see but wanted to.

Jules followed at a distance. She ended up near a school, which he supposed was the one Milly attended. There was a church to one side, and a park on the other, which she ran into. She jogged around in a circle, beside the expanse of grass dotted with leafy trees. He ran in the opposite direction knowing they would meet in the middle. That she would see him coming ever closer.

The dawn chorus started. A slight breeze rustled the trees. Sam saw his agile figure coming towards her and half thrilled, half fearful, she veered onto the lawn, pushed back the strands of a weeping willow, and hid under its cover. Moments later Jules had joined her as she knew he would.

They kissed as though their lives depended on it. He moved her backwards so she was pressed up against the trunk of the tree. Clothes were pushed aside as the need to touch, stroke, and rediscover one another took over. He slid his mouth down her neck, lingering at the scar left exposed in her haste this morning, and kissed the trauma away, like raindrops falling. He made love with a tenderness that sought to erase any hurt he'd caused her. He sought forgiveness. She gave it.

After, they slid to the ground and sat side by side, at peace.

'I don't know much about you,' said Sam.

'I only know about you from the news.'

'Like my already having been married and divorced?'

'He was an idiot to lose you.' Jules kissed her.

She took his hand held it to her cheek. She didn't want there to be any secrets between them. 'Simon used to drink. He lost control and almost strangled me. I had to get away, but it took time to find the courage to do so.'

'My mother left my father because he was violent,' said Jules. 'We escaped to live in England, when I was fourteen.'

'Simon lives in Canada. I don't see him anymore,' said Sam.

'My father's in France. I don't see him either.'

They sat in a shared silence.

Sam fetched out his hanky, always with her. 'You gave me this, remember?'

He smiled. 'Yours to keep.'

She tucked it away.

'Are you still an actress?' he asked.

'No. I don't want to pretend to be someone else. I want to speak my own words.' She hesitated, afraid he might think her foolish. 'Write them actually. I've started a book.'

'What kind?'

'A self-help one about how to overcome trauma. I hope it will help other people as well as myself.' She looked at him. 'You must have seen terrible things in Afghanistan, Jules.'

He looked away from her. 'I have a head filled with images I'd rather forget. It's a weight I carry like all soldiers. But we never speak about it.'

'Never?'

He shook his head, firmly.

'I spent time in therapy after my divorce, talking things through made me stronger not weaker. It might help you.'

'I doubt it.' He cupped her face with his hands 'Loving you will help me more.' He kissed her gently. 'My beautiful Sam.'

A cool breeze whipped through the trees reminding her they couldn't always be this close. And time was running out.

'We'll have to meet in secret until the trial is over,' he said, as he helped her up.

'I could sneak into your apartment under cover of darkness.' The idea of mystique intrigued her now she was a part of it. And Liliana, her cleaner, had already offered to babysit.

'I can meet you on the common in daylight, in the woodland where no one can see us,' said Jules, also enjoying the subterfuge, with her involved.

'Is tomorrow too soon? Early in the morning, after I've dropped Milly off at school?'

'Before I must be at work. Perfect.'

Cautiously they moved out into the open.

No one was around. Sam set off first. Jules followed at a distance. They were so far apart the street cleaners, now arriving with noisy machines, could have had no idea they were together.

At her front door, she watched him drive away. As he disappeared a shiver went through her. Was this how it would be. Snatched meetings and partings, such as her mother had endured with her father, with the inevitable fear of loss in between…

She was still trembling from the reuniting. She had a glow about her that was hard to hide. Once inside she composed herself. Switched into mothering mode before she ventured to Andrea's home to collect Milly. Maybe she could steal her daughter away before anyone was up, and her heightened state wouldn't be noticed.

She arrived to find them already seated around the breakfast table. There was no escape.

166

Milly ran to give her a hug. 'I've had such fun, Mummy.'

Sam was glad to hear this, until she saw Andrea's frosty look. 'You abandoned me last night,' her friend scolded.

'I'm sorry, I didn't mean to.'

'Who was this mystery man?' asked Jeremy, with the air of an accountant suspicious of everyone.

'Someone I knew a while back,' said Sam. 'Someone I had unfinished business with.' She could only hope this would suffice.

But Andrea wasn't satisfied. 'I was left with *Maurice*, the French barman, who gave me too many drinks.' Her evening of freedom had got out of hand.

'I'm sorry, Andrea. I'll make it up to you, I promise.'

'Well, if you're serious about that,' interrupted Jeremy. 'How about taking my wife to that gym of yours, so she can learn how to take care of herself if she's ever again abandoned in a pub full of arseholes!'

Andrea looked worried. The idea of a gym was not to her liking.

Sam ignored this. She smiled at her friend. 'I'd love to take you there. I think you'll be surprised by how much you'll enjoy it.'

Andrea sniffed. 'It seems I have no choice.'

Sam thanked Jeremy for babysitting, took Milly's hand, and was gone before any more questions were asked.

On the walk home Milly was eager to talk about her night away. How they'd stayed up late watching the movie, 'Spirit Untamed,' and how she wanted to be wild like the Mustang was. She also said how lucky Polly was to have Jeremy as her Daddy.

Sam felt guilty at such moments, knowing Milly was deprived of a father of her own. She couldn't help wondering what kind Jules would make. Then feared she was preempting things, and becoming like an untamed spirit herself.

The rest of Sunday was spent playing with her daughter. Flying a kite on the common, feeding the ducks by the pond, and focusing on being a good mother.

Monday morning however, after she'd dropped Milly off at school, mothering took a back seat as she hurried home. A boldness took over as out of the wardrobe she fished a risqué jogging outfit. One she'd bought and never dared wear. She eyed the cleavage, and the crisscross back straps exposing her flesh. She'd no longer be cowed into doubt, and inaction, she'd seize every moment.

On the common were on the track. She waited for Jules in the woodland. When he arrived in his dark blue jogging outfit, he looked so handsome, she stared in awe. He came straight up and took her hand, then led her deep into the thicket. Her ensemble was quickly unzipped. So was his. They slid to the ground and made love more fiercely this time. Each knew what the other wanted without a word being spoken.

Afterwards, they stayed close, wanting to hold on to the happiness they felt.

'I forget about the situation when I'm with you,' said Jules.

I forget about it, too. I only wish the trial wasn't happening.'

Jules didn't say his lawyer had called him to arrange another meeting. That things were moving fast. He didn't want anything to spoil what was happening between him and Sam.

31

Jules was shown into the official office of Tanya Osborne, a smaller, more intimate room than the one in which they'd first met. He walked in to see piles of files on her desk. She was sitting behind it, working on her computer, and she waved a hand to indicate that he should also sit.

When she finally looked up, she gave a harassed smile. 'I'm working overtime. The trial date has been set for the last week in November. The police have been pushing for it to be moved forwards to avoid too much bad publicity. When another case was dropped yours was pushed in.'

Only a few weeks away. Jules felt both relief and anxiety.

'I'll be interviewing witnesses, one by one,' she continued. 'Starting with Sam Elliot, the woman whose life you saved.'

Jules wished Sam was not top of the list.

His lawyer sat back and studied him. 'One question bothers me. Why didn't the actress run like everyone else?'

He couldn't mention Sam's history with a violent husband, or how this had made her actions understandable. He couldn't let his lawyer know that the *actress* was the best thing that had happened to him.

'She froze,' he said. 'She was terrified.'

His lawyer swivelled her computer around for him to see the photograph she'd been looking at. 'Unlike here, where she looks bold and provocative, wouldn't you agree?'

It was of Sam looking not much more than a teenager, exuding a natural confidence, a coltish beauty, and a direct gaze.

'She was only sixteen at the time, a little *Lolita* it's suggested. Might she be someone who courts publicity?' Tanya sat back and folded her arms.

Jules felt indignant on Sam's behalf. 'Are you suggesting she'd put herself in harm's way just to get in the papers. She's not that stupid.'

'How would you know?'

He had to stop himself from answering.

Tanya Osborne narrowed her eyes, then leaned back in her chair. 'The prosecution will use anything against her that works to their advantage. And against you also. I can only hope she didn't captivate you in some way as that would be most unhelpful.'

Jules kept quiet, scared that if he spoke his love would show.

'I expect you've heard of the condition, 'The Victim Saviour Syndrome? Where people, after just such a rescue from the jaws of death, think a special bond has been formed between them?' Tanya looked him in the eye.

Jules shifted in his chair. He didn't appreciate his feelings for Sam being reduced to some psychological label. 'I'm not easily captivated by anyone,' he said. 'I had a job to do, and that was my focus.'

'Maybe it's her I'm more worried about. The prosecution could tear her testimony apart if she had so much as a fantasy about you. Made worse if she'd developed a crush. I gathered from your partner that she tried to find out who you really are.'

Jules remembered Sam had visited the police station and had asked Ted questions. Best he knocked this on the head. 'She didn't succeed,' he lied.

'And she mustn't,' said Tanya. 'A witness and the accused must never meet,' she warned.

The rest of the interview went in a blur. Jules knew he and Sam were taking a terrible risk seeing one another, but he couldn't walk away from her now. Couldn't bear to be left chasing her shadow. He wanted her close. He wanted her all the time. He wasn't sure he could get through the trial without her.

Sam had arranged for Liliana the cleaner to babysit so she could visit Jules in the evenings. Later that week she sneaked back to Putney, under cover of darkness.

Jules let her straight in this time. 'I've prepared a light supper. Ham omelette - French style. And - salade d'accompagnement verte.'

Sam liked a green salad, and liked having a reprieve from always being the one to do the cooking. It gave her time to browse through his bookshelves.

She pulled out, 'The Pioneer of Modern Architecture,' by a Frenchman called Le Corbusier. 'You have an interest in this?' She opened it up.

'I have a dream of becoming an architect myself, one day.'

'Really?' Sam liked the idea of this. She flicked through, impressed by the sculptural forms, and the open planned living spaces. She wasn't so happy with the concrete blocks for social housing. 'They're ugly. More like prisons than homes.'

'Corbusier led the path for social housing. Houses are not just for the rich.' Jules scolded. 'Come sit, the food's ready.' He served out the omelette, two sides folded, soft and runny in the middle, cooked perfectly.

'Which are your favourite buildings in London?' Sam asked in between delicious bites. 'I suppose you like only modern ones.'

'Not at all. I like to see the developments through the ages. I like the Tudor style, the Jacobean, Georgian, and even the more oppressive Victorian. All of which I have learned from. But yes, I also like the challenge of modern buildings that can spiral towards the universe. It's the way of the future.'

Sam could see he was enthralled talking about this. 'It's a pity we can't have a day out together. We could stroll around the streets with you educating me about famous buildings.' She paused, and the idea gathered momentum. 'Why couldn't we? I mean we'd be hidden in the crowds. I could bring Milly along. She still thinks you're just a French tourist so where's the harm? We could be like any other couple for a day…' Her voice tailed away as Jules stayed silent.

He was struggling with the desire to do exactly as she'd suggested. It was only Tanya's warning that held him back. 'I'd love nothing more than to spend time with you and Milly,' he said. 'I've always worried I wouldn't be any good with children after the example set by my father, who was always too competitive, too abrasive, even when he was sober. That day on the beach in Dorset helping Milly with the sandcastle was fun, but…' he shrugged. 'I think we should wait until the trial is over to be seen together. My last meeting with my lawyer was full of admonitions. Legally, as you're a witness, you and I are not supposed to meet.'

'Is that what he said?'

'*She.*'

'Oh.' Sam hadn't imagined it would be a woman.

'You'll be her main witness. The trial set for end of this month.'

'A few weeks away? God, I'm scared, aren't you?' Sam reached out to hold his hand. 'At least we're in it together.'

'Tanya's determined to win.'

'*Tanya?* You're on first name terms?'

He kissed her. 'No need to be jealous, Sam. She'll be calling you, and she mustn't suspect there's anything between us.'

'I wish the trial wasn't happening at all.'

'Best thing would be to find a way to get it cancelled,' he agreed.

They sat, a shadow cast over them.

Sam strived to be positive. She slid her arms around his neck. 'We need something to look forward to for when it's all over and your freed.' 'How about we plan a weekend away? Go to France where you used to live? What city was it?'

'Nice.'

'The hotspot of the French Riviera!'

'My father still lives there. I'd have to avoid him.'

'Don't you miss the lifestyle?'

'I miss the food. I miss skiing in the Alps in winter, and summers spent on the beaches, even if they are covered in pebbles.'

'And the chic French women. I expect you miss them, too.'

He reached for her. 'Not when I have you.' They kissed, skipped desert, and went to bed.

A few days later, Jules met Ted at the café again, his newfound happiness was hard to conceal from his partner.

'You look pleased with yourself,' said Ted.

Jules gave a sheepish smile, and changed the subject. 'I gather you've been contacted by my lawyer.'

'She ambushed me if that's what you mean. Blamed me for the mess you're in. She thinks the teenager and his phone footage could land you in jail. Told me I should have stopped him from recording anything at all.'

'You did try, but he wouldn't listen,' said Jules feeling sorry that Tanya had been so hard on his partner.

'Well, she had a point. It left me wanting to put things right for you, Jules.' Ted cleared his throat. 'I went to see the commander and we talked things through. He decided I should do some surveillance on the lad.'

'On the teenager who took the video?'

Ted nodded. 'I've been sneaking off in the evenings. My wife's not happy about it, but I've made progress. I know where Percy Harris, that's his name, lives, and what he's up to.' He took a breath. 'He's an addict who inhabits a dingy council flat in Tower Hamlets, and owes money to ruthless drug dealers.'

Jules knew this was one of the roughest estates in London.

'The other thing I found out, which is of more concern, is that Jihadists have moved into the same block.'

'Mon Dieu.'

'They came across the channel in dinghy's not so long ago, posing as innocent refugees. Then broke into an empty flat and took it over. No one dared challenge them, and it didn't take long before they'd muscled in on the drug scene. They believe they can weaken society by flooding the market.' Ted took a breath. 'I think Harris may be under their influence.'

'That would explain everything. But how can you be sure?'

'I've started working undercover, getting to know him better.'

'Doing what?'

'He's been attending an addiction group, trying to get clean.'

'Seriously?'

'It seems so. I've been posing as a counsellor.'

Jules had to smile. 'A counsellor?'

'Don't mock. I'm already am one for my church. I have all the credentials.' Ted rubbed his lips. 'Anyway, *Harris* believes I'm legit.'

'Does the commander know about this?'

'He gave me the green light to go ahead. I'm pretty sure Harris feels guilty about what he did. He won't openly admit it. He just tells the group he'd done something he's not proud of. But I can see it's a burden he'd like to unload. I need to see him alone. Pay a visit to his flat.'

'That sounds risky, Ted. Will you have back up?'

His partner didn't answer this. 'I'll get him to admit the video's been tampered with, then turn him to our side. Make him a witness for the defence instead of the prosecution.' He grinned at Jules. 'It could set you free.'

It all sounded a bit too easy to Jules. 'You shouldn't be alone, Ted.'

'I won't be' His partner pressed his hands together, as if in prayer. 'I'll have the Lord.'

Jules was worried about this religious fervor. He offered more practical assistance. 'At least let me be your driver. The Merc can do a fast getaway, if needed.'

His partner took time before agreeing to this.

'It stays between us two, okay. No one must know, not even the commander.'

'Evans doesn't know about the visit to the Towers?'

Ted shrugged. 'He might stop me. Can't miss the only chance we have.' Ted rose from his chair. 'I'll let you know when it's happening, okay.' And he was gone.

Sam picked up the landline to hear a woman's voice.

'This is Tanya Osborne.' The tone was brisk. 'I'm the lawyer for the firearms officer. I'd like to speak to Sam Elliot?'

'Speaking.' Sam, though warned by Jules that this would happen, felt thrown to receive a call so soon. Needing to distance herself she switched to the speaker, and carried on cleaning the sink.

'I'd like us to meet and go through the statement you gave to the enquiry,' the lawyer continued. 'As my star witness we'll need a strategy.'

Both the words *star* and *strategy* had connotations for Sam. One made her feel an Oscar winning performance would be required. The other made her think she'd have to embellish on what had happened.

174

'Won't the truth be good enough?' She couldn't help the sarcasm in her tone.

The lawyer hardly seemed to hear it.

'It's the way you tell it that matters,' she carried on. 'As an actress you'll know that how you present yourself is crucial.'

'I know the prosecution will be tough on me because I'm an actress. That I'll need to be more *real* not less.'

A pause, before the lawyer became more accommodating. 'It might it be easier if I came to your house for the interview, rather than you coming to my office?'

Sam thought it would, knowing she'd feel more in control in her own environment. She tried to delay the meeting by suggesting it should happen next week.

Tanya said time was running out. That she'd prefer they met at the end of this one.

Feeling cornered, Sam agreed.

32

Friday, at eleven o clock sharp, Tanya Osborne arrived at Sam's front door. Jules hadn't mentioned how attractive she was, or comment on the strong perfume the lawyer used. Dior's -*Poison*' always had the effect of giving Sam a headache. She led the way along the hall trying to keep well in front. 'I thought we could talk over a coffee,' she said, over her shoulder.

'I see you're no longer blonde.' Tanya Osborne commented as they entered the light kitchen.

'I've returned to my natural look,' Sam explained. 'I can merge into the crowd better.'

'You didn't relish the attention the papers gave you?'

'What made you think I would?'

'Well you're an actress, aren't you?'

Sam bristled at the cliched view. 'Most actors hate the publicity they receive,' she defended. 'It's usually offensive from the newspapers, full half-baked truths, and gossip.' Pity they'd got off to such a bad start. But it was hardly surprising when there was a touch of rivalry between them.

The lawyer tried to smooth things over. 'Well, we can only hope that your natural look will work in our favor at the trial.' She sat down at the kitchen table and opened her laptop. 'And please call me, Tanya.'

Sam wasn't sure she wanted to. She busied herself making the coffee. Two cups, both black, which she brought over, then sat down opposite the lawyer.

Tanya peered at her computer. 'I've have read the original statement you gave, but it's not very convincing. There are too many stops and starts. Were you nervous?'

'I was still raw when I gave it. I'd seen the news straight after the attack and was upset at the misinformation. I walked into the police station the following morning intent on setting the record straight.'

'You felt driven to help the officer?'

'But of course.'

Tanya gave a thin smile. She returned to her computer and scrolled down. 'I need to go over your statement line by line.'

She asked probing questions. Ones that were harder to deal with now Sam knew Jules was the shooter. Every moment of the attack felt more emotional, every action more meaningful, and more poignant.'

'He was wearing a balaclava. You never saw his face?'

The face Sam couldn't take her eyes off anymore. 'No.'

'How about his physique?'

Unbidden, an image of Jules naked in his apartment came to mind, and Sam blushed. 'I couldn't really see,' she said, flustered. 'He was kneeling, his gun aimed. He was intent on saving me.'

Tanya sat back and folded her arms. 'I can see you're very grateful to him.'

Sam focused on her coffee. At that exact moment her mobile buzzed. She looked down she saw it was a message from Jules, and put her hand over it.

Tanya looked at her supiciously. 'Wouldn't you like to answer that?'

Sam's cheeks were burning. 'Not now.' She picked up the phone and went to the sink and stood looking out onto the garden, trying to remain composed.

The lawyer's voice became a drone in the background. Sam picked up the stand out words, *fantasise* and *obsession*, and concerned, she turned around.

'The problem is,' Tanya Osborne looked her in the eye. 'Victims can be known to have *fantasies* about those who save them.' Sam swallowed. 'They become fixated until feelings of gratitude turn into an infatuation, and a, 'Victim Saviour Syndrome,' takes over.'

Sam felt a rising anger. How could this lawyer reduce her feelings for Jules to a term like this? It made her seem like an idiot.

'The prosecution might suggest that this was the case with you,' Tanya continued. 'I mean have you ever dreamt about the firearms officer?'

Sam came over and sat down at the table again. 'I can't help what my unconscious does. I have sometimes tried to imagine what he might be like, but no more than that.' She lied defiantly.

'My problem is Sam, that you visited the police station in Wimbledon not so long ago, and asked questions about the officer.'

Sam gasped. 'I'd lost my purse. The duty officer recognized me from the news and we got talking, that's all.'

'But you did want to find the man who'd saved you, didn't you? The prosecution could accuse you of stalking him.'

'*Stalking* him?' Sam was outraged. 'That would make me crazy.'

'Indeed, and a psychiatrist could be produced to say that you were.' Tanya continued in her clipped tone. 'Your testimony could be deemed null and void and the accused found guilty.'

Sam was appalled. 'This is a horrible line of questioning.'

'It's no more than the prosecution will do. They will want to extract anything they can from you to use against him. I can't afford for you to have any connection to the officer in any shape or form.'

'Well,' Sam roused herself. 'I've never stalked anybody. I am not delusional. I have a young daughter to ground me, anyway.' She looked at Tanya, curious. 'Do you have any children?' A shadow passed over the lawyer's face, and Sam felt bad. 'I'm sorry, I shouldn't pry.'

'No more than I'm doing.' Tanya's tone had softened. 'I've no time for a child. My career has meant everything to me. The legal profession being the bastion of males hasn't made it easy.' Sam felt a moment of sympathy. She almost caved in and told Tanya everything. But when the lawyer asked another awkward question, she held back.

'How is the scar on your neck? Has it healed?'

Sam's fingers instinctively rose to the scarf covering it. She'd visited the gym a few days ago and the session had been a bit too active. The wound had reopened a little, and the skin around it was even more inflamed. 'It's not good, actually,' she admitted.

'Well, that could be useful. At the trial you could take off your scarf and show it to the jury in a shock and awe tactic.'

Sam looked at her in dismay. 'Like in a horror movie.'

Tanya ignored this. 'I need your testimony to be strong. No weak points.

To Sam's relief she closed her computer. 'Rest assured the trial will be held in a locked courtroom, no members of the public or any journalists allowed in. There will also be armed police on duty so you'll be quite safe.' She collected her things, and rose from her chair. 'I'm banking on you, Sam.' And in a whiff of *Poison* perfume, she saw herself out.

Sam threw away the rest of her coffee. It had turned sour in her mouth. The idea of making her scar a stunt was terrible, the warning about not seeing Jules, like a chill wind. She paced about before switching on her phone and calling him.

He picked up straight away and she told him what Tanya had said. 'The idea of being caught up in some victim savior syndrome has alarmed me. She even asked if I'd been *stalking* you.' Sam bit her lip. 'I shouldn't be seeing you at all. I'm putting your freedom at risk every time. If anybody found out…'

'She's no right interfering in my private life like this. No one need know about us, Sam.'

'If it means keeping you out of jail, we should stop. Not phone one another either as it's easy to trace calls.'

'Hold on, Sam. There may not be a trial.'

'What do you mean?'

'Wait and see.'

This made Sam even more worried. Was he planning something? She reacted by telling him she wouldn't meet him this week, or call him. 'Please don't do anything reckless.' And she switched off.

33

Jules was angered that Tanya Osborne had come between them. It was lucky he had something else to focus on when Ted called to say the visit to Percy Harris was arranged for the following week. Jules drove straight to his garage to make sure that the Merc was in the best shape it could be. Then spent time test driving it for speed.

A week later, on an icy November evening, dressed in dark colours so he would slip into the background, and a balaclava ready to use in the glove compartment, Jules collected Ted in his now finely tuned Merc.

His partner was dressed somberly in a suit and tie for his role as a drug addiction counsellor. 'Glad you're on time, Jules,' he said, as he climbed in.

They drove off. Ted opened his briefcase, and checked it out. Inside was a bible, and pamphlets on addiction prevention. 'I hope I've paved the way by befriending Harris first, otherwise I could be in trouble.'

His partner seemed more nervous now it had come to the time. When he had to halt at some traffic lights, Jules turned to him. 'If you need me to do more than drive Ted, I will.' But his partner shook his head.

'I'm better on my own.' He took a few deep breaths. 'I can do this.'

When they reached the Towers, Jules parked near one of the blocks, switched off the engine. and they sat for a moment in darkness, as Ted prepared himself for what lay ahead.

'Stay at the ready, Jules,' he ordered. And with a determined look, he climbed out of the car, and walked away.

Jules watched him reach the low-lit stairwell at the base of one of the tenements, then take the stairs two at a time, before he disappeared.

Jules was left drumming his fingers on the driving wheel, whilst waiting. Half an hour passed with no sign of Ted returning. Instead some lads cycled up. They climbed off their bikes and propped them against the wall of the stairwell, where they loitered openly rolling joints.

At last Ted reappeared. The lads started speaking to him in what seemed to be a friendly enough manner, and his partner bantered back. His look was one of confidence, as though the visit to Percy Harris had been a success. Jules felt hopeful it would all be over in moments. He rolled down his window.

To his dismay the bantering turned to bartering as the lads pulled out packets of what looked like harder drugs and offered them to Ted. He shook his head but they came after him. One of them grabbed the briefcase, opened it, and searched inside, as if looking for cash or cards.

The bible was held up, and mocked. They started cursing, and humiliating him. The pamphlets were chucked onto the ground. When Ted bent over to pick them up one of the lads kicked him so hard he slumped down. Next thing both lads were beating him up.

No time to put on his balaclava, Jules, switched on the engine, and with his headlights full drove straight at the pair who were forced to leap aside. He screeched to a halt beside his partner, jumped out, and half dragged Ted into the passenger seat. He returned to the driver's side, about to leap in himself, when one of the youths pulled something from his pocket and held it up. Jules feared it was a gun. He didn't wait to check, he jumped into the Merc, spun it around and drove away at speed. The other youth gave chase. He threw a brick which hit the back window and it smashed in a shower of glass. 'Get down Ted!' ordered Jules, as he raced for the main road.

'Little pricks,' said Ted, when they'd reached it He eased himself up and looked in the mirror, saw the bruise forming under his eye. 'It would go wrong at the last moment. Thanks for the quick reaction, Jules. Only hope they didn't get a snap of you on that phone.'

Jules had thought it was a gun not a phone the lad had held up. He felt exposed. His adrenalin pumping, he drove until they were half way home.

He then slowed down and turned to his partner. 'You alright?'
'I'll live.'
'How did it go with Harris?'
'Tricky, at first. He was wary. But it didn't take long for him to tell

me how much he hated living there. How hideous it is.' Ted paused. 'I asked who scared him the most and he immediately said the jihadists. That he had to get his drugs from them and felt at their mercy.'

'What about the attack? Were they involved?'

'It took a bit longer to prize that out of him. But, yes, they ordered him to record it. If he didn't his life would be over. He had to hand it to them after. When it was returned the warnings had been erased. He was told to let Ahmed's family have it.'

'And that's when they got lawyers involved.'

Ted nodded. 'Harris is scared that now he's done what was asked, he's expendable, and that the Jihadists will kill him.'

'They surely will.'

'I told him I could help him to escape.'

'Did you offer him the protection programme?'

Ted shook his head. 'No. He still hates the police. The church is a better route. They do this, often. He could be offered sanctuary far away from here to start a new life. He said that was what he wanted. That he could only tell the truth when he felt safe.'

'He could change his mind,' warned Jules.

'He could. But he'd have to face the wrath of God, and I can see he's vulnerable to that.'

Jules wasn't so sure about this. But when they arrived back at his house he thanked Ted for the effort he'd made wanting to believe it would all work out well.

'I'll have a shiner in the morning,' his partner chuckled, as Jules helped him to his door.

His anxious wife took her husband over. 'What have you been up to?' She gave Jules a dubious look.

'Don't blame him,' said Ted. 'He helped me break up a brawl. These are just battle wounds. Nothing to fuss about, my love.'

Jules went on his way. First thing in the morning he'd book his car into a garage to replace the back window. The Merc was damaged too often on his behalf. He could only hope that this time it hadn't been in vain.

34

Andrea's ventures to the gym had proved more successful than she'd thought possible. She relished showing off the T shirt she'd bought with the words, 'Self Defence Is A Human Right,' boldly imprinted on the front. Never mind that Krav Maga had empowered her.

Sam also appreciated the T shirt. Her own human rights felt violated by Tanya Osborne's warning that she shouldn't have anything to do with Jules. Not seeing him, or even contacting him by phone, had left a lonesome feeling. Spending more time with her friends was her only comfort.

She enjoyed more walks on the common with Aisha. The children enjoyed letting off steam by the pond after a busy day at school, leaving their mothers time to talk. The conversation inevitably turned to the looming trial.

'I'm dreading it,' said Sam.

'I don't think the family of Ahmed are looking forward to it either,' said Aisha. 'It's their lawyers who have pushed them down this treacherous path.'

'Lawyers have a lot to answer for.' Sam couldn't resist a swipe at Tanya.

'I'd like to find a way to stop the trial from happening,' said Aisha.

Sam, already concerned as to what Jules might do, gave her friend a dubious look.

'Ahmed's parents are as nervous as you about the exposure it could bring.'

'They should have thought of that before,' Sam said, a little piqued.

'Maybe they could be persuaded to settle out of court.'

'I doubt that very much.'

Rain was spitting, and she called the children over saying it was time to go. By the time they'd arrived back at their respective houses, darkness had fallen.

Milly, tired out, was happy to go to bed early.

Sam wandered downstairs. Finding the house too quiet she went to her computer in search of company online. She started trawling through Facebook, looking for old friends, ones she'd lost touch with since her divorce. She was about to send off a message, when her screen was taken over and blocked by a hateful warning.

DO NOT TESTIFY OR WE WILL COME FOR YOU. WE WILL KILL YOU AND YOUR DEVIL DAUGHTER. *ALLAHU AKBAR!*

Sam felt a wave of nausea. She ran to the toilet where and threw up. She felt terrorized all over again.

She sat on the seat, with her head in her hands, and wept. The idea someone might kill little Milly was horrific.

After a while she took herself into the kitchen, where she stood in the darkness, staring out at the garden. Might someone climb over the hedge, like that photographer did a while back, sneak across her lawn, and smash down the back door?

She pulled open a kitchen drawer looking for a knife, and a card caught her eye. One for Victim Support that a policewoman had handed to her on the day of the attack. She'd had no use for it until now.

She returned to her computer, deleted the hateful post, and searched for the website of the group.

She found it was run by a man called Giles Edwards, who invited others caught up in the trauma to make contact. Sam clicked on, wrote a few words about who she was, and waited for a response.

Nothing happened. Her mind drifted to Dorset, her safe place, and her two country friends. She picked up her mobile and dialled Chloe. Found she was in the pub with Veronica, enjoying a lunchtime quiz. Laughter came bubbling down the receiver, and Sam was soon drawn in. When she answered a question correctly for them, they cheered.

'We've won!' said Chloe.

Veronica took the phone over. 'See, we can't do without you. Can't you come back?'

'I wish I could,' said Sam. 'But the trial will be soon. I've received some abuse online, which scared me. I just wanted to hear your voices.'

Chloe took the phone again. 'Tell them to fuck off. Just like that Frenchman.'

Sam didn't answer. She couldn't say how everything had changed between her and Jules. That she loved him in a way that they wouldn't understand. After a few more words of support from her two country friends, she ended the call.

By which time she'd been accepted by the support group, who were also sending empowering messages.

You are not alone.

Block them. Defriend. Report to the police.

The threats are mostly bluff, sent to blackmail you into submission and ruin your testimony...

Their advice came thick and fast.

Why hadn't she joined this group before? She felt her spirit returning, and went to bed vowing not to yield to threats.

In the morning, having dropped Milly off at school, she took Aisha aside, and told her what had happened online.

Her friend was upset. 'I'm so sorry. I've had some threats too. You're not alone. But worse has happened to Ahmed's parents.'

'What do you mean?'

'Last night a lighted rag was put through their letter box. It started a fire. They only just put it out in time before the flames took hold.'

'But the family are okay?'

'They're shaken. A right- wing group have been sending them hate mail online, but this is a step further. They are very upset and angry. They don't like being told to withdraw from the trial by Fascists.'

'It will still go on then.' Sam felt hopeless.

Aisha gave her a searching look. 'There's only one way to stop it,' she said. 'Someone needs to speak personally to the parents. Someone who knows what really happened. Someone who was there.'

Sam didn't like the way her friend was looking at her. She felt her legs go weak. ' 'Not *me?* You can't be serious.'

'I'm afraid I am. If they heard it from you they'd have to believe

185

due warnings were given. They'd see their case was based on a lie.'

'Aisha, I cannot meet the parents of my attacker.'

'You won't be alone. I'll ask the Inman to accompany you.'

'I don't even know him.' Sam was still apprehensive. 'Why not you?'

'I'm seen as a trouble maker for speaking out. But I could drive you there, and back.' Aisha put an arm around her. 'Think about Milly. How she needs to be kept safe.'

Sam felt tears spring to her eyes. She blinked them back. 'Do you think I could achieve something?'

'Yes, I do.'

Sam shuddered. She should do this. She took a breath. 'When can it be arranged?'

'I could try for the end of this week.'

Sam went cold. 'That soon?'

'Not soon enough.'

Sam rallied to the cause. 'Okay,' she said. 'I'll do it.'

Jules was taken by surprise when Tanya called with good news. He'd all but decided that Ted's gallant effort at Tower Hamlets had been in vain, when nothing happened.

'By some miracle,' his lawyer announced. 'The teenager who took the film footage has contacted me and is willing to turn witness for the defence.'

Jules was so relieved he couldn't speak.

'Are you still there, *Jean*?'

Tanya's use of his new name always confused. 'Yes. I'm stunned, that's all. Did he say what changed his mind?' He was careful not to let slip he'd played a part in this miracle.

'I don't know the details. I don't want to either. But his evidence should be enough to rip the prosecution's case apart.'

Jules punched the air with his fist. Good for Ted. Good for God! 'So, the trial will be called off?'

Silence. One he didn't like. Or the harsh intake of breath that followed.

'Called off?' Tanya sounded put out. 'Certainly not. It's the only chance to prove you're not guilty. If there's no jury to acquit you Jean, you'll never be truly exonerated and doubts will always linger. We *must* have a trial.'

'But won't the prosecution drop the case when they hear the teenager is on our side?'

'They won't hear until it's too late.'

Jules didn't like the sound of this.

'It's called tactics,' Tanya continued in a more ruthless tone. 'I withhold the information until the last moment giving no time for them to turn him back to their side. I will produce him at the trial in a *coup d'etat.'* Tanya was full of confidence. 'I can win and obtain massive compensation for you.'

'I don't care about money,' he said.' I just want my freedom.'

'Come to my office on Friday afternoon, when it's quiet. We'll go over your statement. I'll convince you this is the right course of action. Come, if only, for a morale booster.'

35

Friday morning, Aisha appeared in her family car. Sam was heartened to see Noor's discarded socks and shoes straggled on the back seat. It made it feel comfortable, and well used.

She covered her head with the dark scarf Aisha handed over, and sank down in her seat.

The traffic through Wimbledon was light for once. She didn't mind going through the high street anymore, which meant they reached the Ahmed's home early. It was all Sam could do not to beg her friend to turn around and take her home again, and not have to do this.

But the house was not dissimilar to hers. A Victorian semi, red brick, gabled, with lots of windows, which would make it light and airy inside. Outside an Audi was parked alongside a run around Skoda. His and hers, like any other suburban couple might own. They were ordinary people.

But how then could they have a murderous son?

Sam was torn between these opposing views. One that wished to understand, the other that wished to condemn.

Aisha walked her to the door. The knocker was shaped like a hand. Aisha explained it was the hand of Fatima, the daughter of Mohammed, known as one of four perfect women in Islam, and seen as a talisman to ward off evil. 'It's there to let people know the family inside are devout.'

'Won't that make them intolerant of me?'

'No. Islam teaches that we follow Allah's example of mercy, justice, and forgiveness in our treatment of other people.'

Sam didn't say it was a pity their son hadn't adhered to this, but now was not the time.

Her friend withdrew to the car. Left alone Sam tapped the knocker timidly, then louder. She had an anxious wait before the door opened to reveal a bearded, elderly man. He was dressed in in a robe, and had a decorative skullcap on his head. He introduced himself as the Inman and coaxed her inside.

In the hall, she removed her shoes and placed then alongside a row of others, big sizes, and small. She took in the dusky, umber painted walls lined with mirrors, and the lanterns lighting up side-tables. Along with the ornate chandeliers hanging from the ceiling, the ripples of coloured light making the atmosphere, lively.

From the far end a door opened and two children ran out. Aged about eight and ten they stared at Sam with interest, until a woman dressed from head to toe in black appeared, and scolded them back inside what must have been the kitchen.

The Inman with his grey beard, and small but bright eyes, led Sam into a room that felt formal and colder, even though he warmly thanked her for coming. 'Don't be afraid. No harm will come to you,' he tried to reassure, before he left her alone and disappeared.

Sam could see that the room was used for fine dining, with high chairs placed around a table. The walls were plum red, with gold cornices, and there were paintings of sumptuous meals. She pulled the Shayla scarf over her head more tightly, and around her neck, hiding the scar until she was ready to reveal it. She wouldn't do this at the trial as Tanya had suggested, like a show, she'd expose it here in a more dignified manner, privately.

When the Inman reappeared and beckoned her to follow, after a moment of panic, Sam rose.

A little way further along the hall he knocked on a door and a male voice called from the inside. 'Udhill.'

She was ushered in to a sitting room full of more colour and finery, where a middle-aged couple sat on two elegant chairs side by side, almost like at a wedding, except their clothes were all black. The mother's Shayla scarf was tight to her face, and her gown flowed to her ankles. The father was suited and had a solemn skullcap on his head. Neither seemed able to look at Sam, and they sat with their heads bowed. A carved wooden coffee table was before them and opposite was a large velvet sofa, with colourful cushions.

The Inman indicated for her to sit. She perched on the edge and looked around, and saw, to her disconcertion, that photographs of their son were on display. As a boy with a beaming smile; as a teenager

189

looking more uncertain; as a young man full of pride at leaving school. All so different from the fanatic of the day, Ahmed was everywhere, and adored. The gilt frames stood alongside other ornate ornaments, Ramadan pendants, wooden and silver jewellery boxes, handsets, gold medallions. The whole room was full of beautiful things. At another time Sam would have liked to study them, but now she felt threatened by each one. How could she bring horror into a room turned into a shrine for a beloved son?

As she looked at the parents Sam could only see grief and bewilderment. It echoed her own incomprehension after the attack, when she'd stood trembling on the pavement, knowing her world had been changed forever.

The mother lifted her head and Sam saw her sad eyes. Ones that contained a web of memories… It was easy to imagine this woman holding her son as a baby, rocking him in her arms, stroking his chubby cheeks as she sung a lullaby, just as Sam had done with Milly. How this mother would have taken her son to school for his first day, watched with pride as he grew up, and passed his exams with enviable results, leading to a place at university. All this before her boy, her joy, her meaning in life, had entered the adult world, and committed a terrible act. How could Sam tell this woman her son had judged innocent people so cruelly? Had handed out his own punishment like he was a God himself. How could his mother bear to hear this? Or see the inflamed scar? It would feel like another attack making Sam no better than their son. When the Inman nodded his head and it was time to begin, she couldn't. Instead she rose from the sofa and said in a teary voice. 'I can't do this. I cannot hurt you anymore than you already are. We are all victims.' And she fled from the room, ignoring the Inman's plea to come back.

She ran along the hall, opened the front door, and raced to Aisha's car, jumped in and cried, 'Get me out of here!'

By the time they arrived at her house she was in a state of abject misery. Aisha could not console her as she berated herself for failing. She hadn't achieved anything. Hadn't helped to make Milly safer. Hadn't helped to free Jules either. The trial would still go on.

Jules headed for his meeting with Tanya knowing none of this. He was only coming to warn his lawyer that Percy Harris might not be trustworthy.

It was disconcerting to be shown into a different room. One that was smaller, full of files and papers, and intimate. Tanya Osborne was sitting behind a desk, but she was not looking conciliatory as he'd expected her to be, ready to convince him the trial was the only way forwards. Instead, she was in a fury.

'Why does good news have to be followed by bad?' she implored him. 'We have the teenager with new evidence reverting to our side. And then our *main* witness does her best to derail everything.'

Jules didn't know what she was talking about.

'I've just had the lawyers for the prosecution on the phone threatening me with contempt of court. Sam Elliot has apparently visited the parents of her attacker. Her intention being to persuade them to call off the trial. I'm working with my hands tied behind my back.'

Jules had to hide his feelings of pride at Sam's effort, and concern at the risk she had taken.

'The prosecution accuses her of being interventionist. Of taking the law into her own hands. She'll be lucky she doesn't get a jail sentence, herself.'

'But is she okay?' He had to ask.

Tanya gave him a withering look. 'What's it to you?'

He shrugged as innocently as he could.

'Well, she's probably humiliated, having run away before any real harm was done.' Tanya let out a sigh. 'I can't waste any more time on her. The best thing we can do is to work on your statement, and put Sam Elliot out of our minds. It is you and I who need to work more closely together.'

Jules felt uncomfortable as his lawyer stood up and came around the desk to be near to him.

She perched on the edge of it and leaned forwards. He could smell her strong perfume. 'I need to prepare you for whatever the prosecution might throw your way. Are you ready?'

He had no time to say not really, as she started firing what felt like abusive questions at him, like in a mock trial. Was he trigger happy? Only trained to kill. An angry young man. Vengeful. A person who could show no mercy. It went on. He was a liar, a wolf in sheep's clothing, a man without remorse. She played the devil's advocate all too well. He felt drained having to defend himself. He was about to walk out saying enough was enough, when she put her hands on the arms of his chair and he felt pinned down.

Her lips were close to his as she whispered, 'A man who likes women too much. A man who wants to please them. A man who knows women also like him. A man who would do anything to save a damsel in distress?' Her breath was on his cheek. Jesus she was coming on to him.

He kept his eyes down. Kept his mind on Sam, determined not to weaken in the way he might once have done for an attractive woman like this.

It was a relief when she pulled back, let out a sigh, and returned behind her desk.

'Okay, test over,' she dismissed as though nothing unusual had occurred. 'I needed to see you could survive such questioning,' she explained it away. 'That you aren't a fool when it comes to women.'

She sat down and opened her laptop, as he struggled to recover. 'You need to persuade the jury of your innocence. Only those twelve good people can set you free. That's why a trial is so important, you do see that, don't you?'

He felt too weak to care. He just wanted to get out of there.

She sat down and opened her laptop. 'You can go now.'

He got the hell out of the building. Took a taxi back to his apartment, where he sank down on his sofa, and poured himself a large whisky.

All he wanted was to see Sam. He'd had enough of being told what he couldn't do. From now on he'd do as he pleased, and to hell with the enforced separation.

36

He waited until dark to drive to Sam's house. A house he'd never been inside. He parked the Merc in the leafy street and only hoped she hadn't gone to bed early.

He didn't want to wake little Milly by buzzing the front door bell, so he went around the side. Sam's car was parked under the ash tree, and finding the garden gate locked, he climbed over. No lights on anywhere. He used his phone to guide him to the back door. It was glass and he peered through, as, at the same time, the hall light switched on and there stood Sam. But instead of looking pleased to see him her expression was one of terror. In dismay he realized she didn't recognize him. That in silhouette he must make a dark and menacing figure.

'Sam! Sam! It's me, Jules,' he tried to reassure her.

Unable to sleep, Sam had ventured downstairs for a glass of water. Hearing sounds at the garden gate she feared jihadists had arrived in a reprisal for her earlier actions. Seeing a figure at the back door she froze, deaf to the familiar voice calling her name. She reached for the heavy stone door stopper, anything to hit the bastard with as she walked to the door, ready to yell, and wake up the neighbors to scare whoever it was away.

'Sam!'

His voice finally penetrated. 'Jules!' Overwhelmed with relief she let him in.

He quickly removed the doorstop from her hands. 'You could have killed me with this.'

'I'm sorry, I've been so scared. It's been hard not seeing you.'

He put it back down on the floor, took hold of her hand, and led her to the table.

They sat down and she told him about the online threats she'd received. 'I thought you were someone sent to kill me and Milly.' She took a breath. 'I also did something foolish. I had a meeting with Ahmed's parents intending to stop the trial from happening, but I failed miserably.' She wiped away a tear.

Jules didn't tell her he already knew. How Tanya had told him. Instead he comforted Sam by telling of his own failure. He explained the effort Ted had made. How it should have led to the trial being cancelled. But how his lawyer had refused to give up her day in court. 'Tanya insists I need twelve good people to find me innocent, or I'll never be truly vindicated.'

Sam took his hand. 'Maybe she's right. Maybe we have to face up to the trial being the only answer.'

He sighed. Then nodded. 'I need to know you'll be safe here alone with Milly. I'll get my commander to arrange protection, until it's over.'

After which, they went upstairs and made up for being apart.

Jules stayed all night, but woke early, and left Sam still sleeping, to avoid seeing little Milly. It was not the time for her to know how much he loved her mother. But one day she'd learn.

He reached his apartment before daylight, and snuck back into bed. He only had an hour of sleep before he was woken again by a shrill bleep from his mobile. He reached for it, and found it was his mate, Leo.

His friend was not his usual jaunty self. His tone was anguished. 'He's gone, Jules. Gone!'

Jules hauled himself into a sitting position. 'Who's gone? What do you mean.'

'Dad. He's *dead*. I hate that bloody word.'

'Mon Dieu, Leo. I'm so sorry. When did this happen?'

'I found him unresponsive in his chair last night and summoned the paramedics who rushed him to the hospital. I followed and stayed at his bedside. At five am I was half dozing when he suddenly came around, sat up, told me he loved me, then had a fit of coughing, and fell back. I still can't believe it's happened.'

Jules had never heard his mate this low. His father had been getting frailer but his death was still unexpected. 'Would you like me to come there?'

'Why do you think I'm ringing at this bloody hour?' said Leo.

Jules told him he'd be arrive before lunch. Then took a moment to assimilate this news. The saying in Afghanistan had always been – That if old Tom was alright, then so was Leo. How would his friend cope without his father?

Jules rose, showered, and packed a suitcase ready. Then called the station to say he was sick and wouldn't be working today.

Next, he called Sam, and told her the sad news. She was full of sympathy for Leo. Jules explained that he'd be away for the weekend in Wiltshire, but would contact her as soon as he returned.

He drove fast along the motorway. He arrived in under two hours and found his mate in the kitchen, slumped at the table, his face wet with tears.

'Thank God you've come. I'm not coping that well. It's brought back my other big loss. Mother dying when I was a boy.'

Jules could see that Leo was overwhelmed and he sat down and just let him talk.

'I had to be the man about the place when she died as Dad went to pieces,' explained his mate. 'Now, I'm following suit. I feel weak as a woman.' Leo wiped his eyes with the back of his sleeves.

'You can't always be soldier strong, Leo. It's a sign of strength showing weakness.'

Leo widened his eyes. 'Oh, and what clever dick told you that?'

Jules looked sheepish. 'Sam, actually.'

Leo blinked. 'Bloody hell, are you two back in touch?'

Jules shrugged.

'I never told her where you lived.'

'I know. But you sent her to some old soldier mates who did.'

Leo scratched his head. 'Was it such a bad thing?'

Jules smiled. 'On the contrary, I couldn't be without her now.

'Does she know who you really are?'

'She does, and it's a relief. Though we have to keep anything between us a secret.'

Leo peered at his friend. 'My God, is Jules Caron in love at last?'

Jules felt the colour rise in his cheeks.

'Life's not all gone to pot then.' Leo managed a wan smile. 'I'm glad for you. I'll keep quiet about it don't worry. It's a good job

Veronica and I are still going strong. Though, I'm not sure I'm much use to her in this state.' His eyes watered again, and blinking back more tears, he rose from the table. 'I need some fresh air before I set about organizing a bloody funeral.'

They set off across the fields. The familiar landscape was a comfort to Leo. 'It's always there, isn't it,' he mused. 'Permanent when everything else feels insecure.'

Over the weekend, Jules walked, talked, ate and drank far too much in support of his grieving friend. He left early on Monday to be back in time for work. The funeral was arranged for the end of the week and he was determined to return for it. He had a wild hope Sam might come with him, that they could risk taking a day away together. Once back in London, he called her.

'I'm sorry but I can't go anywhere on Thursday, Jules,' she said, disappointingly. 'I have my first teaching class and it's too late to cancel it.'

Jules said it was a shame. But she persuaded him it was still not a good idea for them to be seen together, and he let it go.

Thursday morning, he left early in time to arrive at noon. He was dressed in his grey suit and arrived to find Leo in a black mourning one, a bowler hat on his head, a long black coat at the ready, and his black shoes polished until they gleamed.

'Is it very formal?' asked Jules.

'Traditional. Country folk like to do things properly to show due respect,' his mate explained.

He saw Jules was only in a suit, that in his haste he'd forgotten to bring a coat. 'I'll lend you one of Dad's old ones to keep you warm.' Leo gave him a bear hug as he draped one around his mate's shoulders. 'Good to have you here,' he whispered, near to tears again.

Old Tom had asked for a woodland burial on the land he'd worked all his life. Everything was to be biodegradable, the coffin, and any items of clothing. There was to be a wooden plaque to mark Tom's chosen site. An open field lay before it and a copse of ash trees behind, with a breeze blowing through.

People stood about, all the men black suited. The women, also.

196

Except for Veronica and Chloe who had made the trip specially, and stood out in their more vibrant Parka coats. There was no fanfare, each person said a few simple words about how long they'd known old Tom, and confirmed what a character he'd been. A dedicated farmer who loved the land, who'd be now joining the wife he'd so loved.

At the mention of his mother Leo started crying openly with Veronica holding him to her now motherly bosom. Far from minding his weakness she seemed to relish having to be the strong one.

Jules found tears on his own cheeks. The death of his own mother had been too traumatic for such an indulgence. Having nursed her to the end he'd watched her body being slowly destroyed. He'd lost sight of the woman he'd loved. He'd said goodbye to someone who'd deserved only release from her suffering. Now, his feelings of loss caught up with him, and he wept for the child he once was.

Mother's life had been complex. Old Tom's could be valued for its simplicity. There was substance to a man who stayed in the same place, with the same land around him, and the same people to care for all his life. For the first time Jules allowed himself to imagine he could live like this. That he could settle down and be with Sam for the rest of his days.

37

Thursday afternoon, just before her very first client arrived, Sam's cleaner appeared. The robust Liliana, a Portuguese student with strong opinions had come in specially as Sam was nervous of being alone with a man she didn't know. The arrangement being that Lilian would do the cleaning whilst Sam was coaching.

Sam went upstairs to dress in suitable clothing. She picked a slim skirt, silken shirt, and low-heeled shoes, and returned to check everything was ready. That the recording machine was operating. That the chosen book for reading out loud was opened at the right page. That a relaxation mat was laid out on the floor. And that the window looking out onto the street was open, fresh air breezing in.

Sam sat and did a little meditation. When the doorbell rang she had to rouse herself to head into the hall, only to find Liliana was there before her. The front door was wide open, and as Sam peered over her cleaner's shoulder she saw an 'All American Guy.' His sleek fair hair swept back, his skin bronzed, his eyes a sparkling blue.

'I am at the h…house of Sam Jones, yes?' He had a Californian drawl, the flow only interrupted by a jarring stammer.

Sam had to edge Liliana aside to introduce herself. 'Yes, I'm Sam. How do you do.' She held out her hand.

Ben Miller looked at her curiously. For a moment she thought he must have recognized her from the photos that had re-surfaced in the papers of late, but he said nothing. Maybe he had impeccable manners and wouldn't presume to intrude. She wasn't about to enlighten him anyway.

Liliana returned to the cleaning, but not before she'd muttered in Sam's ear, 'My, he's smart.'

Ben Miller was expensively dressed. A Saville row suit, a pristine white shirt, a striped tie and polished leather shoes. Sam surmised he must be successful at whatever he did, the stammer now a hindrance.

She led the way into the sitting room, and indicated for him to sit on the settee.

She sat in the more upright chair she'd chosen for herself, as he explained his accident to her. How he'd fallen asleep at the wheel of a car and had hit another head on. How the driver had been in intensive care for months...'

'Is he alright now?'

'Yes, thank g... goodness. B...but he's suing me for d...damages. It's been a terrible ordeal.'

Sam poured a glass of water which the American drank in one go. She sat assessing his weaknesses. How he spoke too fast. How he stumbled over certain letters. B G and D... How they triggered his stammering. His organs of speech, tongue, mouth, and teeth, would all need work. She knew there was no magic cure, but slowing him down would be a start.

First, he needed to relax.

Easier said than done. Ben needed to be in control and it took a while to persuade him to lie on the mat. Never mind let go of the tension in his body. He lay rigid as a pillar.

The mindfulness routine didn't go much better as he wanted to talk and not listen to sounds coming from outside himself.

She tried some limericks for articulation, but he found - 'She sells sea shells on the sea shore.' And 'Peter piper picked a pickled pepper,' impossible to do.

Only when she handed him Hemmingway's book did he become more engaged. He fingered, 'The Old Man and The Sea,' reverently.

'I only wish people of today could write like him,' he said, 'and I didn't have to publish such mediocrity.'

Sam hadn't known publishing was his trade. She warmed to him as he became more passionate.

'Hemmingway's take on a fisherman and his fight with a Marlin that he catches and loses again, strikes a c...chord with my own ambitious streak. I don't like f...failing.'

No pressure then, thought Sam. But she also wanted to help him.

The funeral was over. Everyone returned to the farmhouse for the wake, where cider, beer, laughter and memories flowed. Chloe and

Veronica had made a pile of sandwiches, tongue and beef, and chicken, which everyone tucked into.

There were a few ex-soldier mates, who'd come to pay their respects. Archie MacLean was one. Jules had last met him on his hike in the summer, when army manouvers had erupted.

Archie told Jules he'd left the army. 'I've had enough of being told what I can and cannot do,' he complained.

Jules could sympathise with this. 'What will you do?'

Archie shrugged. 'Become a trouble shooter, or a mercenary, both are better paid,' he grinned.

He wandered off, and Chloe came up. Her look, was as usual, suspicious.

'Well, if it isn't the vanishing man returned.'

'Is that all I am?'

'Sorry, but I don't like secrets. Maybe I've been involved with too many men who had wives they simply omitted to mention.'

'Well, I think men should be more honest about such things.'

She looked at him surprised. 'Well, that's good to hear. Has something happened to change your attitude, Jules?'

'Just trying to be a better man, Chloe.' He stood up, embarrassed he'd said too much. 'Nice talking to you.'

She gave him a curious look, then offered her hand. 'Nice talking to you too, Jules.'

He shook it gently. Neither of them mentioned Sam. But he could feel her transforming presence as he took his leave.

He went to say goodbye to Leo, who held him back. 'I've had news from Afghanistan.'

'Oh?'

His mate lowered his voice to a whisper. 'I've heard from Abdul and Salim. They're hiking over the Khojak Pass and heading for the Spin Boldak crossing.'

'Mon Dieu.' Jules knew the pass was hundreds of miles of icy mountain terrain, followed by a bleak desert. That the pair of interpreters, must have been desperate to tackle it. 'Who will help them cross into Pakistan?'

200

'Smugglers, who'll demand money.'

'Bastards.'

'Unless,' Leo paused, a glint in his eye. 'We rescue them, first.'

'And how will we do that?'

'Archie MacLean's keen to organize a covert mission.'

'With the army's backing, I hope.'

Leo didn't answer.

'You don't mean go rogue?'

At that moment Veronica came in between them. 'What are you two talking about?'

'Mate-ship, my love.'

She poked him. 'Remember, I come first.'

Leo chuckled, and put his arm around her.

Jules was glad to see his friend's sense of humour hadn't been entirely lost. That the woman in his life could amuse him even at this sad time. He told Leo to take care of himself, and eager to be with the woman in his own life, he headed for his car. The madcap mission to Afghanistan he dismissed as he drove away at speed.

Instead of heading straight for his apartment when he reached London, he'd drive to Sam's house and catch her before she fetched Milly from school. It might be their last chance to be together before the trial.

The lesson came to an end. Sam received a generous payment above and beyond what she'd asked for. 'That's not necessary,' she protested.

'I know, but I want to come again next week. And please call me B…Ben.'

At the front door, she saw the smart Jaguar. 'Nice car,' she said. The chauffer inside was stylish in his peaked cap.

'Pity I can't drive it myself.' Ben gave her a warm smile. 'But with your help I will do, soon.' And he strode towards it.

Sam watched, a little in awe, as he was driven away, the car's engine a privileged purr.

She was thrilled the preliminary class had been a success, and that her first client would be coming for a good while.

She returned inside and drank a large glass of water, before setting off to collect Milly from school.

Jules had arrived in the street moments earlier. He'd parked on the opposite side and had a direct view of Sam as she said goodbye to a man. One with a superior smile on his face as he walked to a brand, new Jaguar, a chauffeur sitting in the driving seat. It was hard to see Sam's look of awe as she watched them drive away, before returning inside.

What chance did he have if she was working with men as wealthy and as good looking as this? He felt overwhelmed by a feeling he wasn't used to, jealousy. He was about to switch on his engine and zoom away, when the front door opened and out she came.

She glanced around, saw him, and gave such a radiant smile, his anxiety faded away. He recalled how it was when they made love. How no one else mattered except the two of them.

She ran over, climbed in, and was in his arms. She stayed long enough to reassure him everything was alright. That he had nothing to worry about.

He gave her a lift as near to the school as he dared risk.

Their last words were about the trip to Nice they'd planned for when the trial was over. How they'd stroll along the Promenade des Anglais as the sun went down, free to do as they pleased.

A week later, Jules quitted his desk job in Putney. A job he'd come to appreciate, having learned the value of listening to other people. He'd made some good friends. Kisi was sad to see him go. Billy Brown from up North said he'd miss practicing his terrible French on him. Whilst duty officer Braithwaite gave a last soldierly salute, perhaps suspecting that the road ahead was an even harder one.

Sam also turned to friends during the final week. She'd come to appreciate words from Aristotle, in her father's books. The idea that there were three forms of friendship intrigued.

The first being the friendship of *utility,* based on a commodity, such as a visit to the hairdressers, where friends were made through a

202

shared usage.

Second, was the friendship of *pleasure,* where common interests connected people, like playing sports, or joining a book club. But if those interests disappeared, so did the friendship.

The last was *true friendship,* which required much more than the others. Where friends needed to be alike in virtue. Where there was a shared sense of goodness and loyalty which went beyond pleasure or usage. These friends stayed around in the hard times like Andrea and Aisha in London, and Chloe and Veronica in the country. Sam knew these women would be there for her come what may, and that this was an unwavering truth.

Mother was also wonderful, arriving to be an extra pair of hands for Milly. Stella Elliot still didn't know the depth of her daughter's involvement with the accused firearms officer. She was simply proud to see Sam upholding British Justice, and wanted to give her all the support that she could.

PART THREE

38

On a cloudy November morning, Sam dropped Milly off at school as usual. Except that today was anything but usual and Milly clung to her. She knew her mother had to stand up in court and - *tell the truth and nothing but, so help me God.* Something Milly strived to do but often found difficult. 'Good luck, Mummy,' she whispered.

The mothers, who were gathered around the gate, also wished Sam well. They said how they liked her hair in a French pleat, and told her how appropriate her navy suit, pristine white shirt, and flat shoes, looked.

The scarf around her neck was also navy. It hid the scar, which, because of the stress building up in the last weeks had flared up horribly.

'Stand firm. Don't be intimidated,' said Barbara, the psychologist.

'Believe in British justice,' said Olivia.

There were a few doubtful murmurings as others expressed uncertainty about what Justice or being British meant anymore.

Aisha came running up. 'Don't let Ahmed's parents put you off this time,' she urged. 'Do what you have to. They've chosen to take this to court when they should have backed down.'

They hugged one another.

When she arrived home, there was a car with two men inside, parked near to the house. She felt safe having these undercover officers around, organized by Jules for her protection.

She went upstairs, put his white hanky into her jacket pocket, and came down ready to go.

A last affirmative hug from her mother, and it was outside to Andrea, waiting, in her electric car. Her friend had offered to act as chauffeur for the day, driving to and from Woolwich Crown Court, the one designated for such terrorist cases.

Andrea was wearing her, 'Self-Defence is a Human Right.' T shirt, and was determined to see Sam safely to her destination. She felt the police car following closely behind them was somewhat unnecessary.

They arrived to see a gun cannon on the lawn, and armed police already in position. Sam knew there would be more security inside the modern building. Tanya Osborne had informed her of this on her last phone call. The lawyer had forgiven Sam's botched visit to Ahmed's parents, and had wanted to reassure her how safe the crown court was. How it had all the mod cons, computers, microphones, and a video screen. She'd also spoken about a special tunnel that had been built underneath. One that led directly to Belmarsh jail, so that when found guilty, villains were taken straight from the dock to their prison cells. Sam had voiced the fear that if the firearms officer were found guilty this might also happen to him.

She was soundly scolded. Ordered not to doubt the officer's innocence for a single moment.

When Andrea dropped her at the entrance and drove away, Sam was left with the problem of how to get inside. The building was indeed modern, with a glass front, which gave it an airy almost welcoming feel. But a group of journalists, banned from entering themselves, were skulking at the entrance. As she walked up they started barraging her with questions, blocking her path. *'Can you still remember the events correctly? Do you still believe the officer is innocent? It could still go either way, couldn't it?'* She felt harassed again.

It took armed police to bulldoze them aside, before she could she could enter.

There were other people waiting in the entrance hall, who quickly introduced themselves as defence witnesses like her. Ones she knew online from the victim support group, but had never met in person. There was the instigator, Giles Edwards, who was determined to see justice done today. There was Simone from Sardinia, who'd been too scared to come forward until his conscience had won through. He was accompanied by Benito, an Indian girl, who, in spite, of a badly slashed arm and many stitches, was smiling and serene. And lastly, a married couple, Iris, still recovering from a stab wound to her side, and her husband Miles, who, his leg not yet healed, had a limp.

206

They were the walking wounded.

Moments later, Tanya Osborne, healthy and striking, came clicking along in her high heel shoes. She was dressed in a formal black gown and a grey wig, which gave due dignity to her role. She thanked them all for arriving on time, and led the way to the court.

The defence lawyer's professionalism now inspired instead of irritated. A male clerk carried her laptops and papers as she strode along the corridors, the witnesses following like a tribe of Israelites. They passed through security, their bags, bodies, and even minds checked out, or so it felt, before they were allowed inside the courtroom.

It had light painted walls, panelled ceiling lights, wooden desks, black office chairs, and computers galore, and felt like a business forum, cold and impersonal. Sam was only cheered at seeing the video screen set up in a corner. At least she'd have a glimpse of Jules when he made his statement.

The clerks, bailiffs and counsels were already present. Only the judge and the jury had yet to appear. Sam knew that some statements had already been given online, so that less people needed to be seen in person. Leo's character reference for his mate had taken place weeks earlier.

Previous days in court had been taken up by the prosecution witnesses. Sam felt sure they'd given unreliable testimonies. Most were passersby, who, she felt, on the day, had either suffered from short sightedness, or were boldfaced liars set on discrediting Jules, and with him, the whole police force. Now, she had the chance to challenge this, and was ready to do whatever was necessary. To answer questions as honestly as she could. Not to botch her way through, or second guess, or try to be clever. She'd be herself, and tell the truth.

Tanya took up her position. The prosecuting lawyers sat along the same row, at an appropriate distance, also wearing formal wigs and gowns.

The atmosphere was solemn as Sam and the other witnesses filed into a row at the back of the court, where they sat waiting to give their statements in turn.

There was a flurry of activity as clerks scurried around handing out last-minute papers to the lawyers, before a bailiff rose to his feet, and intoned, 'All Rise.'

The Judge appeared, not a man as Sam had expected, but a middle-aged woman in a shorter wig and gown, who looked smart and business like. When she sat down, everyone else followed.

Lastly, with a resounding turn of keys, the doors of the court were locked.

Sam studied the prosecution counsel. The elderly man had eyelids that drooped, and a crooked nose. One side of his mouth seemed to be lopsided, which gave him a permanent sneer. He was accompanied by a younger woman, who, Sam surmised, must be his clerk.

Behind them sat the attacker's parents, who looked tense and nervous. Sam hadn't seen them since her failed visit to their house. She decided she wouldn't look at them when she gave her statement today. Saving Jules was her only concern.

The jury filed in, seven men and five women. A fair representation of the British public. Or were they? They were of mixed races, mixed ages, and might well have mixed opinions, too. Could they come to the same conclusion that Jules was innocent and should be freed? Sam knew counsels had spent days accepting and declining people. That these twelve were considered the most suitable. But to her, they appeared too relaxed. She couldn't help wondering if they'd come to the right court, one that was dealing with a horrific terrorist attack. As they settled themselves they were smiling at one another as if this was just a nice day out.

The first testimony came from Jules. Sam felt comforted just seeing him, even though the video screen was darkened so he couldn't be recognized.

His voice was also disguised. There was no hint of a French accent as he recalled what had happened that fateful day. His voice was muffled and robotic, even though his words bore proof that he was a professional officer, trained to be objective.

The prosecution started the cross examination. The old man homed in on Jules's difficult background, suggesting it had turned him into a man full of anger and resentment. That this anger had escalated during his time in Afghanistan and built up into a hatred of all Muslims. The prosecutor turned to check he had the jury's full attention before delivering his final blow. In which he accused Jules of losing control on the fateful day in a desire to exact revenge, and shoot to kill.

Sam prayed Jules would not lose his temper defending himself. But Tanya had drilled him well. He didn't raise his voice as he denied this, and said he'd only felt sadness at having to shoot Ahmed. That it was the last thing he'd wanted to do. But it had been the only way to save another life. He'd been trained to keep the public safe and had done what he'd had to.

His testimony came to an end, and he was followed by his partner. Ted Rowlands's voce was also muffled, and his face darkened. But he clearly stated that three warnings were given and ignored. That his partner had no choice but to take immediate action.

The prosecutor blamed him all the same, claiming he was negligent for damaging his camcorder. Then mocked the idea that his memory of the event could be relied upon. How could anyone's recall in such circumstances be a hundred percent accurate and beyond reasonable doubt? In the horror of the moment it would be impossible to remember much at all.

A few members of the jury nodded their agreement.

Sam didn't agree at all. She could recall every detail, and would do so when her turn came.

One by one the defence witnesses gave their own harrowing testimonies. She had to steel herself against listening too hard, in case she lost her own concentration. When she was finally called, she walked behind the clerk and into the witness box, with a determined step.

Once inside however, her nerve almost failed her. Only when the clerk swore her in and she had to say the words – *to tell the truth and nothing but* - was she able to steel herself.

The dock, usually used by the accused, was opposite to her, but empty. Sam had to imagine Jules was sitting, watching and encouraging her. She looked at the judge with humility. Then at the jury almost pleadingly. The twelve good men and women who would decide the fate of the man she loved.

Tanya Osborne rose and gave a reassuring nod before asking Sam to describe what had happened on that seemingly peaceful summer's day.

Sam spoke quietly. She painted the memory of the event like an artist might. Every detail was coloured by her feelings, as she described the confusion, the shock, the fright, and the final grip of terror as she realized she was about to lose her life. How all she could think of was her little girl. How lost Milly would be without her. How she felt an unbelievable relief when one man did his duty and took the shot that had saved her.

She fished out her hanky and wiped her eyes. The room was completely silent.

39

The prosecutor rose from his seat, straightened his wig, and gave what may have been intended as a disarming smile. To Sam it made him resemble a reptile as his lizard like tongue flicked out words that suggested she was a fantasist, an actress who was inclined to see drama as a means of attracting publicity. How she'd made the headlines in all the papers.

Sam held onto the edge of the box to steady herself before she answered. 'I had nothing to do with any of that. For me the attack was all too real. I could feel the coldness of the blade on my skin, but had to wait for warnings to be given. I'll never forget those seconds before the shot was taken. It was like a bomb was ticking. She looked at the jury. 'I wanted to live for my daughter like any of you would...'

All eyes were on her. She glanced at the parents of Ahmed, saw fear in theirs, but felt no sympathy this time, as in one swift movement she whipped off her scarf and revealed the scar, a red raw jagged line.

There were gasps from the jury at this livid reminder. It was only in the last week that Sam had agreed to reveal it. 'This is where he cut into me,' she continued, her voice trembling. 'It will not heal. It is a reminder of how I almost died. He showed no mercy. No humanity...' She broke down.

The judge gave her a moment to recover before asking the prosecutor if he had any more questions. Sensing it could be counterproductive the old man declined and Sam was discharged from her duty. She returned to the row of other witnesses, emotionally drained.

Simone offered her his bottle of water. Giles Edwards patted her hand, whilst the others leaned across to whisper – 'Well done. Good job.'

She felt no jubilation, just relief her ordeal was over.

Only it wasn't.

Tanya Osborne rose, and announced with a flourish, that she had one more witness. Someone who had decided to put right a wrong.

211

There were puzzled looks as the courtroom doors were unlocked to allow in the teenager who'd taken the mobile phone footage.

Percy Harris had an elderly woman with him. A court guardian, Sam supposed, as he was only seventeen. The woman sat discreetly a way back, when he took the stand.

Sam leant forwards to take a proper look at the lad who was about to become a witness for the defence. A turncoat who'd promised to reveal the truth and set Jules free. She hadn't seen him before. Her back had been turned while he had callously filmed the attack. Now, she took in the cold eyes, the snub nose, the loose clothing, all black, as though he was coming to a funeral. She looked at the prosecutor to see his reaction to this defector, and was disturbed to see the old man looking strangely unperturbed.

She felt uneasy as Harris was sworn in. He was sweating profusely. Tanya started asking questions and his answers were mumbled rather than clear. Instead of cooperating he became surly, and then downright obstructive. To Sam's alarm, he pointed his finger at her. 'Sam Elliot is a liar,' he declared. 'I videoed what really happened. The officer shot without any chance for surrender. No warnings were given. He acted like a coldblooded killer.'

She wanted to shout back, 'You're the liar!' But was afraid she'd only make things worse.

An equally shocked Tanya tried to challenge him, but he refused to even look at her. Instead he smirked at the prosecutor, who gave a satisfied nod, as though he'd known all along that things would go his way.

It was a complete betrayal of what had been promised. Tanya strode up to the bench and explained to the judge this was not the statement her witness had agreed to give. The judge was sympathetic but gave permission for Harris to continue, declaring that his testimony was too important to lose.

Rendered impotent, a furious Tanya accused the teenager of being a lad with no desire to be honest, someone who preferred to double cross people. That his hatred of the police, of the law, of justice, of decency, and of any sort of honour, made him a despicable human being. She turned her back on him and strode away.

Silence.

No one could have imagined what would follow.

People stared critically at the teenager. His face turned slowly puce. Then he let out a guttural howl, and to the horror of the entire court, he pulled a knife from his shoe, leapt over the edge of the witness box, and screamed, '*Allahu Akbar!*' as he ran at Tanya.

She whirled around only to be stabbed in the chest, and then in the neck. She raised her hands in self defence and cried out, 'No! No!' as he kept on attacking her.

People started shouting. Others were stunned into silence. Ahmed's mother, seeing what was happening in front of her very eyes, cried out, 'In the name of Allah, stop!' But Harris was intent on killing the lawyer.

The Bailiff's were too far back, and Sam, without thinking of the risk, went into action. She rushed from her seat, sneaked up behind him, grabbed his arm, poised to strike again, and wrenched it down, twisting hard. The force caused Harris to let go of the knife. It fell to the floor with a clatter, and Tanya slipped from his grasp.

Desperate, he let out a howl and lunged at Sam. His hands went around her throat. He started choking her. Only one move could save her. The one she'd never wanted to do.

She poked her fingers into his eyes.

He gave an anguished shriek and staggered back, straight into the arms of the bailiffs, who'd at last arrived. They dragged him away.

Sam, still struggling to breathe, listened helplessly as he yelled a last deadly threat. *'I know who the murdering firearms officer is – Jules Caron has a fatwa on his head!'*

He was manhandled down the stairs to the basement. Sam could only hope they'd march him through the specially built tunnel all the way to Belmarsh bloody jail! Far from being terrorized by jihadists, Harris had been converted to be one. He'd fooled them all.

The judge was calling out, '*Order! Order!*' too late.

Her pronouncement – *that if anyone shared the revealed name of the firearms officer outside this court they'd be held in contempt,* was hardly heard,

213

before she banged down the hammer.

Pandemonium broke out as doors were unlocked and armed police stormed in, bellowing for everyone to stay where they were.

Sam comforted the distressed and bloodied Tanya until the paramedics arrived to take her away. The courtroom doors were then secured again. An officer explained the attack could be part of a wider conspiracy. That they needed to be protected and the building would be placed in lockdown.

There were horrified murmurs of acquiescence as people huddled together.

'Is everyone, alright?' Giles Edwards asked his group of witnesses. He turned as Sam joined them. 'You were brave going for him like that. Where did you learn those moves?'

Sam didn't say she'd received some training at a farm on the Salisbury Plain. It wasn't the right time. And she was too anxious about Jules, worried he'd seen what had happened and had heard his name being exposed. She was concerned that someone might choose to disobey the judge's ruling about it never being spoken outside the court, and expose it. A high payment could be offered by newspapers for just such a scoop.

Jules had watched the proceedings through the video link set up in the basement of the building. He'd already been appalled by Harris's betrayal. Now he watched helplessly as the teenager physically attacked Tanya Osborne. 'He's going to kill her,' he leapt from his chair.

'Where are the fucking bailiff's,' said the armed officer who was guarding them. Jackson had a Glock pistol in an ankle holder, and a sheathed knife in his pocket. He liked cracking jokes but had stopped mid-flow when he saw what was happening in the court.

'The son of a bitch! He's played us.' Ted Rowlands was mortified. 'It was all an act. If I could have five minutes with the little *shite!*' All Ted's religious fervour was lost.

The three of them stared at the screen stunned to see Sam sneak up and execute a Krav Maga move. One that disarmed the teenager.

Jules felt a rush of pride, only to be followed by a rush of anguish, as Harris retaliated by lunging at her. He grabbed her around the throat and started squeezing...

Jules made for the door. 'I have to get up there.'

But Jackson blocked his path. 'Sorry, but you can't leave this room.'

'Mon Dieu. This is a nightmare.'

Luckily, Sam did another move she'd been loath to use, and poked her fingers into Harris's eyes.

In moments it was all over. The teenager fell back into the arms of the now waiting bailiffs, who dragged him away. But not before he'd screamed out a last deadly threat. Jules heard his name, heard the fatwa being placed on his head, and turned to Ted in despair. 'He's given me a life sentence.'

His partner put a hand on his shoulder. 'Harris is a nobody. The fatwa won't hold. The court case is over, and your innocence proved.'

But Jules couldn't believe this. He watched as armed police stormed the courtroom, shaking his head. When the video screen went blank and any contact with Sam was lost he could only pray she was okay.

'The police will come for you next, Jules.' Jackson gave due warning. 'You'll be taken into protective custody.'

'Protective custody? I can't have that. I have to get out of here.' He tried to reach the door again, but Jackson still barred his way.

'A safe house will feel as bad as being in prison,' Jules pleaded. 'I know where I can escape to.' Leo would hide him at his farm.

'Can't you look the other way, Jackson?' urged Ted. 'And let him escape.'

'Nope. I'll look an idiot if he's not here.'

'But he'll lose his freedom for life, and it will be your fault.'

Ted glared at him. 'Come on, give him a fighting chance. We both know he's innocent. You'd want us to help you in the same position.'

Jackson gave a defeated groan. He pulled keys from his pocket, unlocked the door, and with a sigh stood to one side. 'Go,' he urged.

'I'll not forget this,' said Jules, who with a farewell nod at Ted, fled into the corridor.

40

It seemed an age before the courtroom doors were opened, the building deemed to be secure, and the witnesses allowed to leave. Even then it was only under heavy police escort.

Sam and her group piled into a Black Maria, parked outside the front entrance. She had no time to call to Andrea and explain what had happened. She feared her good friend would be trapped behind some police barrier, feeling frantic.

The van, with a couple of armed police inside, set off on the journey back to the respective homes of the witnesses. Sam was the last to be dropped off.

She found Andrea was already there. She'd been accompanied by the undercover officers, who were still outside the house for ongoing protection.

Mother made a strong pot of tea. The radio news was on, and the main topic - Terror in Court,' recounted Sam's heroic actions. Her mother patted her daughter's hand proudly. Andrea said it was down to the Krav Maga training, of which she was now a devotee.

Sam couldn't allow herself any compliments. She was too worried about Jules. Only when it was announced that the charges against the firearms officer were being dropped did she feel a glimmer of relief.

But it was short lived when they revealed his name had been exposed on the dark web, and that a photograph of him might surface.

'He'll be a target now,' said Andrea, matter of fact. 'Everyone will be looking for him.'

Sam had to hold off a panic attack.

Her mother tried to reassure her by saying that the police would take care of the officer. It wasn't for her to worry about him anymore as she'd shown he was innocent in her testimony. That she'd done all she could.

Sam couldn't explain how much Jules really meant to her. That she was the girlfriend of a man with a price on his head. It was a secret she still had to keep. She feared he'd be placed in a police protection programme and she wouldn't be allowed to see him. That his life would not be his own.

Jules could hear police coming down the stairs and knew he'd have a race to get away.

Outside, he found the security guards in disarray, which made it easy to slip past, and into the nearby streets, without being challenged.

He ran all the way to the Woolwich underground station to catch the South Circular. It took an agonizing hour and twenty-five minutes to reach Putney. He arrived knowing it was only a matter of time before his name would be released and people would start hunting for him.

He took a furtive glance around to see no journalists were hanging around his apartment block, before entering the back way.

Once inside, he called Leo. But his mate was out. He had to leave a voicemail asking for a hiding place. He then called Sam, but she didn't answer either. Not wanting to leave a bleak message he decided to call her later. He then disabled his mobile. He'd use the burner one instead, untraceable, and kept for emergencies.

He packed his suitcase with essential clothes, his passport, which he was relieved he hadn't handed in, and a wad of cash, as credit cards always left a trail. He took a last glance around the apartment he might not see for a very long time, and left. The new life he'd hoped to build for himself was all but destroyed.

He switched on the news as he drove towards the motorway. The reporting was all about the terror attack in the bastion of British justice. How armed police were conducting raids on Tower Hamlets to root out any Jihadists who might have been involved. He was relieved to hear that both Sam and Tanya would be alright. Though the latter would be in hospital for a good while.

When it was said his name had already been leaked on the dark web, he switched off, and focused on his driving, desperate to reach the safety of Leo's farm.

He arrived as dusk was falling. Only the barking of Jock, straining on his kennel leash to be free, greeted him. The menagerie of geese and hens were already locked away from menacing foxes.

He let himself in through the backdoor and entered the kitchen to find Leo sitting in dim lighting.

His mate jumped up when he saw him. 'Thank God you're here. No one followed you, did they?'

Jules shook his head.

'It's all over the internet. What's the world coming to?' Leo shook his head. 'An attack inside a British court and you on the run again. You look fucking exhausted.'

Jules nodded, his drab grey suit, put on specially for the trial, felt damp right through, such was the sweat he'd poured into it.

'Go and take a shower,' urged Leo. 'Make yourself at home in the attic bedroom, while I drum up a sandwich.'

As the steaming hot water ran over him, Jules felt a temporary relief from fear and anxiety. The purity, the cleansing quality, the sense that water both absorbed and dispelled bad energy, released his torment for a short while.

Refreshed, he returned downstairs in an old dressing gown belonging to Leo's father, which had been left invitingly on the attic door.

Leo gave a sad smile when he saw it. 'Glad it's of use.'

Jules sat down and ate his sandwich, realising he was starving.

'It was brave of Sam to tackle that bastard the way she did,' said Leo. 'Is she alright?'

'I think so, but I've yet to speak to her. I left a message before I abandoned my mobile. I'll use a burner from now on.'

'Best not tell her where you are. Or that you might have to leave the country.'

Jules looked at him, the cold reality of his situation dawning. 'You think I should?'

'Only way you'll be safe.'

'I've thought about France. But how do I get there and avoid airports where they'll be scanning for me?'

'I can take you via another route. But first, you need a good night's sleep. We'll talk about it in the morning.'

Sam kept her mobile close expecting Jules to call, but nothing happened. She allowed Mother to fetch Milly home from school, before sitting down to explain things to her daughter. Milly became fearful their troubles would never be over, and it was only when she heard an accolade on the television calling her mother the heroine of the courtroom that she was able to rally. She ran out into the garden and practiced her own Krav Maga, determined to be a heroine herself one day. Andrea, keen to show off her own expertise, joined her.

Sam stayed indoors, glued to the TV news. She was relieved to hear that the defence lawyer was out of danger. That Tanya should make a full recovery. But of Jules there was only wild speculation.

Her mobile rang and she reached for it thinking it was him.

But it was Aisha calling to express her dismay at what had happened. 'The community are divided again. Our mosque wants the fatwa removed, but others, with more extreme members, don't. I hate seeing our religion hijacked in this way. I shall do all I can to fight it.'

Her friend switched off just as the landline started ringing. A journalist wanted Sam to comment. Did she know a photograph of the firearms officer had been released and that people were searching for him? That he'd been sighted in various places and it wouldn't be long before he was found. How did this make her feel?

Sam was sick of feeling anything. Her anxiety escalated. Her mother advised it would be wise to escape to Dorset again and get away from intrusive journalists.

At that moment, as if by telepathy, Veronica called.

Her country friend was reeling from the news. 'Did you know that Jules was the firearms officer?' she asked.

'I only learned recently.'

'Why didn't you tell us?'

'I couldn't. And you mustn't tell anyone that we knew him before the trial. It would only cause more trouble.'

'If that's what you want, Chloe and I will keep Mum. We're your friends, and loyal.'

There was a burning question to ask. 'Has Leo heard from Jules?'

Veronica gave the same old answer. Leo wouldn't tell her even if he had. That a soldier's loyalty was unbreakable.

Sam ended the call telling her country friend that she'd be coming to Dorset soon. That they would talk more then. She had a longing to tell them everything, but knew it still wasn't safe to. Maybe by then it would be.

She was thrilled to check her messages and see Jules's mobile number flash up. It meant he'd tried to reach her. She hardly slept a wink all night, waiting for him to call again.

41

Jules was so tired he slept through. When he woke, he had a quick shower, dressed, and went downstairs.

He found his mate glued to his new computer. 'I see you've invested in technology, Leo.'

'I had to keep up with all the news. Your name's being spread like cow shit, online. They've even got a photograph.'

Jules went over, saw the grainy image was clear enough to make him recognizable. It must have been taken that night at Tower Hamlets, when Ted was having a beating. 'I'll be hunted by all manner of people, now,' he fretted to Leo.

'That's why you should leave the country,' said Leo. 'I have a plan to get you out, incognito.'

Jules bit hard on his toast.

'You must come on the mission to Afghanistan.'

'Mon Dieu, is that really happening?'

'Salim and Abdul are in trouble and need our help.'

'How do you know this?'

'Salim managed to call me. There was a skirmish between the border guards at the Spin Boldak crossing. A soldier on the Pakistan side got shot and they closed it. No one can get through. The pair are holed up in a village a few miles from the crossing at Chaman. They're being protected by locals for the time being, but if the Taliban get hold of them you know what they'll do.'

Jules did, all too well.

'I've got the papers organized for them to come here. And MacLean has organized an operation.'

The last time Jules had spoken to Archie was at old Tom's funeral when the soldier had announced that he'd left the army. Jules knew he'd been in the E squadron, the elite force that did rescue missions all over the world. He could only hope that Archie had kept good contacts.

'He has official backing?' Jules now asked Leo.

His mate looked sheepish. 'Not exactly. But some will turn a blind eye.'

'Who's funding it then?'

'A charity that specializes in such missions.'

Jules wasn't sure about this. But Leo carried on enthusiastically.

'We'll cadge a ride on a transporter plane taking humanitarian aid to a refugee camp near the Pakistan border. We'll land in the city of Quetta, and then be helicoptered, under cover of darkness, into Afghanistan. There'll be two of Archie's ex-commando mates and if you come along the team will be five strong.' Leo grinned at Jules. 'It'll be like old times having my sniper partner at my side.'

'I might be better off heading for France.'

'Well, that's part of the plan. When we've completed the mission, instead of returning to the UK, you can fly there instead, but from Pakistan.'

Jules could see this might be a more discreet route. He saw a glimmer of hope. 'When do you plan to leave for Afghanistan?'

'Sunday, flying from Boscombe Down.'

'That quick.'

Leo nodded. Jules pushed back his chair, walked over to the window, and stared out at the peaceful view. A few sheep were grazing on the front lawn.

'It's in a good cause, Jules,' Leo pressed. 'Abdul and Salim put their lives on the line for us, remember.'

Jules nodded. Half of him relished the idea of some action. The other was worried about Sam. 'I'll have to let her know where I'm going.'

Leo came up behind him. 'You can't. Veronica thinks I'll be on a hike in the Scottish Highlands and will be incommunicado. If I told her the truth she'd be up in arms. It has to remain covert for everyone's safety.'

'How long will the mission take?'

'It should be all over in a few days. I've promised Veronica I'll be back for the Christmas parties, anyway.' He chuckled.

'I'd planned to meet Sam in Nice for the New Year. You think we still could?'

'I don't see why not.'

Jules pulled out his burner phone. 'I must let her know.'

'One call is all I'll allow,' said Leo.

'I'll do it in the back garden.'

'Be quick. My workers will be here soon, I don't want them spotting you.'

Jules slipped outside, pulled out his burner phone and dialled Sam. When she picked up immediately he knew she'd been waiting for his call. 'Cheri, it's me.'

'Jules?' She let out a sob. 'I'd almost given up hearing from you.'

'Never do that. I'll be in touch one way or another.' He needed to reassure her. 'I thought you were amazing in the court.'

'I only did what you and Leo taught me to do. I'm glad it worked. What's happening to you?'

'I'm being shunted around so no one can know where I am.'

'Not even me.'

He didn't answer. She told him that people were out looking for him. That some had claimed sightings. He'd been spotted in churches, buses, trains. Some woman had declared she'd seen him on a beach in the Costa del Sol…

'Last place I'd go.' At least they shared a chuckle. 'I'll be out of contact for a while,' he warned her.

'But you'll call when you're able to, promise me?'

His phone gave a warning bleep. He'd been so tired last night he hadn't charged it and the battery was running low. He needed to keep her hopes up before it cut out. 'How about we make that trip to Nice? See in the New Year.'

'You think we could? I'd love that.'

'We'd have to fly there separately,' he warned. 'Find somewhere to rendezvous.'

'How about the Promenade des Anglais?'

He was about to say that would be perfect, when his phone cut out, the line went dead, and she was gone.

He stood alone in the silence of the countryside, until the

peacefulness had calmed his pounding heart.

He returned inside, his mind made up. 'Leo, I'm in.'

In the following days, they prepared for the mission. Backpacks were filled with critical items; multi tool kits, new burner phones and chargers, medications, extra socks, flashlights, pistols, and escape belts, which would enable them to survive for a few days in an extreme situation. Added to this was bottled water, food rations, sheath knives, sunscreen, fire kits, a few ready to eat meals, and chocolate bars for energy. The British made rifles they prepped ready. Jules only hoped they wouldn't have to use them. His passport he hid in a secret pocket, ready for the trip to France when it was all over. He was glad he'd hung on to it and not handed it in.

Sam, cut off from any contact with Jules for the time being, but at least hopeful she'd see him soon enough, set off for Dorset at the end of the week. Mother had already gone ahead to prepare.

Milly's gloom at missing the Christmas activities at the school she now so enjoyed, luckily lifted, at the sight of the police escort following behind them. She waved at the officers through the car back window excitedly, until, having seen them safely out of London, the two men, their job done, made a discreet exit.

It was freezing weather and a little sleet had started falling, which caused Milly more thrills. By the time they reached the hills of Dorset snowflakes were sticking to the windscreen. When they reached the sea, the clifftops were shrouded in whiteness. The lane leading to mother's cottage was already skiddy, and it was a struggle to stop the car sliding into the ditch.

Once inside, they relished the warmth of the log fire, and sipped drinks of hot chocolate, as it grew even colder outside, the snow falling thickly.

Later, after a light supper, Milly joined Sam in her bedroom., and to keep warm they snuggled together under the winter duvet, Sam, thankful she had her daughter to hold onto. When they woke the next morning, the cottage was snowbound, surrounded in a white void.

42

Leo and Jules were picked up early on Sunday. The van was already occupied by three men, all ex commandos, including Archie MacLean. No one mentioned Jules's predicament. They were too well trained in ethics. They just knew he needed to get away, and one more man was welcome.

The drive to the RAF airport base of Boscombe Down, with the longest military runway in England, should have only taken half an hour. But the roads were slushy from the snow and they were delayed.

Sunday, and the airport was quiet as they raced up the ramp and into the bowels of the transporter plane. The pilot was impatient to leave and moments later, he roared down the runway at full throttle, and lifted the plane into the sky. The team breathed a sigh of relief that they'd made it.

They had on winter protective outfits as the December weather could be even colder at their destination. Jules and Leo sat side by side, their rifles in their hands. Jokes were shared by the other men to ease the tension, until Archie MacLean, suggested they get some sleep on the eight hour flight, so they wouldn't be worn out when they arrived.

Jules dozed only fitfully. He was relishing being a soldier again. Particularly one who was involved in a rescue mission. He felt it might give him a chance to redeem himself.

The plane made a bumpy landing at Quetta airport. The capitol city of the Pakistani province of Balochistan was situated in a wide valley surrounded by mountains. It was a trading centre between the two countries, and famous in the summer for its fruit orchards. But now winter had arrived it was veiled in a cloak of snow.

The plane parked to unload its humanitarian aid. The ramp was lowered and the five men ran down and leapt into a waiting truck. They were then driven for a couple of hours to a helicopter pad nearer to the border with Afghanistan.

A rattling old Chinook was ready to take off. Daylight was gone, and in darkness, the smell of sticky engine oil, and hot air blasting in their faces, they clambered inside the chopper, strapped on the safety stop harnesses, and without further delay the machine ascended into the sky.

As it soared, and pitched forwards through the mountains, the jolts provoked laughter. A feeling of camaraderie formed between the team, as the pilot, an ex- member of the special services group in Pakistan, the SSG, secretly powered them into Afghanistan.

There was no gunner with his heavy machine gun positioned at the open doors in case of any enemy fire. They crossed over without any trouble, unlike during the war, when rocket propelled grenades could come hurtling from the sparse trees on the rocky terrains, able to kill everyone on board.

When they reached the Registan Desert, they put on their visual night goggles and looked down on the eerie landscape of crescent moon shaped dunes, formed by wild winds, and an open plain with sparse shelter, owing to little vegetation.

No snow here, but the night air was still chilly. The landing was made difficult by a fierce wind blowing. The five men had to shimmy down a rope ladder before the pilot could power away. He'd need a different pick up point for when the job was done, and they were ready for collection. Archie Maclean was given orders to find one less windy, and to use his satellite phone to give the correct coordinates so the pilot could swoop in.

The desert was encroaching on agricultural areas, a result of climate change. The interpreters were holed up in one of the few villages left, that had not been submerged by sand storms. The team had to navigate twenty kilometres of harsh landscape, red sand blown in their faces at every step. Nomads were the usual desert inhabitants, but Taliban forces patrolled nearer to the border, and could launch an attack at any time.

They had twenty kilometres to run through, hiding behind rocky outcrops, slithering down sand dunes, and crunching across clay, before they reached the straggle of stone houses that marked their destination.

The village lay near to a riverbed, a trickle of water, and some vegetation. But when they arrived it was night time and no one was around. The streets were in darkness, and all doors were bolted.

It took time to locate the safe house tucked away down an alley, with the coded sign of a shield carved into a side wall.

Leo knocked on the shabby front door three times, the group waiting nervously behind him, hoping no adversaries were around. It was a relief when the password – *rescue* - finally opened it, and there stood Abdul.

Though bedraggled and worn out, he was overjoyed to see them. 'May Allah be merciful to you.' He hugged Leo and then Jules. 'We knew you wouldn't leave us to rot in hell.'

He led the way inside a dark room where the shadowy figure of Salim hung back. In his arms was a bag of rags which he clung to.

Jules went over. 'Are you alright, Salim?' His old friend's eyes were tearful. 'What are you holding?'

From the rags came a cry. With a sorry look Salim exposed a baby, no more than a few weeks old.

"How are we going to deal with an infant?' said Archi MacLean.'

From the back of the room came three more children, and a woman.'

'It's a bloody kindergarten. This could put the operation in jeopardy.' MacLean was worried.

Abdul stepped forwards and explained that they were his family, who he couldn't leave behind.

Salim spoke in a trembling voice to say that his wife hadn't made it. That the Khojak pass was so cold she'd died from exposure. 'We had to bury her in the snow.' The ordeal so terrible he sounded barely alive himself.

Jules knew that in December the fierce winds would have caused perilous drifts, and icy paths that cracked beneath the feet. He knew how desperate his friends must have been to tackle such a terrain to escape from Kandahar.

'We had no food there. No oil to keep us warm, as well as the fear we'd be arrested at any moment,' said Abdul.

He beckoned to an elderly couple, huddled together in a corner, who came over, and bowed. 'These are the good people who have hidden, fed and watered us, in true Afghan spirit.'

The custom of offering food and even gifts to strangers, could cost the pair their lives if discovered by the Taliban. They could have their hands, ears, or even their heads cut off for any generosity to escaping refugees.

'Well, that's brave of them,' acknowledged Archie MacLean. 'But tell then they don't have to worry about us, we have out own supplies. And anyway, we must leave.' He looked at Jules. 'See that baby is wrapped in protective clothing. And the others will need more cover too.'

Lamb skin coats were hurriedly put on before Archie spoke to the three children in the Dari language. 'Keep your eyes on me at all times, and run like you've never run before.'

They nodded, their eyes wide with fright.

Jules gave them each a chocolate bar to help boost their energy.

Night goggles back on, the commando's formed a protective shield around the group of Afghans, and in a body, they crept out of the house and headed for the desert, sneaking through the still silent village streets.

Jules and Leo, rifles at the ready, followed, keeping a distance between them to provide sniper cover. The mission had gone so smoothly they didn't expect any trouble. It came as a shock therefore, when two ghostlike figures came hurtling down a side street, wielding knives. The commandos fled on ahead, and into the desert landscape, whilst Jules and Leo were forced to remain behind to engage in hand to hand combat.

They threw their guns down, and pulled out their own sheathed knives. The fear of being captured, and either skinned alive, stoned to death, or worse beheaded, motivated them to disarm the attackers as quickly as possible.

Jules took a good few blows before he had his in a choke-hold. He knew if he stopped the air flow long enough death would follow instantly. But as the enemy twisted his head, to give a last snarl, he saw the shiny face of a mere boy, and, with a cry of dismay he let him go.

Leo, seeing his was of a similar age, followed suit.

The lads, amazed to be set free, ran off into the darkness, praising Allah.

'They were just kids,' said Jules.

'Unfriendly ones,' said Leo. 'Have we gone soft?'

Jules looked at his trouser leg, and saw blood leaking out. 'Mine left his calling card,' he said, ruefully.

'Is it bad?'

'No, just a nick.'

'We should catch the others up,' said Leo, picking up his gun 'Are you okay to run?'

Jules was looking for his own gun, which he'd thrown further than he'd intended. 'You go on. I'll follow.'

His mate set off at a run.

Jules kicked around the dusty ground, but took a while to find it. By which time his leg was oozing blood, the wound deeper than he'd thought. As he bent down to pick up his gun he felt an acute pain in his side, and more blood spurted out. He realized he'd been stabbed not once, but twice. He tried to stench the flow but it was hopeless. He needed his medical kit, and a safe place to use it. Finding a rusty cellar door ajar, he shouldered his way inside.

He groped around the damp, dark walls, before sinking down in a corner. He frantically rummaged inside his backpack but by the time he pulled his kit out he was too weak to use it. Blood was soaking his trousers, and the pain in his side was now excruciating.

His head felt heavy, as though something was pressing down. He had trouble keeping his eyes open. He feared he was going to pass out...

Leo had thought Jules was right behind him until he reached the group. It was only when he turned and saw no one there that he knew something had gone wrong. He rushed to Archie. 'We have to go back for him,' he said.

Archie shook his head. 'We can't with these children. It will be daylight soon and they'll be lit up like beacons.'

'But I can't leave Jules alone,' said Leo.

'I understand. But I can't give you any man power. They're needed here. There's a better pick up point not far from here. I must call the pilot and give him the coordinates.' He pulled out his satellite phone. 'You have one hour. Go find your mate and then run like hell to join us.'

Leo turned around and raced back to the village.

Jules couldn't believe this was happening. He felt his life was being sapped away. He lay his head back on the stone wall as images started filling his mind, ones that seemed to signal the end was in sight...

Landscapes came first - the rolling hills of England, the majestic alps of France, streams and rivers, the Loir, the Tarn, ones he'd loved canoeing along. People followed, his mother smiling, even his father looking, for once, benign. And his soldier mate Leo striding towards him. Then his partner in the police Ted Rowlands, a bible raised up...Young women came next. Girlfriends he'd had fun with. Others who'd challenged him. Kisi, his co-worker of late, tough but friendly. Tanya, his lawyer, intelligent and formidable. And then there was Sam, honest and open, who had taught him how to love with his whole heart, as well as how to stop running...

He was slipping away... He feared he'd never see her again. That he'd die in this dark damp cellar in Afghanistan, alone, and in pain...

He heard the door being pushed open and for a moment he thought Leo had come to rescue him. Hope rose, but when he heard the local Pashto language being spoke, it was dashed.

Footsteps stomped towards him. He was hauled up, and slumped between two men. He cried out as he was dragged across the stone floor and up some crumbling steps, each one an agony. Next thing he was in a dingy room, laid out on a stone slab, as a man with a dark beard loomed over him like the harbinger of death.

'Batard!' Jules gave a last defiant cry, before darkness engulfed him.

Leo reached the village and returned to the safe house but found he was no longer welcome. The old couple asked him to leave. They said

Jules must have been taken and that this had put them at risk.

Leo searched the alleys for his mate, scoured the ruins and tumbledown houses, but Jules was nowhere to be found. He'd vanished into the darkness.

Leo rushed around in a state of panic as fingers of light started appearing. His own safety in endangered. Time was up. Nothing for it but to return to the desert, and reach the group.

The Chinook was about to leave as he arrived. The pickup point was less windy but he was the last to leap aboard.

With the children and the baby screaming with fright, it roared into the sky, powering them back to Pakistan, and safety.

All except for Jules, who was left behind, his fate unknown.

43

Sam hadn't heard from Jules. She feared that the planned trip to Nice wouldn't happen. That he'd be kept in protection… The best she could do was to keep herself busy preparing for Christmas.

The tree soon glittered with golden baubles, and the small pile of presents underneath, became a source of fascination for Milly. She spent hours trying to work out what lay hidden inside the decorative wrappings.

When the snow blocking the lane evaporated into slush, Sam made a bid for freedom, and drove into Bridport to meet Chloe and Veronica. She intended to tell them the truth about the depth of her relationship with Jules, and to seek their solace. But as they sat in the Harbour pub, sipping wine, she found her two country friends had concerns of their own.

Chloe, had fallen for yet another man, who hadn't told her he was married until she was too involved. 'At least I gave him a bashing, thanks to the Krav Maga training. I hate the way men conceal things from you.'

Veronica commiserated. 'I'm not sure what Leo's up to. He's gone hiking in the Scottish Highlands alone. He didn't want me to accompany him. He's promised to be back for Christmas and he'd better be. I won't be messed about either.'

They clashed their glasses together. 'To women power!'

Sam fell silent. It didn't feel the right time to talk about her own man.

But Chloe surprised her by bringing Jules up herself. 'You know, Sam,' she turned to her. 'I had an interesting chat with the Frenchman at old Tom's funeral.'

'How do you mean, different?' Sam was happy to engage.

'Well, he was kinder, gentler. It's a shame that everything's gone wrong for him when he was trying to be a better man.'

'Is that what he said?'

Chloe nodded.

Sam felt a warm rush knowing this. It encouraged her to think that Jules would be in touch very soon, that he wouldn't abandon her. She decided to wait before saying anything more. To give him longer to make contact. As for the trip to Nice, it could still be on.

She returned home in a more resilient frame of mind, ready for the Christmas festivities.

On the day, Milly was delighted to at last open her presents. She was more than pleased with the roller skates, and whizzed around the cottage all morning, almost knocking Granny down. This didn't stop the Christmas turkey from being cooked to perfection. Or to the ripe pudding being packed with silver wrapped twenty p's. Or to them all listening to the Queen's speech, which, in spite of her majesty's increasing frailty, was truly uplifting.

Which made it more disturbing, when, on Boxing Day, Veronica called in a state.

'Leo's not hiking in the Scottish Highlands like he said he was. He's lied to me!' she cried in disbelief.

Sam didn't know how to respond. Except to say that Leo must have had a good reason for not telling her the truth.

'Oh yes, a crazy one,' said Veronica. 'He's taken himself off to Afghanistan.'

Sam was shocked. 'Afghanistan? How do you know this?'

'When he didn't return in time, I pestered one of his soldier mates, who let slip that Leo was on some mad mission to rescue people.'

'What people?'

'Interpreter mates that he once worked with. Now that the Taliban are back in control their lives are in danger, and they need to be brought to the UK.'

'Well, the army is good at such things. Special forces can sneak in and out of countries with nobody knowing they're around.'

'Except that the army isn't involved. It's unofficial. They're a group of ex-soldiers on a rogue venture.'

Sam fell silent. This was of more concern, as they'd be operating outside the control of any authority.

'Who will rescue them, if they get into trouble?' said a now forlorn

Veronica.

Sam tried to stay positive. 'I'm sure they'll be back safe and sound.'

'That's the problem. The others *are* back, but Leo isn't with them.'

Sam felt a shiver of anxiety. 'Why not?'

'One of the team went missing and he's waiting at the border, hoping he'll reappear. I can only hope Leo doesn't slip back into Afghanistan to look for him. He must be a very good mate for him to wait this long, as it's been weeks.'

The name that floated into Sam's mind was too distressing to contemplate. She felt her heart constrict. 'What are you suggesting, Veronica?'

'I'm not sure.'

Her friend said no more, except that she'd call back as soon as she'd heard something.

Sam was left with a fear she couldn't yet process. She could only pray it couldn't be, it just couldn't be… He'd told her he was in protective custody, and she believed him.

But by the time she received another call she was beside herself with worry. Made worse when it wasn't her friend's voice coming down the line, but Leo's, his voice laden with guilt.

'I have some difficult news, Sam.'

She couldn't speak, couldn't breathe.

'You must have suspected it was Jules who came with me.'

It was as she'd dreaded. She felt a wave of anguish. 'What's happened to him?'

'There was a skirmish.'

'Was he injured?'

'Not seriously.'

'What does that mean?' She felt a rush of anger. 'He might be lying somewhere, bleeding, and alone…'

'I searched everywhere for him, Sam. Even the hospitals…'

'You should never have taken him to Afghanistan.'

'Leaving the UK was his only option with everyone looking for him.'

'You made him lie to me.' She heard Leo's sharp intake of breath.

234

'He couldn't tell you, Sam. It was covert. It was successful, too. The Afghans are safely in the UK.'

'But not Jules.' She stifled a sob.

'Don't give up hope, Sam. Scouts are still searching, at risk to themselves. They won't give up until they find him. I'll call as soon as I have news.' He paused. 'Veronica's standing next to me. I've told her everything. She'd like a word with you.'

But Sam didn't feel able to talk to her friend. She switched off her phone and threw it down as if it were a snake.

Her mother came in. 'Whatever's wrong? You're ashen.'

Sam shook her head and went from the room, knowing that if she spoke, the tears would flow.

She waited days for Leo to call again, but he didn't. She felt suspended in time, waiting, hoping for good news.

A whole week later, on a freezing afternoon, there was a knock on the cottage door.

In trepidation she went to open it. There stood Leo and Veronica. One look at their distraught faces and her fears were confirmed. She let out a howl of such anguish it brought Milly and her mother running.

'What's wrong Mummy?' said Milly, looking scared.

'Darling girl?' Her mother put an arm around her to hold her steady.

'I've brought grim news, I'm afraid,' said Leo, his eyes red and watery.

Milly was sent back to the kitchen, and given a drink and biscuit, while they moved into the sitting room.

Leo, explained in a more formal manner, how a soldier Sam knew had gone missing in Afghanistan. That scouts had searched high and low for him but no trace was found. That they'd had to presume he'd been captured by the Taliban,' Leo hesitated before whispering the final words, 'and *executed.'*

Sam cried out, 'No! That cannot be!' She broke into sobs.

Her mother knew all too well that it could. Knew that any soldier caught would be tortured and then killed. What she didn't understand was why her daughter was drowning in such sorrow, or who this man really was.

Leo tried to offer comfort, but Sam was too angry with him. And fearing they were doing more harm than good, he and Veronica retreated.

Sam's mother took charge. Milly was given a light supper and put to bed, assured that all would be explained in the morning.

The rest of the evening was spent in the sitting room by the fire, as she coaxed her daughter to tell more. When Sam finally spoke, it was in stops and starts, as she revealed the truth about the man she obviously loved. The man she had first encountered in the Wimbledon attack, the firearms officer who had saved her life.

Her mother was astonished to hear this. And to discover he was also the man who'd appeared at the music festival. Sam explained that she hadn't known who he really was for a long time. How they'd met again in London and had fallen in love. How she'd only found out his real identity then.

The rest her mother knew. How the court case, and another attack, had led to this same officer fleeing to Afghanistan, only for him to go missing and then be killed. It was heartrending.

'But if he was dead, surely I'd feel it here.' Sam placed her hand on her heart. 'All I have is anger and disbelief.'

Her mother didn't say she'd felt similarly when Sam's father had died. How she too had been angry and in denial. She also knew that being a soldier meant risking one's life so that others might live freely. That death was always a part of it.

Sam would not give up the hope that Jules was still alive, and would reappear at any moment. That if she tried hard enough she could summon him back, love being all powerful.

Milly kept giving her mother hugs after it had been gently explained by Granny, that the Frenchman they'd first met on the beach, had tragically died in action. Even at her young age the child could relate to loss and grief.

But without a body no funeral could be held.

Leo, wanted to hold a small gathering at his farm in memory of his friend, and he begged Sam to attend.

Wanting to make peace with the gentle giant, and not hold a grudge against him, Sam agreed. Veronica and Chloe came along for support, the pair now understanding how much Jules had meant to her.

It still felt surreal as she stood amongst a group of people, out in the field where Leo's father was buried, as they stepped up one by one to speak of a soldier they believed was lost in combat. A dead hero.

She was dismayed to see a small wreath had been sent by Jules's French father.

Leo explained he'd had to inform him as the only living relative.

'But he was violent towards Jules,' she protested. 'He never showed him any love.' At least she could console herself that Jules could be in no doubt of her own. That she loved him, body and soul.

44

(January. 2022)

Jules opened his eyes to find he was still alive. He couldn't believe his luck. Slowly, he took in the white walled room. Saw the drip fixed to his wrist and knew he was in a hospital. He felt drugged and unable to move, a leg hung limp in a sling, and he feared he was a prisoner. He tensed as the door opened and in walked a white coated man.

The man fiddled with the drip, and then tightened the sling around the leg, which caused a searing pain. '*Mon Dieu*. That hurts,' Jules cried.

'I'm sorry. It was necessary. But it is good that you speak English and I can talk to you.'

Jules stayed silent, fearful of revealing anything about himself.

The man informed him of his condition. He had a soft Pakistani accent as he told Jules he'd almost lost his leg from one of the stab wounds. How the other had pierced deeply into his side and caused internal injuries. How he'd needed hours of surgery. How septic peritonitis had set in post operation and had made him very sick. That he'd been in and out of consciousness for weeks, jabbering only in French.

'Am I in a prison hospital?' Jules dared to ask.

'Goodness, no. You are in Quetta, Pakistan. I am Doctor Hassan. I have taken good care of you.' The man beamed.

Jules felt relief he was no longer in Afghanistan, but was still wary. 'How did I get here?'

'By the courage of two young men who found you in the cellar of their home. Who patched you up, and then risked their lives ferrying you across the border and into Pakistan. You were placed in an old ambulance usually used to fetch medical supplies.'

Jules could remember none of this. Only being laid out on a cold slab in a dingy room. 'I was sure they'd kill me.'

'The border guards nearly did. There have been fights breaking out on both sides. But when they were informed you had a severe case of Covid, untrue of course, they didn't even look at you, but just waved you through.'

'How long have I been here?'

'Well, we've seen in the New Year.'

Weeks had passed. 'Has anyone come looking for me?' Leo must have tried to find him.

The doctor didn't answer.

'Where's my backpack?' Jules asked. The burner phone was inside. He'd call Leo immediately.

'I'm afraid your pack, isn't here.' Hassan looked a little nervous. 'I needed to know who you were so I rifled through and found your passport.' So much for the secret pocket, thought Jules. 'When I saw you were French I called the Embassy in Islamabad. I informed them that one of their countrymen was badly injured and they sent someone to visit you. But you were still unconscious, so they left, and took the pack with them.'

'Mon Dieu.'

'I'm expect they'll return it when they come again.'

'Did they say anything about me?' Jules felt worried.

'It's been a while since a French National arrived from Afghanistan with stab wounds. They asked me to keep your presence here a secret, until they have the full story.' The doctor left the room.

Even if Leo had come to the hospital he'd have been sent away, patient unknown. Jules felt trapped.

A few days later, a woman appeared, the backpack on her arm.

She drew up a chair, leaned closer, and spoke in a quiet voice.

'Bonjour. Je suis, Sophie Dupont. And you,' she reverted to English, 'are Jules Caron, yes?'

He stayed silent, still uncertain who *she* was.

It was a shock when she informed him she was from the DGSE, the French Intelligence Service. He knew they had thousands of agents working all over the world. What could they want with him?

He was dismayed when she told him they'd learned about his trials in England from their counterparts - MI5.

'MI5? But I'm not a spy.'

'No. But you were the firearms officer involved in a terrorist attack, were you not?'

No point denying this. He nodded.

'One that led to you fleeing the country?'

He nodded again.

She gave him a sorry look. 'There's no easy way to tell you this, but everyone in England believes you are dead. That you were captured in Afghanistan and executed by the Taliban. Unfortunately, someone leaked this to the newspapers.'

Jules knew it would have come from Salim or Abdul, thrilled to be safe in the UK. But he was horrified to hear that everyone thought he was dead. He couldn't bear to think of Sam being told this. Couldn't begin to imagine how she would have taken it. He lay in a panic.

Dupont kept talking. 'For your continued safety we think it should stay that way.'

'I should stay *dead?* Mon Dieu.' How could they even consider this? He tried to raise himself, but too weak, he fell back.

'Fatwa's are never completely removed. If any jihadists thought you were still alive they'd come after you. And, reprisals could be sought from anyone who was close to you.'

Jules felt a coldness grip him knowing this could put Sam and little Milly in danger. As well as Leo and the team.

'You must not contact anyone in England, ever again,' Dupont damned.

He might as well have been executed.

Dupont just held up his passport. 'Look, we can give you a second chance in life. All you need is a new identity for repatriation in France. We can even organize a flight to your home city of Nice.'

But Jules didn't want to go to there anymore. Not without Sam. He didn't want to see his *pere* either. 'I can't pretend to be someone else,' he said. 'My father still lives there.'

'Not anymore. He's moved to Argentina.'

'What?' Dupont knew more than he did.

'There was trouble with the criminal fraternity. Henri Caron sold up his businesses and left in a hurry.'

Jules was relieved he'd gone, but also appalled. It was typical of his father to just disappear.

She continued to say that the hospital bills would be paid for by the DGSE. That they'd take care of everything.

He felt spooked, fearing what they might want in return.

Dupont read his mind. 'We may use your sniper skills to protect visiting dignitaries from the rooftops of our cities, but that's all.'

He didn't want to be a sniper anymore. He just wanted peace.

'The rest of the time you can live a quiet life. Become an architect if you so wish.'

She even knew of his dreams.

'But you can no longer be Jules Caron,' she said, as though losing his identity was nothing. 'You'll need a new name. Have you any preference?'

The name he'd used for his lawyer slid from his lips as though it had been waiting there all the time - *'Jean Bailey.'*

'That will do, *bien.'* Dupont smiled for the first time. 'I'll have a new passport for you by the end of the week.' She rose from her chair, and before he could make any real protest, she'd left.

It was a *fait accompli*. He felt that the English and the French intelligence services had conspired to have him banished as if he was an embarrassment. An ex-soldier gone rogue in Afghanistan. One who'd been left for dead...

At least his backpack had been returned to him. He could still call Leo and let him know he was still alive, and scupper Dupont's plan.

He fiddled around for the burner phone, but to his dismay it wasn't there. She must have taken it. He let out a howl of frustration, thrashed about and swore loudly, until Doctor Hassan came running in. An injection was administered, and in moments, Jules was asleep again.

The New Year was celebrated in Dorset, but Sam couldn't show any enthusiasm for it. She was still unable to accept Jules was really gone. She stayed in an almost dream like state.

It was time to return to London for the start of Milly's school term. She said farewell to Chloe and Veronica, who made her promise to call them on a regular basis, to let them know she was okay. They'd done their best to make her face reality, but could see she was only going through the motions of living.

Sam's mother decided to come too, for extra support. She hoped that when the school routine took over, and her daughter returned to work, that things would return to normal. But not long after they arrived life took another turn, one that threw Sam back into despair.

A story was leaked to the news about the rogue operation to Afghanistan. Jules Caron made the headlines as a hero, yet again. A dead one.

Interest in him returned with a vengeance. When people learned that he'd died trying to rescue people, strangers started mourning him as if they knew him personally. Sam felt he belonged to the public more than her. She felt left out in the cold.

She lost all purpose in life. The drama students she was supposed to be coaching did their best to draw her attention with their audition pieces. Hamlet's famous speech - 'To be or not to be,' was performed over and over. But she sat, hardly listening. The idea of questioning one's purpose in life was of little interest to her now.

It took Ben Miller, the American, returning for his public speaking classes, to rally her. He'd conquered his stammer, and full of gratitude, he wanted to help. On discovering the notes for her book, left forlornly on her desk, he couldn't resist looking.

At first, Sam scolded him for snooping. 'I'd rather you didn't look at those, Ben. I've lost my motivation for writing the book, anyway.'

'Well, that's a shame,' he said in his American drawl. 'I think it has potential. Self Help is popular right now.' He tapped the notes with his finger. 'This is just the sort of material my company wants to promote.'

Sam had forgotten he was in publishing. Not that it mattered. The book would never be finished. 'I'm sorry, but I wouldn't know where to begin.' She showed him to the door.

Her mother told her she was being foolish, that Ben was offering her an opportunity, not to be missed.

It was only when the nights became sleepless, and Sam took to wandering downstairs, did she absentmindedly start flicking through the notes.

This led to new ideas. Words were conjured up. She started writing phrases in snatched moments as exquisite memories returned, images she could describe, until she couldn't stop. She felt an urgency to record of all that had happened, with nothing held back. The love affair was hinted at in every page in a dream like narrative, if only, to keep Jules alive in her mind.

When she finally stared down at the words - THE END – she felt every emotion she'd ever felt had been wrung out of her. She had no feelings left.

Her mother told her she should hand the book over to Ben.

Sam wasn't ready to do any such thing. She hid it in a drawer as a keep sake, away from prying eyes.

But Ben persisted. 'You can't let all that work go to waste. At least let me read it and give you my honest opinion.'

Her curiosity finally got the better of her, and she handed it over.

'I'll get back to you with an answer.' The American walked out with it under his arm.

A week later he returned saying he loved it. That he would take care of everything, the marketing, the publicity. He even had a title for it - 'Surviving Death.'

At first Sam wanted it back. Unable to let go of this last connection to Jules. 'I don't think I can bear to lose it,' she said.

'Oh, come on,' Ben pleaded. 'In the spirit of Carp Deim, let's do this.'

The gauntlet thrown down, Sam changed her mind. She'd publish and be damned.

As the first signs of Spring appeared, white Hawthorne blossom arrayed like a veil over the common, her hope for a life with Jules faded. She felt driven to return to the land of the living, an embattled survivor, without him.

Jules had recovered enough to make the specially organized flight to France. Strapped onto a stretcher, he had a nurse accompanying him, instead of an air hostess. In case of turbulence, he was sedated.

He'd tried to contact Leo. He'd begged Doctor Hassan to allow him to use *his* phone, as well as asking some of the nurses for theirs, but no one would oblige him. They were under strict instructions from Sophie Dupont, not to. The DGSE had taken complete control of his life.

On arrival in Nice, he was driven by ambulance out of the city to a small private hospital in the Alps.

There, he endured weeks of physiotherapy, and work outs in the gym, until gradually his old fitness returned. Only a slight limp gave away what he'd been through, physically.

His mind was a different matter.

He felt brain washed by psychiatrist's who wanted him to embrace his new identity, and answer only to the name of - *Jean Bailey*. He was told over and over that this was imperative to keep him safe, as well as those who'd been close to him.

He kept wondering if Sam believed what she'd been told, and if not, had she tried to find him? He hung onto this hope for as long as he could.

But the knowledge that he could bring real harm to her and little Milly made him finally give up the fight. He felt he had little choice but to become another person. Jules Caron slipped to a dark recess at the back of his mind, buried.

As the first signs of spring arrived, the Oleander bushes bursting into colour on the boulevards of Nice, Jules sacrificed the chance for a life with Sam. He felt driven to return to the land of the living, an embattled survivor, without her.

Epilogue

45

(Six months later)

On a bright September morning, Sam slipped out of her house and climbed into the car hired by Ben.

The black Mercedes had a friendly driver. As she sat in the back seat, he handed her a newspaper, opened at the review page, with a heading that was hard to miss. Her book, 'Surviving Death,' had made it onto the best seller list, all due to her amazing publishers, 'Miller and Parker.' Once a small boutique affair they were set to conquer the world.

Ben's idea of promoting the love element, the dream like narrative intended to keep the memory of Jules alive, had captured the imagination of the public. Sam had spent the last months attending book launches all around the country, and felt almost burnt out. When Ben had suggested this weekend away, and Mother had offered to take care of Milly, she'd leapt at the chance to escape.

She folded up the paper and sat musing on her change of fortune. Far from being damned for bearing her soul, she was being celebrated as a Superwoman. The books vivid description of the self defence training, had led to half the females in the country signing up for classes in Krav Maga.

Milly, along with half the girls in her class were already devotees. Her daughter was able to speak her mind as well as having enviable physical energy. Life at school was pleasant. Noor was still her best friend but there were lots of other friends, too. Gone were the days of division and animosity. Wimbledon had returned to being a peaceful suburb, the cafés were full, and the traffic was no longer at a standstill. Life was almost back to normal, whatever normal was.

Sam arrived at London airport to find Ben waiting inside the business lounge. He'd told her they'd be flying to Europe, but to which country he wouldn't say. He had this boyish desire to surprise her, which was both intriguing and irritating at the same time.

It was bumpy as they flew over the channel. Ben tried to distract her by talking about how 'Miller and Parker,' were determined to crack open the European market. How her book would lead the way. She knew that a small amount of work would be involved before she could throw off her shackles and relax.

A little nervous about his insatiable ambition, she looked out of the plane to see the landscape of France unfolding beneath her. The valleys, the forests, the low lying plains, and finally, the majestic snowcapped Alps.

She suspected they'd fly on to Germany, where the largest book fair in the world was held. Or maybe it would be to Italy, in Venice, a known city of book lovers. Or to Spain, Barcelona was a ripe setting for thrillers.

She was taken by surprise, therefore, when the plane swooped down to a lower altitude, and the shimmering waters of the French Riviera lay before her. She stared out of the window in shock. 'Ben? We're not going here, are we?'

He shrugged. 'When an offer to launch your book in Nice came, I took it.' He gave her a challenging look.

She stared back in dismay. Fearing this was deliberate on his part. A way of making her lay the ghost of Jules once and for all. To stop her having imagined sightings of him, ones Ben had grown weary of. Her publisher had often said it was time she related to other men, like him, she now supposed.

As the plane glided towards the airport, winging its way low across the sea, she felt a wave of sadness. *Nice* - The city of painters, Matisse and Chagall, of jazz, and sunshine, and romance. The city she'd planned a trip with Jules to see in the New Year. A trip that had never happened. A trip she'd tried to forget about but had failed to.

Ben was full of enthusiasm on the taxi ride to the hotel, whereas she sat huddled beside the open window, unprepared for how she would cope with what lay ahead. She was only vaguely aware of sunshine, warmth, and French speaking people.

It was only when they reached the hotel, *Le Negresco,* that she could start taking in her surroundings. The doormen in their red-plumed postillion hats that harked back to the eighteen-century were hard to ignore. Along with the artistry and style of the décor in the foyer. Plush carpets, ornate tables and chairs, sculptures, a fine bust of Renoir, an accolade to love. And a showy portrait of Louis XIV, that dominated. And amid all this was a stand, on which there was a poster with a large photograph of her.

Startled, she went over, and read the elegant writing that announced her appearance at the hotel that very evening. That her book *'Surviving Death,'* translated into French as, *'Survivre à la Mort,'* would be available to buy, with the author signing copies.

Ben, having checked them in at reception, came over, with a proud look on his face.

'Did you organize all this?' she asked him.

He nodded. 'I'm glad to see that they've followed my instructions to the letter. You're in famous company, Sam. Elton John featured this hotel in his video - 'I'm Still Standing.' And Liz Taylor, and Brigitte Bardot, and the Beatles, stayed here in their hey days. And now here you are following in their footsteps,' he beamed at her.

She should have been pleased, instead she was embarrassed. 'You don't think this hotel is a trite ostentatious?'

This only invited Ben to give a lecture on how the owner was a philanthropist who gave half the yearly profits to rescuing endangered animals as well as homeless people. That during the horrendous truck attack on the Promenade des Anglais, only a few years back, she'd opened the foyer to the injured.

Unfortunately, the reminder of this terrible attack, far worse than her own, had an adverse effect on Sam. She felt desperate to reach her bedroom and she hurried to the lift.

Ben came after her. 'I didn't mean to upset you. I was just explaining.'

She told him that she needed some peace and quiet, and slipped into her bedroom, thankful to be alone.

It was sunny inside. The blue and white striped wallpaper, a testimony to life on the beach.

Sam opened the French windows and went out onto the balcony, let the still warm September air drift over her. Eyes closed, she listened to the sounds around her. The rustle of palm trees, the light traffic idling by, the excited cries of children, the splash of waves on the pebbly beach, happy sounds.

She opened her eyes but was dazzled by the sun's brightness. She put on her sunglasses, and looked across the boulevard. Oleander bushes were in their last bloom, shadowy clouds feathered the azure sky, and the sea was a deep blue. Nice was in the dying glory before Autumn arrived.

Tourists were making the best of this by parading along the Promenade des Anglais. Some were stylishly dressed and looked like Parisians, the women in flowing dresses, the men in chinos, and panama hats. Others wore more garish clothing, Americans, with glitzy sunglasses. And then came the English, more careless, calling out to one another, their children skipping along beside them, ice creams dripping onto the concrete.

Rallied by their joyful spirits, Sam felt an urge to embrace this beautiful city. She was about to go inside to change into a sundress and go for a stroll, when a man caught her eye.

He had a slight limp as he dodged about the crowds. He was wearing casual jeans, and trainers, and had a certain energy, his dark hair ruffled in the breeze. She leaned over the balcony for a closer look. Felt a tightness in her throat…It couldn't be… could it?

A commanding knock on the door interrupted her reverie. She felt impelled to go and open it.

Ben's fair hair was swept back, his eyes even bluer in the Provence light, and dressed in his suave white suit it was hard not to see him as every woman's ideal.

'How about a light lunch in the Negresco bar? I shouldn't have kept you in the dark. I was worried you wouldn't come if I'd told you the truth, and it was such a good opportunity.' He smiled at her, apologetically.

He could always win her round. She should be more grateful. She told him she was a bit on edge. That after she'd changed into something lighter, she'd join him there.

She closed the door, but unable to resist, rushed back to the balcony for another look.

The man was no longer there. He'd been swallowed up by the throng of people. It was just foolish imaginings anyway, her eyes deceiving her. She really should stop doing this.

She returned inside her room, slipped on a sundress, picked up her sunhat, and glasses, ready for a stroll, later.

No need for a scarf around her neck. Ben had organized a plastic surgeon, and after a small operation, there was nothing to hide anymore. Her skin was smooth and unmarked. The ugly reminder of the attack, vanquished.

Jean had arrived in Nice for his meeting with Sophie Dupont of the DGSE, a little early. He took the chance to visit the beach for a quick dip in the sea, before he made his way back along the Promenade de Anglais. What he hadn't bargained for was tourists crowding his path, ones he had dodge around so he wouldn't be late.

He felt unnerved that the French intelligence service had summoned him back to the city of his youth. He'd become used to living quietly in a nearby town doing what he'd always wanted to do, train to be an architect. He'd found a job as an apprentice in a small firm and his dream was at last being realized. He could only hope Sophie Dupont would not make demands that could sabotage his progress.

He arrived at the small and somewhat dingy office, unlike the grander headquarters in Paris, and found she was alone, not even a secretary in sight. It seemed he was still considered to be a man with secrets, a man who nobody could really know.

He could hardly contain his relief, when, Dupont, pleased to hear that he liked his quieter life, told him that he'd earned his freedom. That the agency was willing to leave him to his new existence and would not be using him.

He left in a hurry, before she could change her mind, and with a buoyant air he returned to the Promenade des Anglais feeling like a normal person. One who could enjoy lunch at a café overlooking the sea.

He ordered a glass of Rose, and a Salade Nicois, which was the best he'd ever tasted, and the Pain au Chocolat that followed, was superb. After a leisurely café creme, he sat back, and allowed the sun to warm him, a free man.

The Negresco bar had subtle lighting, and the soft walnut woodwork of the walls, lavish with paintings, gave it a romantic style. Ben had already ordered her a glass of champagne, and it wasn't long before the fizzy zing had Sam in a relaxed frame of mind.

'I believe they play jazz here in the evenings. We should come here after the launch, to celebrate,' Ben enthused.

'Sounds good to me,' Sam agreed, much to his delight.

He ran through the agenda for the launch, and asked her how she wanted to open things.

She said she would the mention the attack that had happened here a few years back. Then hold a minute's silence out of respect for the victims. After which she would do the usual readings, followed by questions, and the book signings, lastly.

'The hotel will roll out the red carpet,' said Ben. 'There'll be journalists mobbing you.'

Sam still felt fearful of such people, even though they'd been complimentary of late. 'I wish I could sneak in, do the work, and sneak out again,' she said, not wanting to feel like an actress about to give a performance.

'The days for an author's anonymity have long passed, Sam. Your fans want to know everything about you.' Ben lifted his glass. 'Here's to the French kneeling at your feet.'

Sam suspected the French would never kneel to anyone. But being an American Ben thought anything was possible.

His lunch finished, he had a string of meetings arranged, hoping to sell more of her books. 'I'll see you at six, dressed and ready to inspire.' And with a smile of confidence, off he went to promote her.

She knew he meant well, and that she should thank him for his efforts. He was sometimes just too enthusiastic to bear.

She felt like some fresh air, and her lunch finished, she made her way to the foyer.

The receptionist gave her a smile.

The two doormen gave her bows. 'Bonjour, Madame Elliot,' they chorused in unison.

Buoyed by this show of appreciation, she walked out into the street protected from the sun by her beloved sun hat, and with dark sunglasses perched on her nose, she felt ready to stroll along the Promenade des Anglais.

The cafes were finishing lunches, and waiters on roller skates were whizzing about clearing the tables. They were so skilful, that finding one free, she sat down to watch the spectacle. She was about to order a *café du crème*, when a sudden breeze whipped her sunhat clean off her head. It flew into the air like a lost balloon. For a moment she froze, fearful it would take someone's fancy and they'd waltz off with the treasured item. The one with memories she couldn't bear to lose, of a Dorset beach, and building sandcastles, and dancing at a music festival...

She rose, and pushed her way through the crowds to try and reach it. But as the breeze changed direction it fluttered to the ground, lost to her, about to be trampled on, her memories crushed to dust...

Desperate for the sanctuary of her hotel room, she made a dash across the boulevard. She was blind to the danger of cars coming towards her. Deaf to the driver's horns as they swerved to avoid her. It was a miracle she reached the other side, unscathed.

She rushed to the hotel and swept past the doormen with barely a glance.

In the foyer the receptionist gave her a concerned look. 'Are you alright Madame?'

'I...I lost my hat.' Sam patted her empty head, before hurrying into the lift, trying to hide her tears.

Jean, his lunch over, was walking along when the sunhat tumbled

251

through the air and landed at his feet. Like a gift, or so people around him teased, as he bent down to rescue it.

He swept it up, saw the red ribbon, felt his nerve ends tingle at its strange familiarity.

He moved outside the crowd to examine it, ran his fingers around the wide rim, felt the softness of the straw, and his mind started drifting back to another time, another place, to Dorset in England, where a woman had lain sunbathing on a beach with a similar hat covering her face, her lovely face…

Hearing horns blaring, he raised his head, and saw a woman running across the boulevard. French drivers were not the best at avoiding people and it was a relief to see her reach the other side safely. He watched as she hurried inside the Hotel Negresco.

He looked at the hat again. Then shook his head. It couldn't be hers, could it? But at the thought it might even remotely be, a tsunami of emotions hit. Seeing the traffic on the boulevard had slowed to a halt, like a man possessed, he crossed over, and followed her into the hotel.

The doormen raised their eyebrows at the sight of the hat in his hand, but he ignored them and marched inside

His eyes scanned around foyer but there no sign of the woman, just a stand with a poster. He felt impelled to go over, and stood, unable to register at first who the woman smiling back at him was. Her eyes were luminous and even more challenging than he remembered…

It wasn't until his heart started hammering in his chest, that he knew, without a shadow of doubt, that it really was Sam.

His Sam. His hands started to tremble. He had to hold onto the stand to steady himself, as he read that she'd be appearing this very evening, in this hotel, to launch her book, *Survivre à la Mort.*'

He remembered it was the work she'd talked about, now an acclaimed success. He felt a rush of pride, knowing how hard she must have worked, what a fighter she was. How much he loved her for it. He felt better just thinking this, until a disturbing thought impinged. Maybe she'd overcome the loss of him now that she was such a success, and that was why she could smile so winningly. Maybe she'd accepted that he no longer existed and was just a memory, a loser, who'd fled to Afghanistan without telling her and had never returned.

Doubts piled in. What right had he to be here? He was no longer the person she'd known. He was Jean Bailey, a man doomed to walk alone, whose presence could only cause her pain.

In anguish he turned away. He was about to leave the hotel when the receptionist called to him, 'Monsieur. Est-ce Madame Elliot's?' And she pointed to the hat he was still holding.

He explained how he'd come by it. 'Il a soufflé dans la brise.'

She smiled. 'Donnez-le-moi et je le rendrai à Madame.'

If only he could give it to Sam himself. He held onto it, unwilling to let go. But the receptionist reached out and took it from him. Then asked if he was coming to the book launch that evening.

He couldn't answer, couldn't speak, he felt like an intruder. He fled from the hotel and was back on the Promenade des Anglais before he knew it, limping away.

Inside her room, Sam lay on the bed and scolded herself for being sentimental. She shouldn't hold onto memories. The hat was but a foolish memento.

She closed her eyes and almost drifted off to sleep before a loud knock on the door had her sitting up with a start. She thought it must be Ben again and went to open it, but there stood the receptionist with the hat in her hands.

'Someone brought it in, Madame.'

Sam gasped, forgot her resolve, and took hold as though she was being offered the crown jewels. 'Who found it?'

'A good Samaritan,' said the receptionist. 'Who left.'

Sam nodded. It was good to know they still existed. Just holding her hat felt reassuring. She thanked the receptionist for her trouble, and popped the memento back into the wardrobe. Memories weren't meant to be lost. They were meant to be enduring. You shouldn't try to erase part of your life.

She returned to her bed, and fell into a deep and relieved slumber.

46

She woke to find it was time to prepare for the evening. She took a long bath, wrapped a towel around herself, and sat on the upright Renaissance chair to do some mindfulness. Then she dried her hair and pulled it into a neat French pleat, put minimal make up on, and dressed in a black trouser suit, a silk grey shirt, and low-heeled sling back shoes. The result made her look smart and professional. Somewhat like Tanya Osborne used to look. Only now Tanya wore floral printed dresses that were loose and feminine. She was engaged to be married and hoped to become pregnant soon. Or so she'd informed Sam in one of their regular phone conversations. They'd had a lot to share. Drawn together by the courtroom drama, they'd united against terror.

Sam checked her bag containing the necessary items. A comb, a compact, lipstick, the usual clean white hanky that once belonged to Jules, a notepad, and a pen for the book signings. Then she sat waiting for Ben's knock on her door.

Quarter to six on the dot it came.

He looked very American in his stone coloured linen suit. He asked Sam to do a pirouette and told her he thought she looked better than he'd ever seen. How coming to Nice had been the best thing for her. He offered his arm. 'Let's go conquer the French.'

They arrived in the foyer to find a red carpet laid out. The Paparazzi appeared and crowded around them, cameras flashing. Questions were called out - *Did Sam love Nice? Was there a message for its people in her book, seeing as she too had suffered from a terrorist attack?*

She smiled without answering and moved closer to Ben, who put a protective arm around her shoulders as he hurried her along. The feeling of being hounded was all too familiar.

Having wrestled with himself all afternoon, Jean, returned to the hotel in time for the launch. He would see her perform, and leave. But to his dismay he found the event had sold out. The foyer was packed with people holding onto their prized tickets. The best he could do was push his way into a smaller room, adjacent to the main event, where he at least found copies of Sam's book. He just managed to buy one before the room turned into a scrum, as the audience piled in.

He was backed into a corner, where a small sofa looked out of a window onto a garden area. He sank down, and stayed hidden. Only when he heard a hullabaloo did he lift his head to peer across the body of people to see what was happening.

An entourage had appeared. It was like being at the Cannes film festival. Cameras flashed and journalists called out questions to a smiling and gracious Sam, who looked more like a film star in a movie than the woman that he knew and loved. He was taken aback by her elegance and composure. He even felt a little intimidated. Only her eyes gave way a glimmer of anxiety that there might be a price to pay for her new-found success. The loss of privacy perhaps, something that together they had relished. He felt a wrench seeing another man place a protective arm around her as he hustled her into the main room.

Jules felt gutted that she must have found someone else already. He should leave but his legs had gone weak. He sank back onto the sofa, his mind in turmoil.

The room quickly emptied. He heard the doors to the event closing. He was alone with only Sam's book for company. He stared down at the cover, and taking a deep breath he opened it. When he saw the dedication – 'To Jules *without whom none of this could have been written. To whom I owe everything…*' he had to fight back the tears, as his effort over the past months to become an entirely different person, crumbled. Jules Caron returned, and like a man starved, he started reading.

There was loud applause as Sam walked in. All the chairs were taken. There was an excited murmur from the audience as she walked down the aisle to reach the small platform at the far end of the room. It was startling how different these appearances were to the time spent writing a book. Time spent alone with only her own thoughts. Unlike the almost gladiatorial experience of a book launch, where the work often felt owned by other people.

She walked to the chair provided for her. A lectern was set up, and

255

a glass of water made available. Reading aloud always left her with a dry mouth.

Ben introduced her in his American drawl, his stammer conquered. After which he sat down, and she stepped forwards.

She spoke of how a terrorist attack in a leafy London suburb had led to the writing of the book. How she hoped it might help others to recover from similar traumas. How humbled she felt to be in Nice, where they had suffered even more. She then asked for a minute's silence out of respect for those who'd lost their lives, those who were injured, and those still in distress.

After this she started reading, her tone, subdued.

The first extract described the moment of horror when she'd frozen and been unable to run. How she had stood seemingly helpless to her fate. The audience seemed gripped as she read about her journey back to living again, her imagined love, and her survival through writing the book.

She sat down to applause.

Then came the questions.

How hard was it to write about such a horrific event? Was it hard to find the discipline? Was she drained when she reached the end? Would she ever find such an intense love in reality?

She didn't answer the last one. She knew audiences wanted the firearms officer to remain a dead hero. The love between them only imagined. That the loss of him had led to her rising from the ashes to make a success of her life. An example they could all follow and leave any trauma behind. Believe that they could be as free and independent as she was...

Sam thanked the audience for their attentiveness. Then told them she'd be happy to sign copies of her book. She returned to her chair and sipped some water, while the room emptied. Then, with Ben leading the way she walked down the aisle and into the smaller anti-room, where a table and chair had been set aside for the signings.

Ben went to assist staff still selling copies, while she sat, pulled the pen from her bag, and started meeting the people who'd already formed a queue.

She did her best to engage with each one. Ben had made her practice her signature until it was an eye-catching logo, swirly and stylish. The French loved it and she signed until her fingers ached. But it was a relief when she came to the last copy. She wrote with a flourish and sat back in her chair eager for the weekend of leisure that lay ahead.

With his usual enthusiasm, Ben was busy at the book counter, calculating the sales of the evening, his face flushed with success. Sam smiled to herself, collected her things, and rose ready to leave.

But a sudden movement in the corner of the room caught her attention. A dark-haired man, sitting on a small sofa, facing away from her, had, '*Survivre à la Mort,*' held up before him. There was something endearing about his focused posture, as he read it.

She was roused to call out, 'Excuse me, but I could sign that copy before I leave, if you would like.' She sat down again and waited for his response.

Hidden in his corner, Jules was stunned by the book. He could see, in the dream like narrative, how Sam had kept him alive in every page. He had a desperate wish to speak to her, to explain how he'd only become someone else under duress, because there was no other way to keep her safe. He hadn't even noticed the event was over and that she was in the same room. The sounds of social exchange had gone over his head. It was only her uplifting English voice that broke through his reverie.

Even then his head told him he should stay hidden. But his heart was too full to do any such thing. He had to give this a chance to find out if she still wanted him. He rose from the sofa, and turned to face her.

Sam tried to take in the stranger. Dark haired, handsome in a raw edged way, his eyes fixed on hers. Eyes that saw right through her.

She felt the breath ripped from her as she registered the achingly familiar features. Ones imprinted on her mind forever. The eyes still as arresting, though there was a certain fragility, a desperateness, as though he was afraid of her, as she stared in bewilderment at a ghost come alive.

She willed him to come over. He walked with a slight limp and she knew he was the man she'd seen this morning, that her eyes had not deceived her, and that he was very much alive.

Gently he laid the book on the table, opened it, and pointed at the first page.

Like an automaton, she reached for her pen, and scrawled her name, just as she had for all the others. Except this time, it meant so much more.

He picked up the book. Neither of them could speak. He gave her a helpless look and turned to leave.

She couldn't let him go like this. She managed to whisper. 'Where can we meet?'

He turned back. She saw the flash of hope in his eyes.

'At the pergola on the Promenade des Anglais,' he whispered back. 'I'll be waiting for you.' And the book held close, the man she had thought was dead, left.

She sat watching as he disappeared, his agility less assured, as though he too had been through much.

Ben came up and saw she was trembling. He stared after the retreating figure. 'Who is that?'

'Oh, a last customer, that's all.' She couldn't begin to describe what had occurred. Ben wouldn't believe her. He'd say she was imagining things again.

But this time she wasn't. She rose from her chair, feeling more like a ghost herself. 'I'm in need of fresh air. I'd like a walk on my own, if you don't mind.'

Ben frowned at the rejection of his company, but quickly rallied. 'Well, don't be long. I've arranged for some celebratory champagne at the hotel, remember.'

'Don't worry, I'll be there.'

It took time for her to reach the promenade, where tourists were now taking an evening stroll. Mostly it was couples in thrall to one another. She followed behind them, a lone woman searching for a man she'd also been in thrall to.

She knew it couldn't be the same as before, that too much had happened, but needed to find out if he still wanted her.

He was standing on the edge of the Pergola, his head down, as if he too, was anxious. Maybe he'd turn back into a ghost an evaporate into the thin night air. But then he raised his head and smiled at her, and she felt the old stirring.

As she came up close, without a word, he took her arm and led her down the promenade steps to the beach.

At the water's edge they sat on the pebbles in silence. The waves lapped at their feet as the sun disappeared, it's light dying in a blaze of glory, with the promise of a new dawn…

Jules spoke quietly as he told her his story. She saw the pain in his eyes and understood the sacrifice he'd made to keep her and Milly safe. The pain he'd felt at having to be someone else. 'Jules Caron was buried at the back of my mind,' he said.

She laid her head on his shoulder. 'Except in my book.'

'Except in your book. Reading it brought the real me alive again. I can't bury him anymore. Or, how we once were.' He ran his finger down her cheek. Saw that her neck was healed.

Sam felt a yearning to be kissed. For it to be the way it was. But doubts hindered her. They were leading separate lives in different countries, how could they really be together? What if she took the risk and lost him again, it would be unbearable, and the hope inside her faded.

He saw her eyes dim, and the hope inside him faded too. How could he ask her to give up her new life? Nice, the city of love and romance could blind one to realities. Maybe being together was but a foolish dream. He should savour this last moment, and let her go.

Sam remembered the celebratory champagne Ben had ordered at the hotel. She felt guilty for keeping him waiting. 'I have to meet somebody,' she said.

They both felt powerless to stop this. They were doomed to meet and part, the fear of loss like a barrier between them they could not overcome.

They returned to the promenade, where they stared into one another's eyes, each trying to read the other, but failing.

Jules tried to harden himself to losing her forever.

Sam found it hard to tear her eyes from his.

'Go quickly, if you must,' he urged her.

She began walking away, but crowds of people milled around her. She felt suffocated. She felt life was being wrenched from her at every step. Her heart started pounding like a death knoll. How could she walk away? She couldn't resist turning back for one last look...

But he wasn't there. She was too late.

Jules felt his as though bones were disintegrating as he walked in the opposite direction. The Pergola was amassed with people, shoulder to shoulder. He had to push his way through trying to ignore their happy faces, trying to stifle his own desire to be happy too. Having just found Sam, losing her felt unbearable. He couldn't resist turning back for one last look...

But she wasn't there. He was too late.

Desperately he looked again, his eyes scanning the crowd, their faces bland in the darkening light. Except for one, unique and true to herself, Sam stood out like a shining star, the tears streaming down her cheeks, a look of desolation on her face.

He fought his way back to her, knowing that this was their last chance.

He took her in his arms. 'I'll do whatever it takes to be with you,' he whispered.

'And I, with you,' she whispered back.

Nothing else mattered. Not fame or fortune. Or being a superwoman, or a superman. It was love they had survived for, over and over again.

THE END

ALSO BY CARI DAVIES

On the Border

A coming of age, family saga set between two opposing worlds, rural Wales and London in the swinging Sixties.

ISBN: 978-1-8384289-4-5